THE HEART OF THE RENASCENCE RUBY

WHEN DARKNESS FALLS: BOOK 2

ANGELA M. JOHNSON

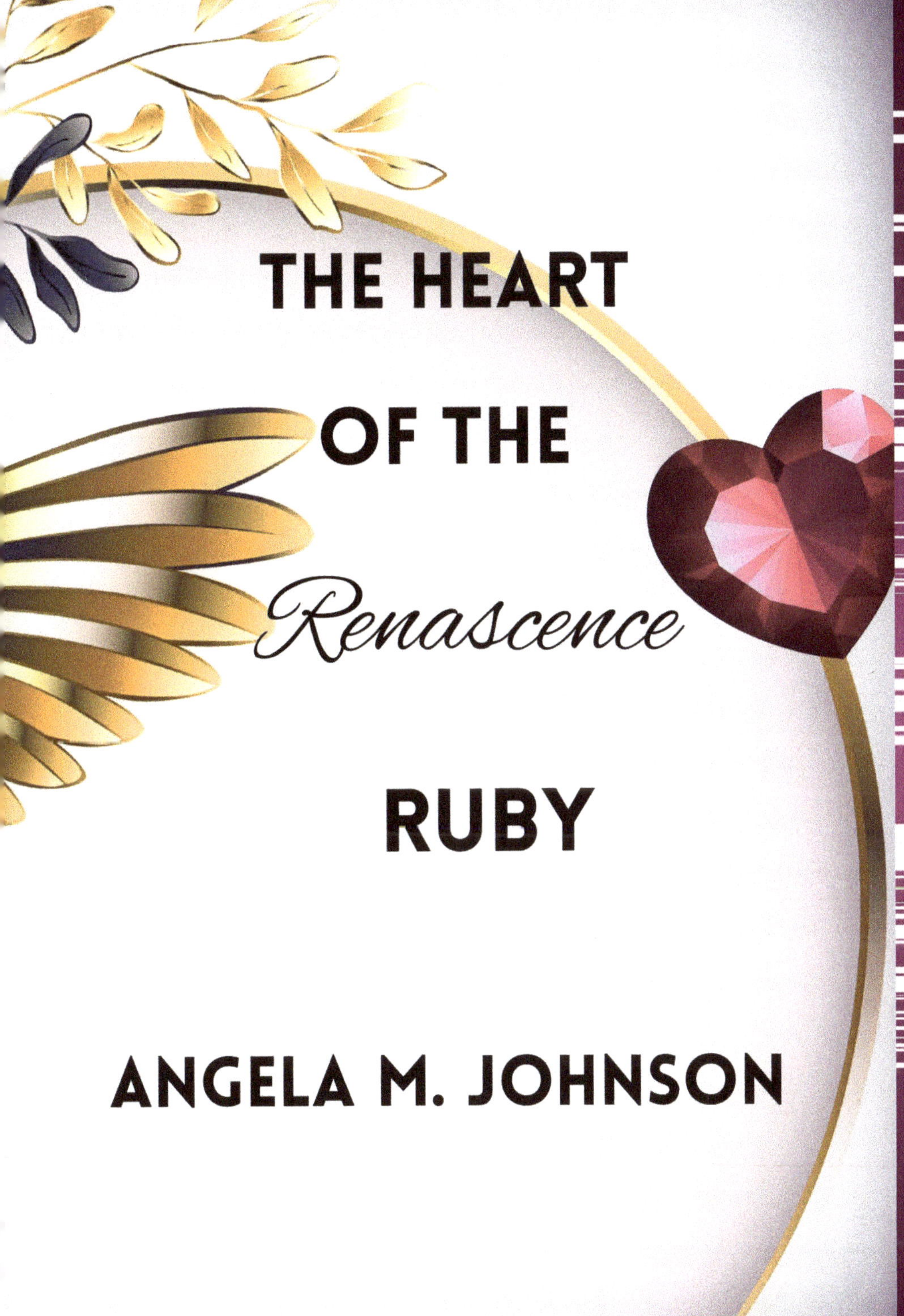
THE HEART
OF THE
Renascence
RUBY
ANGELA M. JOHNSON

AMJ Publishing
Prairie Grove, AR 72753

CONTENTS

Dedication

Content Warnings

PART ONE

1. Nightmares of a Fractured Mind (Melody) — 3
2. Endless Pursuit (Hades) — 11
3. My New Normal (Melody) — 18
4. Saving Grace (Melody) — 26
5. My Undoing (Hades) — 35
6. Blood of the Gods (Melody) — 42
7. Power of the Dead (Hades) — 49
8. Aftermath (Melody) — 59
9. Washed Away (Hades) — 65
10. Windows to the Soul (Melody) — 72
11. Small Victories, Big Hard-On (Hades) — 80
12. Tethered (Melody) — 87
13. Take a Walk (Hades) — 96
14. And so it Begins (Melody) — 102
15. Out of Tartarus and Into Elysium (Hades) — 109
16. Temple of the Gatekeeper (Melody) — 116
17. Goddess of the Rose (Hades) — 124
18. The Acolyte (Hades) — 133
19. Affair of the Heart (Hades' Memory) — 139
20. Essence of the Divine (Hades' Memory) — 145
21. Death or Dishonor (Hades' Memory) — 154
22. Golden Tears (Hades' Memory) — 164

PART TWO

23. What Lurks Beneath (Melody) — 183
24. Sands in the Hourglass (Hades) — 191
25. Collector's Delight (Melody) — 199

26. Revelations (Hades)   206

27. Tread Lightly (Hades)   213

28. Gut Feeling (Melody)   222

29. Unexpected Savior (Hades)   229

30. Wielder of the Remnants (Hades)   236

31. New Identity (Hades)   242

32. Returning to the Scene of the Crime (Melody)   256

33. Appetizers Before the Main Course, Always (Hades)   265

34. Half-Past Seven (Hades)   272

35. A Woman Marked (Melody)   276

36. Golden Temple (Hades)   286

Epilogue: Aphrodite's Plea   294

About the Author

DEDICATION

For those who wonder if getting busy with a god would blow their back out.

CONTENT WARNINGS

Some of the themes in this story may not be suitable for all and, as such, read with caution.

This telling has graphic intercourse scenes, narcissistic relationships, ritualistic killings, alcohol and drug use (non-consensual and consensual).

Playlist

These songs inspired me as I wrote. I pictured each scene as they played in the background; scored like a movie or tv series.

Pronunciation Guide

gorget (gȯr-jət)

pteruges (pteri-yes)

Gigantes (ghee-ghan-dez)

Algea (al-ghee-a)

Ichor (ai-kor)

Orpheus (or-fee-uhs)

Eurydice (yr-i-duh-see)

zoí (zoh-ee)

kykeon (kuh-keh-ohn)

Hecatoncheires (hek-a-tón-khei-res)

loukoumades (loo-koo-mah-dayz)

tiganites (tee-gah-nee-tes)

souvlaki (soov-laa-kee)

Underworld
Lethe
(Waters of Oblivion)
Elysium
Asphodel Meadows
Mnemosyne
(Waters of Memory)
Acheron
(River of Woe)
Taenarum
(Gates to the Underworld)

Tartarus
Pyriphlegethon
(River of Flame)
Hades' Palace
Scales of Judgement
Stables
Cocytus
(River of Tears)
Charon's
Temple
Styx
(River of Hate)

PART ONE

"Deathless Aphrodite of the spangled mind,
child of Zeus, who twists lures, I beg you
do not break with hard pains,
O lady, my heart..."
SAPPHO

CHAPTER 1

NIGHTMARES OF A FRACTURED MIND (MELODY)

"I think I like you best this way." The words ring out in a menacing tone, with hatred dripping off the tip of my tongue. It is my voice, low and resonant, but I don't recognize the words as mine. And looking down, I see a woman's face, her mouth gaping as if trapped in a scream. There, lying in the grass, now brown and golden from fall's emergence, Jen's dead eyes bulge. Her face is contorted from the torment marring those once teasing features while the night creeps in around us and her body lies still beneath me.

But... I skipped past this. I know I did. I fast-forwarded through Jen's torturous last moments and resumed following her passing, just as her soul left her body. Then why can I see my hands coated in her blood, holding her face longingly as I lean down for a... *Oh, gods!*

I jerk awake, eyes wide and searching the darkness while I draw my arms to my chest. Sleep falls away and my vision clears, allowing me to focus on the mercury-colored orbs shining from the other side of the bed. Bright silver eyes gleam, reflecting like a predator in the night, and I startle at first before realizing it is just Hades watching me. He's always watching me.

Reaching over, his delicate touch trails slowly from my elbow to where my hands are clenched over my chest. His fingers are warm when he squeezes, confirming he is real, *here*, and a shuddering sigh escapes as I let out a sob. Then, easing across the bed, he pulls me into his arms, cradling me. "Shhh. You are okay, Melody. You are here with me. You are safe." He places a kiss on my head, and his lips are soft where they linger at my temple.

"I was back there and—" I choke back a whimper, hiding my face in his hard chest.

"It will be okay. This will pass with time." Hades' insistence is soothing, and I allow the low rumble of his breathing to calm me. I surrender to his warmth as it surrounds me like a chrysalis, protecting my delicate wings while they form within my cocoon.

I thought I had been born anew in this place, but despite that rebirth, I have yet to feel quite myself since my arrival. My eyes flutter closed, and the beating of his heart lulls me back to sleep, only to stir several hours later when I awake alone.

Hades' warmth is long gone, so I grip the cold sheets from his side of the bed in my hand, bunching them. I trail my fingers along the indentation his body made in the mattress as he held me, unnerved by the sheer size, and breathe in what little of his sandal-wood and black tea scent remains. Once again, he has departed to begin his day and left me to sleep, knowing I have been struggling to do just that.

My first night in the Underworld, after being carried off the ferry and past the throne composed of twisted bones at the edge of the river, guards corralled souls into one twisted line and gawked at me in Hades' arms. Whispers arose amongst the departed about who I was, while overlapping conversations of the guards full of conjecture followed us as we strode toward the stone castle looming in the distance.

Hades stopped at the gated entrance to the seat of his power, where my head turned, following a long wall that spanned as far as my eyes could see. And then, after tilting my head up and up some more, I gaped at all that was before me. There were twenty foot tall alabaster walls adorned with gold seals that separated the palace from the scales, with a structure rivaling the Arc de Triomphe in Paris at its center.

After he set me down, Hades never left my side as we walked toward the white marble archway. He seemed to be on high alert, with his head twisted like an owl as he scowled behind us. It was odd because it was his domain after all, so what would strike fear into the heart of the King of Death?

My eyes fixed on where Hades' were trained on the gates on the other side of the river. I cleared my throat, and he scanned the line awaiting judgment before turning his attention back to me. *Smooth,* I thought. *Make it seem intentional.* But it wasn't.

Facing the archway once more, I studied it more closely. Yellow-tinted striations meandered over the surface, scoring the stone like gilded claw marks, with renderings of him sitting atop his throne carved on each side. Blank eyes seemed to judge me from beneath unruly brows as I waited, and eventually metal hinges creaked in opposition when he pushed the gates wide for us to pass through.

The gates clinked noisily as it closed behind us, separating us and his palace from the rest of the Underworld. Then, Hades and I walked across a dusty courtyard, where his heavy footfalls crunched over pebbles and sent puffs of dust skyward with each step. But when we finally reached the keep, the castle appeared less opulent than the previous structures I'd seen, and stretched out where it seemed to meld into the mountain beyond.

Two columns stood prominently on each side of the entryway at the top of the stairs, and proud statues of what I assumed were Cerberus with his three heads baring elongated fangs guarded the bottom. They faced inward like the Sphinx gate from an eighties movie I saw once. Luckily for me, when I walked before the statues of the hellhound, the eyes didn't open and shoot lasers at my feet. If that had been my test, I am certain they would have deemed me unworthy.

As I study the keep, where every other structure had appeared to be carved from marble or alabaster, shimmering with smooth lines, Hades' castle was composed of porous stones. Chalky beige and cream bricks were stacked one atop the other, making up the single level of the castle, before joining the base of the mountain range where it rose into what looked like the night sky.

Stars twinkled high above the range, but no constellations could be seen beyond the peaks. It looked real enough, but really we were deep within the earth, and when asked about it, Hades explained that the Underworld was encapsulated within a deep cave. So, what I was seeing was nothing more than his will projected onto the ceiling—distant memories from his time in the mortal realm, when he would lie peacefully staring up at all that glittered above.

His face fell, and he looked away as what might have been familiarity shifted into... *What is that, longing?*

Once we ascended the steps, he pushed open a large wooden entry door with crossed bidents etched into a brass shield at its center. The hinges creaked noisily, and torches sparked to life down the corridor, where their crackling rose to greet us as they burned brighter.

The flames of the torches danced, emitting a sapphire glow, and sent our shadows bounding off the walls as we walked on. Hades' shadow was monstrous—imposing—and loomed over mine as it shrank back, cowering. The whole scene reminded me of a puppet show with marionettes I saw as a child. One where a beastly creature with spindly legs and arms stalked an innocent girl before swallowing her whole.

Is that Hades' intent? I thought, studying his face for any indication of danger. I found none.

After a short walk down the hall, we reached a door on the left side, and Hades pushed it open. More hinges creaked, and as his shadow disappeared, my shoulders relaxed. I hadn't realized I had been so tense, and cringed at the sound of the door as I thought, *No WD-40 in the Underworld, apparently.*

Hades beckoned me to enter, so I crossed the threshold, taking in all that lay before me and scanned the room; it was rather dark despite the torches sparking to life along the walls.

A large bed sat in the center of the room, with the most luxurious dark purple coverlet draped over the edge and billowing to the floor. It wouldn't have been my color choice, but I was a visitor here, so I couldn't complain about what was offered.

There were piles of pillows in lavender hues stacked at the head of the bed, a small vanity sitting beside it, and a console table with a basin and an armoire along the far wall. It should have been inviting, but considering the events of that evening, it was hard to find comfort in anything. Besides Hades, that is.

My eyes narrowed on the simple wooden table with the basin. After living in a world that advanced with time, being somewhere trapped in the past and lacking basic comforts—electricity and modern plumbing—I wondered what other antiquities I should expect. *I swear to the gods, if he asks me to shit in a hole, I am out of here!*

I ran my fingers across the fur draping the end of the bed after stepping to its edge and turned to face Hades when he cleared his throat. "This is your room for as long as you wish it to be," he offered, his feet shifting anxiously just outside the door in the hallway.

"My room? I thought... never mind," I said, shaking my head. "Thank you."

"I am sure you are exhausted, so I will leave you to rest. If you need anything, and I mean anything, I will be just down the hall." He hesitated outside the door, his eyes raising to meet mine before falling once again to the floor.

That version of Hades was perplexing because everything I had seen through Persephone's eyes didn't match the god standing before me. This god was unsure of himself. Almost skittish.

"You're right. I am a little tired, so maybe I should try to sleep. But I do have one question, though. You don't honestly expect me to shit in a bucket or anything, right?" I stepped to the head of the bed and tossed the covers back, turning to face him once more.

Hades was about to leave when my question halted him. His eyes widened. "I had not considered—" He paused, his features twisting as he worked through something. Then his eyes flickered, and he continued, "The facilities are down the hall. Fourth door on the left. And the grotto—bathing chamber—is down around the corner. You will know it when you see it."

The door latch clinked as it fell closed, and he was gone. Nothing more was offered, not another word spoken, and I was alone in a strange place with no fucking clue what the future held. Or if I even had one.

Sleep evaded me that night, for the most part, and I awoke terrified some hours later with tears streaming down my face. The darkness seemed to breathe along the walls, where shadows lurked from being cast by a mostly melted candle burning across the room. I did not want to be alone, and could not find peace in a foreign space, so I padded toward the door, searching for something known. But the only thing known there was him, and he said if I needed anything...

The hallway was pitch-dark when I opened my door, but slowly the torches flickered to life, one by one, until the path to my left was dimly lit. He would be just down the hall, but how would I ever know which door was his? *Not the fourth one, obviously.*

Unsure where to begin, I started down the hall, stopping at each door on my left and listening for sounds within. The hall was mostly stone, and I ran my hand along it, my fingertips rambling over the sandy surface. *This is so fucking surreal*, I thought. Just like the feel of the ancient ruins from my trip to Mexico my senior year—withstanding the test of time but haunted by echoes from the past.

Finally, I reached a set of doors where the sounds of heavy breathing and labored snores sounded. On the outside, the same brass shield with crossed bidents adorned the center of each one, and I knew the room must be his.

I opened the doors, and rusted hinges groaned as I pushed with all my might. They were heavy, and creaked open gradually as I put my shoulder into them. But before I stepped inside, the snoring ceased and a rumbling growl, deep and filled with warning, rang out, stopping me mid-step.

The light from the hall broke through the darkness and illuminated a bristling Cerberus lying at the foot of Hades' bed. With two heads raised from his paws and a snarl baring two sets of terrifying fangs, he alerted as I stepped inside.

Seeing it was me, Cerberus huffed, licking his lips before each head settled back down. One head had not even bothered to rise, despite never meeting me before, and instead glared at me with one accusing amber-colored eye as its toppled head let out a harrumph.

"Excuse the shit out of me," I muttered, closing the doors behind me before hesitantly taking one step and then another into the room.

Cerberus allowed me to pass, padding his large, outstretched paws into the rug at the base of the bed. He yawned as his claws caught and tore into the floor covering, and then his even breaths filled the room once more as I creeped toward the head of the bed.

Embers from a dying fire glowed red in a familiar hearth along the left wall, and several candles flickered wildly on the bedside table as they melted down. They washed the room in an ominous glow, but the familiarity of the space ended there.

The rest of the room was nothing like what I had seen in Persephone's memories. There were no "toys" threatening me from the nightstand, no chairs of torment in the corners, and Hades wasn't the scary, sadistic being she had known. His face lacked the twisted scowl that had been etched into my mind from all the times she had writhed in fear as he towered over her. Now, he was nestled under a large duvet, shifting and turning away from me in his sleep.

Curled up on the left side of the bed in the fetal position, he looked peaceful. Handsome, even. I eased back the covers and slid in, not wanting to disturb his slumber.

Once I settled, I closed my eyes and was soon fast asleep. I would love to say that it was as peaceful as his, but it was not. Because more torture awaited me the moment I drifted off, but this time absent Hades. He wasn't the cause, nor the focal point. Now Persephone was my tormentor, and I fucking despised that bitch.

CHAPTER 2

ENDLESS PURSUIT (HADES)

"Any sign of her soul?" I call out to Charon when the ferry draws nearer. The flailing arms of the tortured Nevermore rise above the waterline, reaching for the splintered hull of the vessel as it cuts through the water. Their decrepit fingers grasp, trying to gain purchase, and the guards bat them away with an oar as I stand watching impatiently beside the dock.

I slide my hands to my hips in irritation when Charon finally steps ashore. He sloshes through small pools of water and emerges with his sandals covered in muck as the smell of sulphur rises with each step.

Once we stand together at the edge of the river Styx, he reaches for my hand in greeting and replies, "Not yet, my friend."

Ignoring his offered hand, I turn my back on him as I growl out, "It has been eight days, Charon. She could not just disappear again, could she?"

Not allowing my slight to faze him, Charon clasps his hand on my shoulder, squeezing it. "Not disappeared, just not here." His weathered fingers dig into my flesh.

"As if there is a difference?" I grumble, shrugging him off.

"She will turn up, eventually. They always do," he insists.

"Tell that to the fourteen people she slaughtered. Where are their souls, huh? Still trapped in that Titan-forsaken stone. She is out there, Charon. She may be lying low, but she is out there," I warn.

I look over the river toward the entrance to the labyrinth. My vacant stare is trapped on the sealed gates on the other side, where the skulls of Gigantes curve along the top of the iron and trail down the obsidian gate piers, facing toward me. Hollow sockets peer out from each one and seem to assess me, but I do not fear their judgement, however, because mine is the only one that matters here. But if any soul remains inside the labyrinth, it is not their judgement they should fear. Those now soulless eyes will not look upon them, and they will have to contend with the horrors lurking in the shadows. I shudder.

The Algea are not as forgiving as I, bombarding the souls within the labyrinth with unimaginable pain and suffering before claiming them as their own. After the gates close, they will subject the souls locked out of the Underworld to physical and mental torture. Grief, sorrow, and distress will be loosed upon those trapped on their side, and who knows how their souls will fare while waiting for the gates to reopen in the morning. What will remain? That is, if anything remains at all?

The gates used to remain open with arrivals streaming through non-stop, but that was before we realized how easy it was for mortals to sneak in amongst the masses. It was a dangerous undertaking, sure, but too many made it past my guards and my wards, threatening the sanctity of the afterlife. I could not chance their peace, and so, now we close the gates, protecting the souls on my side from what lies within the labyrinth, and whoever tries to enter without cause from me.

Stomping away from the docks, I leave Charon staring after me as I make my way to the throne at the edge of the river. The line awaiting judgement is already long, curving along the bend, and if I do not start sorting all the souls, I will be here well into the evening. Plus, it has been days since I checked in on Tartarus, so a visit through those gates is long overdue.

After sitting on my throne for hours, sending what seems like equal numbers of souls in both directions—half to Elysium for peace and half to Tartarus for penance—I become restless. The task is exhausting—viewing the lives each soul has lived to determine their afterlife—and I want to cut my day of weighing short. So, I decide to finish the line to the tenth soul, maybe check in on Tartarus, and then spend the rest of the evening with Melody.

Melody's transition has been less than satisfactory, and she has not been sleeping. I tried to give her time. Hell, I even tried to give her space. But on that very first night, she decided that my room would also be her room, and now with it being *our* room, she still has found no comfort. I am at a loss, because with all my power and everything I can offer, the one thing she wants, the peace she deserves, I cannot seem to deliver.

Nine souls later and after the flashes of their lives flooded my mind, I have seen so much: pain, confusion, malice, and sometimes downright evil. I have seen everything from atrocities to heartbreak across the ages, but nothing prepared me for a glimpse into the life of that tenth soul.

I never thought I would take a walk through the remnants of a mortal life in this age and see Aphrodite, but as that tenth soul stepped onto the scales and I gleaned her life, I saw makeshift altars with offerings to a goddess who, as far as I knew, slumbered. Aphrodite should be nestled far beneath the depths of Mount

Olympus with all the gods and goddesses, waiting for a time when her reverence brought her back to power. Instead, there she was—the golden goddess—walking through the memory of that woman when she should appear only on a page in the annals.

I grip the arm of my throne, crushing it beneath the force of my hand. Bones crush, wood splinters, and anger ignites my flame, turning the bone fragments and wood shards to ash. I stand and address the woman, shouting one question: "How⁇"

The woman's body shakes, her knees knocking together as fear courses through her. "How what?" she mumbles, refusing to raise her eyes and meet mine. She wrings her hands in the skirts of her simple lavender gown, her eyes fixed on her slippered feet.

I seethe, "How is it I see your memories of her when I should not⁇" I step down from my throne, my skirts swishing and sandals flopping as I stalk toward her.

The wrinkles on the woman's withered face are prominent as she scrunches her brows. "I don't know—"

"Tsk, tsk, tsk. You are thinking about lying." I step onto the scales, dwarfing the woman with my presence. She is flummoxed—her soul fragmented and memories jumbled—and I shake my finger in admonishment, circling her like a predator stalking its prey. "I can see your falsehood forming on your features," I sing. I stop, placing my finger under her chin where her crepey skin gathers along her neckline. "She cannot protect you here. Here you stand, and I alone control the outcome, so choose wisely before you answer," I command, my nail lengthening to a point as it presses into her wrinkled flesh. "What role did you play for her?"

"I was just an Acolyte, and one of many. I know only what you have seen. I was of the lesser order," she cries.

"A lesser order⁇" I bark, dropping my hand. "From what I saw… no, I do not truly understand it. It is all too discombobulated." I wince, breathing out. "There are so many colors and patterns I am unable to get a clear picture. Looking through your mind is like looking through a kaleidoscope, but there is another way." I step into her, and she flinches. She then takes a shuddering breath as she drops to one knee before me.

A droplet of her soul's essence beads from where my fingernail pricked her, and it is almost magnetic. Resonant. *God's power? But it cannot be.* I can barely hear the faintest tone—like a tuning fork echoing over a great distance—as it trails down her neck.

When she finally speaks again, she says, "There are several echelons. You earn your right to ascend to a higher order: Acolyte, Devotee, Anointed, and Priestess."

I cock a brow as I assess her with scrutiny, all while she blabs about a hierarchy I have no knowledge of. "And how does one *ascend* to a higher order?" I mock the woman with a flourish of my hand.

"The goddess alone decides," she answers, looking down at my feet.

I tap my foot in agitation. "You are old, no offense, but if you served her for years, how is it you have not ascended to a *higher order*?"

"I... I was unwilling to sacrifice. Without a sacrifice, she deemed me unworthy, and my belief alone was not enough to appease her," she recounts, finally allowing her eyes to rise. They stop when they reach the crossed bidents stamped into the medallion on my pteruges, and she stares at my waistline, her eyes bulging when they reach the muscles of my abdomen.

I reach down, placing one hand on each side of her temples, and then tilt her head back, forcing her eyes to mine. With silvery ether sparking behind my irises, I ask, "What sacrifice were you unwilling to make? Show me!"

My flames spark to life as I clutch her head in my hands. Her skin sizzles beneath my fingertips, and the pungency of burnt flesh fills the air while she screams in agony as my hands imprint on her flesh.

Power radiates, surging as I dive deep within her mind where I see flashes of rituals: women by the dozens adorned in Aphrodite's colors, moving within a temple of sorts. And then a woman rises, motioning toward someone beside her.

With my hands on her flesh, her memories are no longer laid out haphazardly. They are ordered—sequential—and play out before me like a movie reel. The shuttered illusion is like that from an old projector, and through the eyes of the woman before me I see her rise, looking at the goddess with trepidation. Then, she walks into the loving embrace of Aphrodite, who takes her face in her hands and gives her a kiss of acceptance. She and Aphrodite stroll to the rear of the temple, looking behind them only once before leaving a woman standing with tears streaming down her face.

They are not tears of sadness, but ones of elation, I realize.

The old woman, once the young girl in whose memory I walked, collapses, staring up at me from where she cowers at my feet. "She wanted a daughter, all daughters. Someone to carry on the burden. But when it was time for me to offer mine, I just couldn't." Her words rush out between sniffles as she averts her eyes. "My mother gave me away freely, offering me up to serve as so many others had before her. She was proud to do so." She looks up at me again, shaking her head from side-to-side as the brands from my fingertips glow red. "All of them died. One by one, I watched them," she whimpers. "I watched them ascend, watched them serve, and then I watched them die. And each one was absorbed into that Titan-forsaken stone when she no longer had use of them!" A sneer lifts the corner of her lips.

I crouch beside the woman, placing my forearms on my knees. She looks away, wiping her nose with the back of her hand. Then, once again placing my finger under her jaw, I force her face back to me. I stare into her sage green eyes, my features softening, and I sigh. "You are going to tell me all about this rite." I pause, squeezing her shoulder in reassurance. "And when you are done, I will see you safely to Elysium," I soothe. Standing, I motion to my guards. "Take her to Charon's temple. I will question her at my leisure. Understood?"

"As you wish, my king," a guard answers.

As they lead her away, I ascend my throne once more, returning to the tedium of my responsibilities. I then cycle through five more souls, but my mind never leaves the woman or what I have seen. Because how could I possibly think of anything else when I now know Aphrodite, that golden bitch, is out there denying me what is rightfully mine—the souls of the departed and my revenge on Persephone.

CHAPTER 3
MY NEW NORMAL (MELODY)

Each night, I awake drenched in sweat, muscles tense as I either scream or come to with tears stinging my eyes. The images of Persephone's misdeeds while controlling my body continues bouncing through my memory, tormenting me, and from what I have seen, Hades was right when he said things in the mortal realm were "pretty fucking bad." I mean... I died, and it gets no more fucking bad than that.

As I lie alone tossing and turning, my mind wanders back to a memory of my own—lying in Hades' arms as he stepped onto the ferry—when he said I had to decide. Even though I did not know then what I know now, I stayed, choosing a life, *well... whatever this is*, with him and by his side. And even if it had not been "pretty fucking bad" or I had not been dead, I would have made the same choice given the option, right?

Tired of all the what-ifs running through my mind, I rise, stretching my arms above me as I sit at the edge of the bed. *Our bed.*

A strange feeling washed over me the first time he called it that. Almost an unease. The concept of there being an "our" anything felt so foreign because, never in my wildest would I have thought I would share a bed with none other than "The Hades," King of Death, ruler of the Underworld, and be doing so willingly. None of my period romance books, filled with page after page of witty banter and happily ever afters, prepared me for that kind of plot twist.

In the past, when reading, I forwent the sub-genres of romantasy and paranormal romance. Seeing enough chaos in the world around me, I stuck to period pieces and harlequin romances like my mom used to read while sitting at our kitchen table. Those were my bag, and Desire and I devoured them time and time again.

Now I find myself at a severe disadvantage because, within those sub-genres mortals and gods came together in blissful unions, enemies became lovers, and often the lead was forced to choose between a life of magic and that of the mundane. Outcomes like that were prevalent. Expected. But despite all the chaos, and the trials and tribulations the characters were subjected to, somehow the villain in those stories eventually got the girl.

In my story, however, Hades is not a villain. Not mine, anyway.

Standing, I walk over to the wardrobe on the other side of the room and throw it open. I grab my pale chiffon robe from inside and drape its billowy softness over my skin before padding toward the door. I open it and then make my way down the torch-lined hall toward the grotto where a good soak will wash away all the dried sweat coating my flesh. Plus, the soothing waters will do wonders for the tightness that has set in my muscles, and I need that.

I forgot my sandals in our room again, as I have the many times I traversed about the keep, and considered going back to retrieve them. But then, when I pressed the wall and the grotto entrance stone slid back, sending heat billowing out of the opening, I forgot about my sandals completely.

Inside the cavern, sconces flicker to life along the walls and illuminate the space with their amber-like glow. The fragrant aroma of jasmine fills the air from creeping vines that wind their way along the crystalline walls and ceiling, where their tiny tuber-like petals drape down like white bells. Again, it is so fucking surreal, *ethereal*, and I can't believe this is my life now. *Or death as it were.*

Once I walk to the back of the space, I drop my robe, placing it on a stone seat along the wall near the pool's entrance steps. My feet are black from walking through the ash dropped by the torches lining the hallway, so when I take those first steps entering the pool, dark grey spreads like watercolor on a page as the dirt washes off my soles. But even with the bottoms of my feet now clean, and the cloudiness inks the surface of the water, my soul feels just as dark and just as murky as it had when I entered the pool; forever stained by the evil Persephone committed with my hands.

I do my best to shake off the guilt from her actions still plaguing me, and submerge myself before wading toward the lounge chair carved out at the side of the pool. Once there, small ceramic containers of lavender soothing salts and aromatic jasmine soaps line a small ledge, and I take a handful of the salts, arcing them out around me. They plop like raindrops in the water, with each drip and drop sounding off the walls as they make contact. The surface of the pool clouds as they dissolve.

I lean back onto the seat, extending my legs along the chair, and allow the warmth of the pool to envelop me. My face remains above the waterline, and when pressure fills my ears, I hear my heart pounding and thrumming loudly with each pulse.

The water in the pool is hot, not boiling, but warm enough for my muscles to relax as I breathe in the soothing scent of the lavender. The tempo eventually slows—the thudding of my heart quieting as calm washes over me—and I melt into the marble chaise beneath me while steam billows into the air.

Reminded of home by the scent of lavender, I think back on that little apartment I shared with Desire. The place where I had appraised my naked form in the moisture-draped mirror of my bathroom, and pleasured myself in the shower as steam wafted about when my fingers went wandering—trailing through satisfaction delivered by thoughts of *him*. But the *him* I remembered from my mortal life is not the *him* I now live with. And though that apartment held many memories, that is all it is now. All it will ever be. That life—my life—is over, and now I am... *what the fuck am I, anyway?*

Forcing my thoughts elsewhere, I ponder if Hades can get me lavender baby oil or something like it. Just as the thought enters my mind, a bottle of oil appears on the ledge next to me, tinkling as the glass teeters back and forth before settling. I look around and see no one, so I call out with a hesitant, "Thank you?"

My response is met with silence.

Lying back in the water, my hair floats along the surface, spreading out and reminding me of a painting by John William Waterhouse—the one where the nymphs found Orpheus with his face bobbing up and down as it floated in the water. Ripples curved out around his severed head, while his auburn hair drifted with the current. I chuckle at myself for the comparison.

Orpheus. His story was legendary, but I wonder if it came to pass. I need to ask Hades when he returns whether the tale holds truth. Had Orpheus traveled to the Underworld to retrieve his wife, Eurydice?

No. Surely not. Well, maybe... Hell, I don't know. I thought Hades was a myth, so it is quite possible that tale, too, is based on actual events. There is only one way to know for sure.

That is love, isn't it? Braving the Underworld knowing you'll face untold horrors, all on the off chance you might rescue the one who makes your life complete. How I long for a connection like that. A love like that. Perhaps a connection, or dare I say *love* like that, can bloom between Hades and me? *But at this rate, how can it?*

I know Hades liked me and enjoyed having sex with me as Aaron, but he has not laid a finger on me since arriving in the Underworld save a chaste kiss or steadying caress here or there. And yes, I know that sex alone does not equate to love. Thoughts like that faded away with the failed relationships of my youth. Even so, the fact that he has lain by my side night after night without so much as a grope is maddening. Because I am with him, chose to be so, and he is keeping me at arm's length. But why?

His sudden lack of need for me, and his overall lack of physical response, is making me second guess my decision to stay. And despite falling asleep with his warm body beside me, most times I still feel so... *alone.*

After washing my hair and body with the jasmine wash, I rinse off before exiting the pool. I then pat dry with a towel from a small table poolside and slather my body in the oil that appeared. It is lavender as I hoped, and it tingles when I smooth it across the surface of my legs.

My legs—my "stems" as I once called them—still bear Hades' mark, just as raised and dark as when I first saw it. He claimed me, saving me from an eternity of nothingness in the wailing river, but now... nothing.

Ugh! I have got to stop dwelling on his indifference, or the frustration from it will drive me mad. We're all mad here, I think, my mind flitting to the Cheshire Cat's last words before he vanished into thin air. *Will I just disappear one day too?*

Once the oil is liberally applied to my skin, I don my robe, my wet hair dripping down my back. Then, I head toward the entrance of the grotto where, remembering my forgotten sandals, I sigh aloud. "Any chance you can magic me up some sandals so I don't muck my feet on the way back to our room?" I call out, shaking my head.

Just as I step toward the opening, a pair appears to the left of the entrance, halting me mid-step. Like before, I look around, and again there is no one. So, offering another "Thanks," I slide on the sandals before exiting the grotto.

Stepping through, the stone shifts closed behind me, and the wall sconces dim as it does. It is only then that I begin my trek down the long hall back to our room.

As I am passing by a doorway on my right side, a gaping hole dead center with splintered edges and singe marks around the casing catches my eye. Unsure of how I missed it all the times I passed it before, I survey the door.

The edges of the door jamb are charred from where flames licked their way across the surface, and the scent of burnt wood faintly lingers in the air. I scrunch my nose when the smell accosts me, and a memory flashes before my eyes—a room, an archive of sorts, where torches flickered, illuminating rows of chests as they spanned the back wall.

Still immersed in the memory, I trip over something, not realizing I have stepped over the threshold and into the room. I catch myself before I face plant, and now, lying on the floor, ash coats my robe. My damp hair dangles over the stone, and my hands are filthy, scratched, but at least I spared my face. "Fucking gods!" I curse. "Damn stones tried to take me out."

As I push off the floor, a thought causes me to smile. *I can just see it: Hades returning from a day at the scales to find me laid out flat, half in the hallway and half in the room. Victim of what juts out from the floor. Those things are going to kill somebody. Lucky for me, I am already dead.*

I finally rise to my feet, scowling down at the jagged stones. Then, looking about the room, I walk to the far end where a chest lies haphazardly with trays resting neatly beside the debris. It is the one from my dreams, and the trays hold sparkling gems and other items nestled in their dividers with little slips of paper beneath each one.

I pick up a familiar stone—a large ruby in the shape of a heart—and hold it lovingly in my palm. It is cool in my hand as I trace the facets with my index finger, but heavier than I remember it being when it first appeared to me. "This is the stone," I say to no one in particular. The same one I lifted into the air as I was being dragged toward the river's edge after I... *after I died.*

Sadness washes over me. *It seems like a lifetime ago now*; I think as I stare down at the gem glistening in my palm. But it really has only been a matter of days. A week tops.

Remembering the look on the guard's face, and the way his skeletal jaw gaped wide when he saw the stone in my hand that day, I smirk. Then, I slide the stone into the pocket of my robe. *It's mine,* I think, patting my pocket and pulling the sash of my robe tighter, tying it at the waist.

Hades had gifted the stone to me, so he should not be too mad when he finds it on the bedside table when he gets back. Besides, I still have so many questions, and the stone will be a good starting point for our discussion. *Or so I think.*

CHAPTER 4
SAVING GRACE (MELODY)

Panic and pain, *so much pain*, radiates through me. Every muscle constricts and tightens, my teeth gritting so hard my jaw aches from the tension. I feel like I am being torn apart, with pieces shorn free as a deep feeling of loss washes over me. I have never experienced anything so excruciating. Not even when I dislocated my shoulder and the overwhelming burning sensation spread throughout my left arm and down into my fingers.

My pain now is one thousand times worse, as if my skin is being sliced free of the muscle with a bread knife. Those jagged teeth on its serrated edge saw back and forth, back and forth, as mangled chunks of me are slashed off. And I can feel my essence—Persephone's essence—as it is cleaved free once, twice, twelve times over while the lifeless eyes of the departed flash before my vision.

I see bodies of men and women stacked side by side, blood soaking their garments as its color spreads out from their centers. Like roses when they bloom, there is a beauty in the details when they go from cupped to flat as their petals unfurl. And even though it is a bloodbath, a scene where crimson pools beneath each corpse and seeps into the earth, I cannot seem to tear my eyes from what is before me.

Ruby-red blood spatter paints twisted arms, the spray decorating their skin as I wait for them to wilt and die. A final death. But those departed will not lie dormant through the winter like a rose. No, regardless of feeding and pruning, there will be no reawakening come spring. Their lives are at an end, fuel for the stone and for her. Their essences will feed Persephone, and their power—their souls— will remain within the stone until she is ready to feast.

With wide eyes and heart beating wildly, I take in the hands raised above me and gripping the blood-streaked Infinity Stone. Then, one piece, two pieces, twelve pieces of what feels like my soul tear off and entwine with that of Persephone's victims. More power fuels the stone, adding to the trapped smorgasbord of life within, where it will wait to finally be called to action.

A scream gets trapped in my throat and pressure builds, as if hands encircle my neck, constricting when the fingers cinch tight. My body spasms from the shock of the contact—back arching while my muscles twitch uncontrollably—and my spine curves into a comma.

I am levitating, with the surface beneath me supporting my shoulders as the rest of my body is drawn upward. Then, tight bands encircle me, crushing my ribs and bringing me down, down, down.

I fall into nothingness.

I can't breathe! I panic, and the air trapped in my lungs flutters like hundreds of butterflies as they bounce around within. A burning radiates from my chest and I gasp, over and over, clawing at my neck as I attempt to release myself from those hands.

Just when I think I will blackout, and the flickering and flashing of my vision is much like those first moments in the cavern after my death, I awaken.

Drawing in a large gulp of refreshing breath, I choke, my body shaking as an uncontrollable sadness settles deep in my bones. My lip quivers when I attempt to hold back my sobs, but I fail miserably, my short whimpers turning into an embarrassing wailing. Tight arms encircling me are now the only things holding me together. If it weren't for those arms, and *his* strength, I would shatter to pieces.

Once again, like the many nights before, Hades shushes me, soothing and calming as he holds me to his chest. He returned from his dealings at the scales, and now his lips trail whisper-soft kisses across the top of my head, the heat of his breath caressing my hair as I curl into him.

I needed his embrace, his warmth. I needed the safety of his arms and the comfort of his presence after that one. Because that nightmare—no, that memory, *her memory*—was the worst one yet.

Resting my head on his chest, Hades runs his hands up and down my arms, sending the much-needed blood flowing back to my extremities. My hands were fisted so tightly that my fingers tingle, my muscles screaming for release.

My mind is fractured, and there is no definitive separation between what was hers and mine. Because I know she no longer lingers within, and that her essence—her soul—is gone, but I am unprepared for the moment when I am barraged by the feeling of loss as the last image from my mortal life flashes before my eyes. I look down and can swear I still see a gaping hole in my chest; the final blow that ended my life.

Despite the absence of Persephone's soul, the remnants of memory she left bouncing around inside my head are a far worse punishment than her deeds while controlling me ever were. And I need to feel some semblance of control—recapture what autonomy I have lost. But how do I do that? How do I take back what was mine after she dug her grimy little fucking fingers into my entire being?

I do not want to think anymore and do not want to remember. I only want to feel something other than what I do in this moment.

Something other than this bullshit powerless feeling of being trapped by Persephone.

Reaching up, I place my hands, one on each side of Hades' face, and make circular motions, sweeping my fingers from the edge of his lips to the lobe of his ears and then back again. The repetitive movement soothes me, and I draw in his scent—that overpowering cedar and sandalwood essence.

A groan escapes his lips and, drawing in a sharp breath, his eyes flutter closed. Staring intently at him, a pained look adorns his face, so I tilt it down toward me.

I hold him there, waiting, and study the lines of his face— sculpted cheekbones, elegantly sloped nose, and full, sensual lips. He is stunning.

His eyes remain screwed shut as I rub my nose up and across his cheek, trailing my lips over his before tracing my nose to the other side. Stopping at the edge of his ear, I whisper, "I need you."

"I should not—"

"No," I assert. "No, Hades. I fucking need you," I plead, my lips brushing across the shell of his ear. I nip his lobe, pulling it between my teeth, and then let go. "Please," I beg.

I can see him fighting against his body's reaction to me, gripping my shoulders as he grits out, "I do not want to hurt you." Static electricity pulses around him like an aura.

"You won't," I say, offering words of certainty, even though I have no fucking way of knowing for sure.

"If I ever—"

"You won't!" I proclaim, gripping his jaw tight.

He opens his eyes, the pupils blown, and a fire burns within them. Cobalt blue flames flicker around the irises, circling like a whirlpool, and silver pulses around the edges as I stare into his godly orbs. Then, his lips crash onto mine, and our eyes shutter closed once more as we lie clinging to one another.

More than lust, more than longing, seeps into our kiss. There is more than need, more than hunger. There is a desperation and a pleading in that one kiss that we both share. Our kiss—that glorious, tumultuous kiss—is a desperation to be wanted, a desperation to be accepted, and a desperation to be fucking loved for once. It is a plea for it. A yearning that has gone unsatisfied for far too long. For us both.

Hades had tap danced around me, keeping me at a safe distance, and for what? I am not fucking fragile. I will not break. Nothing he can do will scare me away. I chose him and thought he had chosen me, but maybe I was wrong. Maybe what he offered is only a small mercy, and what he proposes now is his penance for the percussion grenade that fucking Persephone so callously threw into my life.

Or maybe he just feels obligated. *Perhaps he feels nothing for me at all.*

Feeling my hesitation in the tightening of my shoulders as I am barraged by maybes, Hades pulls back. "We do not have to," he offers, his eyes dancing wildly while he searches mine.

"No, I want to. *I need to*," I draw out.

"Then, what is it?" he asks, his arms slacking. He allows me room to collect my thoughts.

"Do you even want me?" I ask, my voice quivering. "Because I thought I knew, but now..." I shake my head.

"How can you even ask that? Of course I want you," he asserts.

I look away, heat flushing my cheeks as my insecurity builds. "It's just..." I trail off, releasing an exasperated sigh, "I don't want you to feel obligated." *Gods, I sound so needy!*

Hades takes my face in his hands, cupping my jaw, and stares into my eyes. "You are not an obligation, Melody. You are not here out of guilt or spite, or anything of the sort. I want you *here*," he exaggerates. "I want you more than words alone can express. The hesitation you feel has nothing to do with you directly."

"Then what is it?" I demand.

"I am afraid..." Hades sighs again as he trails off. "I am afraid her memories will alter your opinion of me. As frequently as they are coming, I fear you will see me through her eyes and hate me just as fervently as she did. *Does*." His throat bobs as he works a swallow.

Laying my head on his chest, my fingers trace over his collarbone. "I have seen you through *her* eyes, yes. But the man I know you to be, the god I know you to be, is a far cry from the one she remembers. I saw you at your worst, and anyone else might run in the other direction, but where am I?" I ask as I look into his eyes.

"Here," he answers, a smile creasing his lips and finally reaching his eyes.

"That's right, I'm here. I'm in your arms and in your bed. Not down the hall and not in Elysium. *Here*. I choose to be here. I choose you, and I'm not changing my mind. You're not getting rid of me, like it or not," I tease, caressing his nose with my own.

His hold on me tightens, and I look expectantly into his eyes. "I want you here too," he offers.

"Good," I say. "Then how about you start fucking acting like it?" I quip, snaking my hand up between us and flicking his nose.

"You want me to act like it?" he asks playfully, tossing me over and flipping me onto my back.

Hades tickles me, and I giggle uncontrollably, attempting to twist from his grip. He stops, and there is an intensity in his eyes as our chests rise and fall in unison.

My billowy gown gapes open in the front from his jostling, leaving my cleavage on display, and his arousal peaks, his excitement pressing into me. I am caged within his arms, and his weight presses me into the bed while his eyes flicker back to life when the dark blue ignites.

With an almost autonomic reaction, his hand trails down the side of my body, and he bunches my soft gown in his hand. The skirt rises slowly over my hips, and I moisten in anticipation of what will come next.

Demanding fingers, hot against my bare skin, slide effortlessly beneath me, gripping my ass in his palms as he pulls me flush against him. A tightness coils in my belly, and a heat washes over me, rambling its way down, down, down and settling at my center.

Taking a deep breath, his nostrils flare as he scents me. "So needy," he purrs, his fingers dancing across my legs and lingering when he reaches the soft flesh of my inner thigh.

Placing his knees between my thighs, he spreads them apart and then rises. Now, looking down upon me, his linen skirt tents where his erection begs to be acknowledged. He was impressive as Aaron, but now...

Unwrapping his gown, his glorious cock—*gigantic cock*—springs free as the constriction of the fabric releases him in all his glory. Every ridge, every vein is prominent as he wrestles free of the fabric. And after he throws it off the bed, he butts his knees between mine before sliding his hands beneath my thighs.

He's too big and I couldn't possibly—my thought is cut short as he hauls me up, wrapping my legs over his shoulders. My gown falls over my face, and I slide it down my arms, tossing it away like the unwelcome distraction it is.

Hades leans back onto his calves, scooting my ass up his chest. His face is right above my pussy now, and I can feel his hot breath teasing across my center while my head hangs above the bed. All the blood is rushing to my head as he keeps me waiting, teasing me with light brushes of his lips over my most sensitive flesh. He speaks to my pussy, "Still want me to act like it?" Then, not waiting for my reply, he swipes across my sensitive flesh with his tongue.

I shiver from the contact when his warmth slides through my crease, collecting my decadence on the tip before drawing my lips into his mouth where he sucks. The languid strokes as he probes my fiery center send me into a free fall. Gravity shifts, and I am left floating, dangling from his shoulders as he feasts upon me, one glorious lap after another with his tongue.

With my ass gripped firmly in both hands, he holds me to him, savoring me bit by bit. I am delirious and unable to moan despite the pleasure he's delivering when all the blood rushes to my head. Starbursts appear in my vision as a high-pitched ringing echoes in my ears. Then, a tight pressure settles behind my eyes, and I am so close—on the precipice—as if at the edge of a cliff, ready to bound forth and send myself hurtling through the air without a parachute. "Fucking gods!" I cry out.

Hades growls into my pussy; it is a feral sound, and I can feel his throbbing cock tapping against the top of my head with every bounce off his body.

Finally, my climax crescendos and my body vibrates, sending tiny electric-like shocks through me from head to toe. With my satisfaction dripping off his chin, Hades plops me back onto the bed, slides my legs off his shoulders, and once again settles his knees between my thighs. And just when I think he will take me, just when I think he will take that beautiful cock and place it at my entrance, he takes two fingers and plunges them deep inside, searching for that oh-so-special place.

Gods, how I hope he will find it. For as impressive as he has been thus far, if he finds that... I am done for.

Pulsing forward and curving his two fingers in and up, he holds that position. Rubbing back and forth, in and out against my special place, he takes me to a plane of existence I have never known. Forget Elysium and all its peace, Tartarus and all its torture. Hades' movements deliver me beyond death, beyond the afterlife, just so far fucking beyond.

The building pressure, the culmination of his efforts, bursts forth on command, and I scream out in ecstasy as Hades delivers a guttural, "That is my fucking good girl. Yes. That is it. Give it to me."

Gods, the yell of triumph from that man—my Hades, my King of Death, my ruler of the Underworld—is the most beautiful fucking music to my ears, and I geyser my satisfaction everywhere.

Hades finishes me by splashing my release, sliding his palm back and forth across my pussy. And the rubbing over my clit that happens as he summons the genie from my magic lamp once again? *Ugh!* He delivers me the most excruciating pleasure, and I know I am fucking ruined forever. *Done for.* Chosen, claimed, and taken, never again to be the same.

When I think that is all he will offer, finally, he takes himself in his hand, and, *fucking finally,* places the head of his cock at my entrance. His shit-eating grin widens, and he growls, holding himself back as he says, "Last chance to change your mind." Tapping the head of his dick on my clit before sliding it through my slick and down to my opening, he stills.

I cannot speak, still drowning in the mind-altering pleasure, so I offer the only consent I can by pulsing my pussy against him. My limbs are numb, heavy, and my netherlips smack as a hunger and need for his cock consume me.

CHAPTER 5
MY UNDOING (HADES)

Grabbing Melody's hip in my right hand, I grit out, "Just remember, you asked for this." Then, pushing inward, I breach her entrance, and her opening stretches to accommodate me. Her lips are so warm, so welcoming, that I am finding it hard to think straight as they threaten to swallow me whole. And I want to let them, but she is not ready. Not yet.

Melody mewls when the pressure from me filling her sends a jolt through her pussy. And that sound—her garbled moan—causes my head to weep, seeping pre-cum from the tip as my cock practically cries out in response to her whimpers.

Gasps escape parted lips, forming an "o" when I tense from holding back the thrusting my body wants so desperately. At this point, I am not sure if the gasps were hers or mine, but we are *both* on edge. Both craving. Both anticipating the moment when the carefully crafted barriers I have constructed to hold myself back come crashing down so we can revel in the destruction.

My cock thumps, and I want to rut into her, burying myself deep, but she has only taken my first few inches thus far. My head is still the only thing inside her, and regardless, a feeling of pride fills me when that alone seems enough to take her breath away.

"She is almost ready for me, baby." I offer a devilish smile as I place my thumb on her flesh, making small circles around her clit, priming her.

Her pussy throbs around my head as my torture twists her features. Her lips curl back into a snarl, and she bares her teeth as a hiss escapes, but still I keep her waiting. Wanting. Salivating. Creaming all over the head of my dick as her pussy and clit beg for more.

Cock pulsing, and veins swelling painfully as blood surges forth, engorging me, I have got to move. Need to. So, allowing her to adjust to my size with each forward thrust and successive withdrawal, I press in, but am gentle. So gentle as she welcomes me and I apply pressure to her clit with my thumb, holding it there.

My patience wanes, and my cock yearns to be seated fully inside her, but still, I keep my movements slow, inching forward as she studies me. With my face contorted—eyes screwed shut and gritting my teeth—I know I look anything but in control. I am holding back, I admit, but I am sparing her the ferocity of the feral beast that is howling, scratching, biting to break free of its gilded cage.

I know she does not want me like this—collared, tethered and being jerked back mercilessly by the metaphorical chains wrapped around my throat. She wants me to release the reins, unshackle the creature, and turn that dial all the way up. And she does not care if it gets messy or rough, because she wants me that way. She wants me hard and erratic, and just as untamed as she is. She wants me ravenous. Needs me to be. And for the first time since she chose to be here, I realize she wants *all* of me. Not just the perfectly put together gentleman with polished manners and perpetual patience I have shown her thus far. She wants the unrelenting brute who will take his fill until there is nothing left but ashes and dust when the fire of our passions burns out.

I will eventually glide the curve of my thick head into her, touching her in all the places no one has ever been—places she didn't know she needed to be touched—before filling her with each excruciating inch of my wide shaft. *Gods, she wants it so bad now, I can see it. Feel it.* So, with her hunger for me burning in her eyes like a wildfire, I let her show me just how badly she wants it.

Melody allows her legs to fall open, and finally letting go of my restraint—my control—I remove my thumb from her clit, grab both of her hips, and slam into her. Once to gauge her comfort level. Twice to gauge her pleasure. And then the third time to find her depth before I will even consider letting the beast within emerge.

"Not yet, little one. You are doing so good, taking my cock, but you are still not ready for all of me," I say as I keep a steady pace. It is a one-two-three rhythm. Flowing, graceful, and timed like the waltz I am humming in my head so as not to lose my shit and cum too quickly.

"Please," she pleads. But then her next plea is halted when she exhales with a *gasp* as I go deeper.

My pace quickens, hands grip, legs tense and tighten as my ass cheeks clench together, and it is not long before I am putting more force behind each thrust so I can fuck into her with wild abandon.

She is cresting again, her insides quaking as they tighten around me, and despite my counting, I am so close I can feel it. I throb and pulse inside her, just for her, *only for her*, from now until forever, *or at least until she tires of me*, and I cannot get enough. Neither can she as she lifts to meet me, granting me entrance deep, deeper, until I am filling her so fully I do not know where she ends and I begin.

"Do not give up," I pant, placing my hand beneath her jaw and gripping tightly. I slam my hips forward into her. "Make me work for it." *Slam.* "Make me earn it." *Slam.* Starbursts flood my field of vision, and I can feel the fight within me.

Hold back, Hades. Hold back. It is a mantra, a battle cry, and I will prove victorious.

Melody's hand shoots up, and she grasps for my neck. She flails as I apply pressure, her nails scratching across my chest, and a hiss escapes my lips. "That is more like it. Make me pay. Take all your frustration out on me, little one."

Looking down, I grin at her scratch marks beading with golden droplets. My god's blood strobes with power and calls out to her. I can see her fighting the need to taste it—to taste me—as she dislodges my hand from her neck.

Turning her head, she bites down into the fleshy part of my palm hard, and I cry out. Then, raising my hand, I shake it from side-to-side. "That fucking hurt, you feral bitch." I chuckle, reaching for her throat again.

With me still inside her, she bucks her hips, throwing me off balance. As I tilt, she rolls, flipping me onto my back, and I slip out of her. My cock is trapped between us as she straddles me, and she locks her ankles under my thighs, sitting triumphantly atop me. Then, she raises her hips slightly, hovering above me as she slides her folds teasingly up my length and then back down again. "You want me to make you work for it?" she taunts, sliding back and forth, enjoying the friction.

Lowering her hips, she squishes me, and half my length peeks between her thighs, pressing into my abdomen. Her right hand rises, and she spits into it, grasping the head of my cock. She rotates around my velvety tip in agonizingly slow circles, and I curse, "Fuck!" I close my eyes, my neck tensing as I arch beneath her.

"You want me to make you earn it?" she coos. Stopping, she squeezes hard, and my eyes go wide as my mouth drops open in surprise. "Huh?"

I do not answer fast enough, so she pulls her hand away, crossing her arms over her chest. "Yes," I grit out. "Yes." I grip the sheets gathered beneath me and snarl, "Make me pay."

She lifts her hips and slides her palm through her slick. Then, once she lowers again, she grips my head in her hand. Pressing her pussy against me now, she rotates her hand, drawing it down my length to where our bodies meet. "You know…" she utters, never stopping her movements, "from this angle, it looks like I'm jerking myself off." She squeezes my shaft and taps the head against my abdomen, chuckling in amusement at her intrusive thoughts.

Grinding her hips against me, she shuttles up, and then down my shaft. It becomes a pattern, the movements like a dance as she rocks her hips forward, sliding her pussy along the base of my shaft. She revels in the friction against her clit as she fists the top of my cock in her hand, drawing it toward her just to bounce it off her pelvis when our bodies meet.

I watch her intently, my chin pressed to my chest as I strain my neck. "Just like that," I urge, lifting my hips.

She bounces onto me, pressing my ass into the bed. "Not yet, my king. You haven't paid nearly enough for all the waiting you've made me do. Do you know how horny I've been?" She glides forward as she rotates. "Do you know how *hard* it's been lying next to you each night without so much as a fucking fondle?"

Bouncing off, she grips as she shuttles up to my head. I grip the sheets tighter, and the fabric singes from my heat as I fight against my need to rock into her. "Tell me," I pant.

"I thought you didn't have it in you," she goads. "That the way you fucked me as Aaron was all you were capable of. Is that the case?" *Grip and rotate, glide and bounce.* She pauses.

I grab her hips, sliding her back and forth as I draw my cock through her pooled satisfaction. I stop when my head rubs against her overly sensitive clit and she gasps. Then I pulse, the slight movements targeting her bundle of nerves. "That mortal form has nothing on me. The *real* me," I assert.

She bends her knees and unlocks her ankles from beneath my thighs. Then, I rise to a seated position, and she wraps around me, placing her feet flat on the bed as I adjust.

Placing my cock at her entrance, I glide her forward onto me. I slide in with less effort this time, and she tightens around me. "You want me to show you what I am capable of?" I ask. I jerk her down my length, her ass slapping against the top of my thighs when I bottom out.

She cannot hold back this time and cries out.

"Where did that cocky bitch who wanted me to pay for her frustration go?" *Slap.Cry. Moan.* "Where is that unquenchable fire you said was burning?" *Slap. Cry. Moan.* It takes so much effort not to cum, so with every ounce of my resolve I deny myself the release, allowing it to build as my searing heat fills her so completely.

"I never said I burned for you," she quips, her eyes burning so brightly with her passion that I feel her melting my insides.

But she sure as hell is burning now, I think, her mouth falling open as what should have been a scream escapes silently when I tweak a nipple.

My control is waning again, and I can feel her on the verge of shattering into a million pieces. *I better have a fucking mop and bucket for the mess I am about to make, because damn!*

Pulsing, tensing, straining, I feel her walls closing around me, bearing down for my next surge—the one that will have her bursting like an overfilled water balloon.

I can feel the rapture, so close, yet so far. The end, the culmination of our efforts, the rhapsody as it were, is barreling its way through our barricades, sending us both ping-ponging off the guardrails as we careen toward the cliff's edge. It is the edge of oblivion, and we open our arms wide, welcoming it with a surge of power that sends ripples throughout the room. A percussive ringing and a bright light accompany that burst of overpressure. Then a pitcher across the room shatters, and what fragments there should have been disintegrate into nothing but dust and settle on the floor.

Looks like we will need a broom and a dustpan as well, I think, my eyes shooting back to her from where they were drawn to the destruction.

With eyes that I am sure are pure molten silver, and with cobalt flames engulfing my entire head and shoulders, my skin sloughs away, leaving nothing but gilded bones. Then, as ashes swirl around us, the charred deposits gather in the fissures of my skeletal form.

My dark, emotionless orbs hold her stare, and I burst, filling her with what feels like lava flowing from my engorged tip. Spurt after spurt, I release, her walls clenching around my pulsing length. And when her dam bursts wide open, seeking to put out the fire within, the most beautiful fucking sound I have ever heard—Melody's moan of pure satisfaction—escapes her slackened jaw.

Staring at me as the burning subsides, my skin reforms over every inch of my being right before Melody's sated gaze. Finally, my storm-cloud eyes peer back at her as she sits straddling my muscular thighs. I am completely in awe of her. Her satisfaction— that unrelenting satisfaction—is unfathomable, but I want more. Yearn for it. More of her and more of that feeling. It is seductive, all-consuming, and I do not think I will ever tire of it. *Or her.*

CHAPTER 6
BLOOD OF THE GODS (MELODY)

Falling back onto the bed, Hades pulls me down with him, my core quivering as the rest of my body goes limp. My toes tingle as blood rushes its way back to their tips, and my calves cramp from how hard I had them flexed. *Too long.* I had my toes curled for too long. And despite feeling boneless, I can feel every strain placed on my muscles from our little... session.

As we lay in silence, my heartbeat, that sharp snare drum raging to escape my chest, gradually slows. What was once a driving rhythm now patters with the steadiness of a dripping faucet. And my cheek, resting on his chest, feels every reverberation as his heartbeat eases to match my own.

In sync. Our breathing and the thrumming of our hearts are in sync as he caresses my bare back with one hand. My hair flows over my shoulder, cascading onto the bed, while Hades' fingers of his other hand twist and twirl through the ends. He holds me close, and I nuzzle into his chest as an intoxicating scent—indulgent like honey—wafts to greet me. It is decadent, ambrosia-like, and I cannot resist anymore.

My tongue darts out and laps at Hades' golden essence from where my scratches marked him. One lick, two, and then I freeze. Lips tingling and tongue plumping, swelling as if stung by a bee, my throat constricts—a lump building that swallowing alone cannot quell. I jerk in Hades' arms and my hand flies to the column of my neck.

He pulls back, the panic in his eyes mirroring mine. "What did you do?" His tone is a mixture of irritation and terror. "Melody?" His eyes lower to where the tacky residue of his blood paints my pout like a shiny gloss.

Then, with preternatural speed, he hauls me up and we are moving. Without a stitch of clothing, Hades in all his naked glory sprints to the door and tears it open, carrying my exposed form into the hallway where an agitated Cerberus stands. The scruffs of his three heads are raised, teeth bared with fangs dripping saliva, and Hades veers to the side. "Out of the way, boy," he barks, shoving by the hound and bounding down the corridor.

I do not know where we are going or what is happening to me, and I cannot focus on anything other than getting air into my lungs as I lay naked in his arms. My vision is flickering in and out, my head pounding and heart racing as fear-induced adrenaline courses through me, when delirium sets in. *I guess this is what happens when a mortal fucks a god*, I think, wishing I could chuckle. Leave it to me to embrace a comedic thought instead of succumbing to terror like a normal person.

"Stay with me," he pleads. "We are almost there. Melody?"

I do not answer. Cannot answer. What little effort I can exert, I use to breathe through my nose. But that too is becoming more diffi-cult as every fiber of my being expands, and I feel like a button on a pair of overly-restrictive pants, ready to burst free. With each moment that passes, less and less oxygen remains within my lungs, and I can feel myself fading. *I do not want to go through it again—do not want to die.* I played that game once and somehow lived. At least, I think I did. I do not know what I am where living or being dead is concerned, but that is a question for when I get through whatever is happening.

If I get through it.

Teetering on the edge of succumbing, darkness attempts to wrap its torturous tendrils around me, beckoning me to follow it farther from the light. *Follow us into nothingness, the eternity where even Hades' control is stifled*, it whispers. The whispers from the darkness are seductive, and I drop my hand from my throat, reaching out to them.

"No!" Hades contends with the darkness, pulling me taut against him as he pushes back the force with his fire. It sparks to life, his anger flaring that bright cobalt, and sends the shadows scurrying back to the corners of the hallway absent illumination with almost a hiss.

Hades holds the darkness at bay as we race by, only slowing when we reach the scorched entryway to the room with the chests. Then, blasting what remains of the door to pieces, the shards disintegrate, leaving particles suspended in the air before dancing to the ground. I am transfixed by their movements, unable to tear my eyes away from where they drift toward the stones at his feet.

His feet? The shadows reach for his ankles, trying to trip him up as he steps over the threshold. But it is the stones, the same ones I tripped on earlier, that halt our progress. He topples forward but rights himself, and as he does, the shadows slam against an invisible barrier.

Unable to enter, the shadows creep up the wards obstructing their entry. Scratching like impatient fingers tapping against a windowpane, the darkness demonstrates its frustration at being kept at bay. *Being kept from me.* Their scraping is high-pitched, ear-piercing, but I do not have the strength to cover my ears, so I hang limply, being tortured by every shrill note.

"Fucking Algea," Hades grumbles, kneeling next to the ramshackle chest I took the heart stone from earlier. With me still cradled in his arms possessively, he shifts, digging through the contents of a different chest, tossing slips of paper and their corresponding items to the side. "Where is it? Where is it?" I hear him mumble, so much like a plea. "There! Fucking finally," he revels, the words spoken like a prayer answered just in time.

I do not see what he pulls from the chest; I only know that whatever it is, he squeezes my jaw to open my mouth and pours the contents inside.

"Swallow it," he commands. "You have got to swallow. Melody?" His voice pitches up as his tone goes from hope to horror. "For Titan's sake, swallow! I need you!" His body shakes, his arms cinching around me like a vice. "Zoí," he mutters, holding me as if I alone am the reason for his existence, and within me lies the very fate of the Underworld, but without me he is lost.

The swelling that closed off my airway dissipates, and when the tightness lessens enough, I gulp down lungfuls of air. The labored sound causes Hades to shudder in relief, followed by a whispered plea to the highest power. "Thank the Titans, I thought I had lost you," he murmurs, his forehead resting on mine.

My mind still races from the whole ordeal, and unsure of what just happened, I stay silent. I lay motionless in Hades' arms as he caresses my hair back from my face.

He cradles me, rocking back and forth as his eyes narrow on the doorway where the darkness once raged. When I can finally speak, in a ragged whisper I ask, "What was that?"

"The darkness?" He pauses. "It was the Algea. They sought to feed off your terror. If they had been allowed, they would have torn your soul from me and dragged you back to the labyrinth where they would have happily feasted on whatever remained."

"Algea, your guards, Persephone, those fucking stones!" I point to the threshold, my anger rising as I glare at the uneven doorway. "Is there anything in the Underworld that isn't trying to end me?" I pull my hand back, wrapping my arms around my middle. I sigh.

"I am not trying to end you," Hades assures me.

I tear my eyes from the stones and glance up to find Hades' look of concern. He draws me to his chest, and I breathe in his scent. It calms me, and I nestle my head, resting it on his chest. "Well, at least there's that." I force a smile.

"You are safe here. I promise. I would never let anything bad happen to you. Not if I can help it, anyway." He squeezes me harder.

I swallow hard, trying to ease the pain in my throat. "I'm tired. Can we just go back to bed now?"

"Whatever you need and whatever you want. I would do anything to see to your happiness," he insists.

"Can you turn back time and take back everything Persephone has done?"

He stiffens. "Unfortunately, that is something that is not within my power."

"You can take over the body of a mortal, save me from death, and somehow provide a magic castle that sees to my every whim and want, but you can't undo the past? Seems like a fucking waste, if you ask me," I grumble.

"The castle is not magic; it is powered by the souls of the Underworld. It understands wants and desires, delivering what you need."

"Sounds a lot like magic to me," I quip.

"I could help you forget, if that is what you wish? I could take away your memories and allow you to write your story however you want?" he offers.

"To what end?"

"To grant you peace. To allow you to sleep. Hell, we could fabricate the most glorious of memories, if you willed it." He looks down at me expectantly.

"That sounds great and all, but what if there's something I want to remember? Do I get to pick and choose the memories, or is it an all-or-nothing situation? Like, if you wipe my memory, am I even me anymore? Or am I a blank slate?" Confusion and frustration lace my tone.

"I wish it worked like that, but it does not. You would be required to offer up every memory, casting them away willingly," he explains. "You would have to shed yourself of their burden, and then you could be filled once more."

"Then, no. That is definitely not something I want. My life wasn't all shit, just the last little bit. If it's all or nothing, I choose to keep it all. I want to be myself. *Need to be*. You understand, don't you?"

"I do." He grimaces.

"You're not mad, are you? I mean, I wish it were that simple. I wish I could choose to wash myself fucking clean of all the darkness she's imparted on me and become anew. But if I did, it would be like you never saved me at all. I might not be trapped in the wailing river for eternity, but I would still be trapped." I shudder.

His tone softens. "I understand, and I apologize if my offer was insulting."

"I'm not insulted, I'm frustrated. There's a difference." I force a smile. "Please, can we go back to our room now? I feel like I haven't slept in days."

"Because you have not." He chuckles. Rising, he stands and walks toward the door where an agitated Cerberus waits, bristling.

Trying to lighten the mood, I joke, "Who knew death could be so exciting?"

As we reach the threshold, he says, "You are not dead. At least not in the literal sense. Your life-force in the literal sense has departed, but you remain in possession of your soul. Your essence lives on, but your mortal form, your mortal life, is no more."

We venture into the hallway, and a heaviness washes over me. My eyelids droop, and a yawn escapes. "Here's to living it up after death," I say, closing my eyes. Once again, I fall back to sleep.

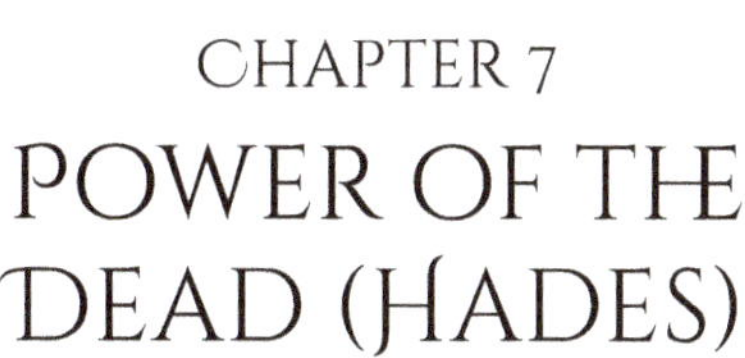

CHAPTER 7
POWER OF THE DEAD (HADES)

With Melody cradled in my arms, I trudge back to our room, my panic dwindling with each step down the corridor. Cerberus walks beside me, two heads on high alert as they scan the hallway beyond, while the other looks expectantly at me. It has been a tense evening, so I offer the hound a smile to ease his nerves, and he brushes against my side.

The Algea have never ventured that far into my domain before, so why did they this time? I saw them waiting at the gates to the Underworld on the day of Melody's arrival, ready to claim her for themselves. And perhaps they would have if I had not intervened just as their gnarled hands with talon-like nails tried to wrench the gates open.

Seeing them seething and so ready to encroach on what was mine... Well, that image has been plaguing me ever since that day. And then, this afternoon, while I was walking through the memories of the Acolyte, the cacophony of the Algea's cries echoed across the river like a chorus of wailing souls. Their monstrous forms bristled with hunger, rattling the hinges and dislodging stones from the archway, as once again they attempted to enter my kingdom despite my presence, and I did not know what to think.

My power and the barrier of the gates have kept them at bay for centuries, but there is just something about the Acolyte and Melody that dared them to chance my wrath for a taste. It had to be them because their souls are the only variables that make sense for the Algea's behavior. And it is not as if anything else has changed within my realm. The wards remain as far as I can tell, but perhaps their power has dwindled somehow?

Looking down at where Melody lies peacefully in my arms, I thank the Titans I acted in time. If I had hesitated, the Algea would have feasted on her soul, and I would have lost her forever. Not to mention that a mortal, even the essence of one, consuming ichor—a god's blood—is a death sentence. The final kind. I could not have that, would not have that, so I need to do a better job of safe-guarding my charge.

No, not charge. Charge is too impersonal for what she is to me. Or for what I want her to be. Because Melody is the warmth I craved, that was never reciprocated by Persephone. She is the need burning deep within me, not to control or possess, but to share this existence with. I need her, not only by my side but for me to hold a special place in her heart. I wanted all those things with Persephone too, but denied her choice; she did not want me. This time is different because I gave Melody a choice, and despite what memories she has seen; she chose me.

It is a unique feeling to be chosen, to be wanted. Though my craving for her is strong, my need to dominate her as I had with Persephone is not, and not that given the right situation, I would not dominate her. I say only that domination is not the result I am looking for. Because I would dominate the shit out of her if she begged me to. *Begged?* I scoff. *Would she really have to beg, or would she simply have to say that is what she needed?* Point taken. I push the thoughts aside as I reach for our door.

I am hard after picturing all the ways I could dominate Melody, but now certainly is not the time for any of that. She will be fragile while she recovers from ingesting my blood, and after the trauma of her near annihilation. I do not expect she will seek comfort from me anytime soon, and temper my arousal.

Once I open the door, I cross the room and gently lay Melody on her side of our bed, tucking her in. The ruby lies on the nightstand on her side, pulsing with power, and a crimson glow emanates from the stone.

I place my hand on Melody's chest, feeling a hearty thrum beneath my palm, and my brows furrow when I realize the strobing of the stone matches each beat of her heart. It is strange. The stone never reacted in this manner with Adonis. It housed his essence and kept him what is considered "alive" within my realm until his end, when his soul was freed, but it never did... this.

Confused, I stand watching the stone pulse as my hand rises and falls with each breath Melody takes. Her essence seems to be more than just contained within the stone; it seems to be one with it. I lift my hand off her chest and step back from the bed, but the power of the stone does not waver; it just glows steadily as she slumbers.

Cerberus followed behind me when I entered our room and took a position on the fur rug at the foot of the bed. "Watch after her, boy," I say, stopping to scratch behind his ear, mussing his wiry hair the way he likes before heading to the door. I close it behind me as I step into the hallway.

After I exit our room, I search the castle for any signs that the Algea remain. They should not have been able to make it as far as they did in the first fucking place, but seeing as they did, I am taking no chances where Melody is concerned. If it were just me, I could

have ignored their trespass completely. But with her in residence...
let me just say that their intrusion borders on an act of war.

Now, do I want to go to war with the Algea? Absolutely fucking
not, but it is not just my safety I have to consider. To me, they are no
more than a nuisance, but to anyone else—everyone else—they
would be an undoing. They would feast on every available soul, be
they in Elysium or Tartarus, and then they would turn their hunger
to my horses, my guards. Hell, they would even take a crack at
Charon, as brazen as they are at the moment. Not that it would do
them any good.

Charon would drive them back into the labyrinth and remind
them of their place, leaving them to do as they wish on their side.
That is, if he did not wipe them from existence for the audacity of
their challenge. The Algea are playing with fire, and useful or not, I
am all too willing to see them burn. At my hands or within the
depths of Tartarus.

I step off the ferry with Charon at my side and survey what remains
of the gates to the Underworld. The iron has been bent, the hinges
nearly torn from the piers, and faint cries of the Algea sound off the
walls in the distance. Their menacing cries plague me while I direct
the repairs that need to be made.

The foundation stones have shifted, and the gates are twisted
inward from where they broke through, so I place my hands, first on
one gate and then on the other, calling forth my fire to heat the
metal.

Once the iron is glowing red, the guards slam their hammers, a
loud clang sounding with each strike as the gate is forged anew.
Because fixing the metal is the easy part, and reinforcing the stones
also takes little effort, but it is the creation of stronger wards I loathe

the most. The amount of power I will have to imbue, and the toll that will take is something I dread with my entire being.

When I first created the wards protecting the Underworld, I had the reverence of all those who believed in me and could draw on that power. Now, in a time where I have been relegated to a myth, the only source of power I have to draw on is what I gain from the souls who enter. Whatever essence I meld to the gates will weaken another part of the Underworld, because there are no longer vast amounts of power to create in the land of the dead; there is only the power that is and has been. And it is not like I can choose where the power is taken from. No, the cost will only be revealed in time.

With the gates mended and stronger wards in place, I wipe the sweat from my brow and turn to face Charon. "I think it is time we had a little *chat* with the Acolyte," I grumble.

"That can wait until tomorrow," Charon utters.

"No, it cannot," I state matter-of-factly. "I need to know exactly what Aphrodite is up to and how, or if Persephone also has a part to play in her plans."

"As you wish." Charon motions to the ferry, and I stride forward, stepping onto the vessel so we can depart.

Once we reach the other side of the river, I head straight toward Charon's temple with two guards in tow and my ferryman a short distance behind us. He stops to give directions to the sentries, then meets me at the base of the steps.

Charon's temple is built from marble and alabaster, with several rooms partitioned inside once you step through the entryway at the top of the stairs. We ascend, and my two guards step forward, taking their places on either side of the entryway. They are tall, bare-chested, with muscles rippling over the expanse of their bodies as they stand awaiting their orders. "No one enters the temple," I command.

"Yes, my king," they reply.

"And boys…" Charon starts, "see his majesty and I are undisturbed. You have my permission to handle any unrest at your leisure."

A smirk lifts the corner of one of the guard's lips as Charon runs his hand across his biceps suggestively. "As you wish," he supplicates.

Charon walks into his temple and tears off his robe, tossing it over a chaise. I follow behind him, my eyes drawn to the smoke billowing at the back of the chamber.

Incense burns in large, ornately carved, hanging censers, and there is an earthy scent—like fresh pine needles and moss, with a hint of vanilla. Then, columns, equidistant to one another, span the length of the chamber, four on each side, where sconces burn brightly on each one. "Rather lavish, do you not think?" I ask, my eyes widening as I take in the finery.

"Old habits die hard," Charon quips, motioning toward the dais. "As if there were any doubt as to what I prefer."

"Yes, but you do not need to burn an offering of worship, Charon. If you need the ear of a god, I am well within walking distance." I chuckle.

"Not all of us have forgone the old ways, my friend," Charon answers.

"I have been made abundantly aware. This Acolyte has proven to me just how right you are. Now, where is she?"

"Lenore?" Charon calls out.

A woman adorned in robes resembling Charon's walks from the left side of the dais and kneels before us. Her cream-colored hood is covering her face, and Charon's symbol—a circle positioned above a crescent—repeats down the front and around the sleeves of her robe.

"Allow me to present my new attendant, Lenore." Charon smiles up at me.

"Your attendant?" I lift a brow.

"Don't mock me, Hades," Charon scoffs. "It has been a long time since I have had anyone who knew how to tend my temple."

"Indulgent much?"

"Perhaps, but good help is hard to come by these days." Charon places his hands on his hips.

"I suppose I can grant you this one... *accommodation*."

"As you should." Charon crosses his arms, lifting his chin with all the obstinacy of a petulant child.

I climb the dais and take a seat on a long marble bench. Charon places a tufted pillow atop it and takes his place beside me, resting his hands in his lap. "Come, Lenore. Regale the king with the tales of your time as an Acolyte." He beckons her toward us.

Lenore rises from where she knelt and walks up the steps, taking her place before us on the dais.

Charon reaches out, pushing her hood off her head, and she raises her eyes to meet his gaze. I watch in rapt fascination as a much younger woman than I had previously set eyes upon stares directly at Charon, not moving an inch or saying a word.

Leaning toward Charon, I whisper out of the side of my mouth, "What have you done to her?"

He turns his head, a smile lifting the corner of his lips. His answer is hushed. "It's nothing, really. I just thought she would be more comfortable this way. And more forthcoming if I gave her a little... *push*."

"Charon?" I admonish. "It is not her appearance I was speaking of."

"Okay, fine. I may have allowed her an amphora of my sacramental wine. It is her last journey, after all. Besides, you wanted her mind open, and now it is."

"Opened how?"

"Don't be mad, but I may have slipped a little honey into her libation." He shrugs his shoulders.

"And?" I growl.

"And? Why must there be an *and*?" Charon's cheeks flush as he fails to hide his amusement.

I glower at him.

"Yes, *and*... I may have added a *smidgeon* of kykeon." Charon coughs after his admission, guilt written all over his features.

"Titans be damned, Charon!" My voice rises in agitation.

"Hear me out. Your methods are far from pleasant, and I just thought..." Charon motions to where Lenore sways before us, "this was a more enjoyable option."

"Enjoyable for *whom*?" I grumble.

Charon and I watch as Lenore frolics across the dais, recounting her time as an Acolyte in a singsong voice. With arms swinging about her as she dances, her practically see-through gown billows around her calves as she tells us all about the gatherings where Aphrodite graced her worshippers with her presence.

All of Aphrodite's followers, dedicated at birth, would congregate at the place of her power, and one would be chosen from among them to carry the burden.

"Wait. Wait!" I bellow, gaining her attention and ceasing her incessant blathering. "What burden? You speak of a burden, but have made no mention of what it is exactly."

I start to rise, and Charon halts me. "A different approach." Charon forces my hands to lower, and I fist them at my sides, my power bristling at my fingertips. I stay my hand and spare her the unpleasantness of my intrusion into her mind.

"Only one brimming with the essence of the goddess and pure in faith can withstand what resides within," she says, shaking her head as if it is knowledge we should possess. "They alone can wield the power to rid the world of the *one unseen* by harvesting the power of the dead."

"Harvest the power of the dead," Charon and I mumble in unison. Our mouths slacken open in surprise, and we turn, facing one another, our eyes widening when her meaning becomes clear.

"She means to siphon the power from the Underworld and end your reign once and for all." Charon gasps, and I shoot to my feet, closing the distance between me and Lenore.

I grasp her arms and shake her, trying to clear the fog from the kykeon. It is of no use, however, and she giggles as she pulls away, beginning to dance once more.

"Once the harvest is complete, she will take her place as queen and do away with all the false gods." Lenore takes her skirt in her hands and twirls, bowing when she completes the turn. Looking up, she continues, her tone dripping with foreboding. "Her daughter is the key. The seed who yearns to be sown so that she can burst forth from the earth and yield a crop of plenty. Her power will abound, and there will be none to strike her down." She pauses. "Or so they say." And then she passes out, her body slumping to the ground in a heap.

I stand, stomping down the steps of the dais before stepping over the still form of Lenore. Then, stopping at the doors of the temple, I turn, pointing one finger in Charon's direction. "Next time we do this my way."

Charon sighs from where he remains seated atop the dais, and as I exit, I hear him call out, "I still say that my way was more fun!"

CHAPTER 8
AFTERMATH (MELODY)

I am unsure how long I have slept when I am roused by a loud banging coming from the hallway. I slip out from under the covers, stand, slip on my robe and then my sandals, before gazing briefly at the stone glowing next to the bed. It was not doing that before. Or maybe I was not paying enough attention when I placed it there.

I pick up the stone and hold it in my palm. It is warm, but I am certain it was cool when I pulled it from the chest earlier—yesterday? Honestly, I am not sure how much time has passed after everything that has happened since.

I walk to the door and jerk it open, stepping into the hallway where the banging gets louder. It is frequent, evenly paced, and I walk down the corridor to where the sound seems to come from.

As I turn the corner, I see Hades on his hands and knees, bringing a small hammer down on the stones at the threshold of the room full of chests, over and over. The chisel meets stone with one loud clang after another, and then crunching sounds when the stone fractures.

Hades does not notice me walking toward him, so I watch him intently as he peels back the stones, cursing the shards as he tosses them into a small pail. "Doing some light renovations, are we?" I joke, leaning against the far wall and pulling my robe tighter around me.

"Would you believe me if I said this is something I have been meaning to do for quite some time?" Hades wipes the sweat from his brow and leans back on his ankles, peering over at me. His muscular legs are bent at an unnatural angle, his gown cascading over his thighs, and the stones beneath his knees could not be comfortable as they dig into his flesh.

Fuck, he is beautiful. Hades is all taut lines and rippling muscles as his chest seems to dance before me. Hair sparsely lines the crease between his pecs, drawing my eyes down his tanned abdomen to where fabric gathers above his waistline.

"I believe that if you hadn't already been dealing with those fucking things, I would have gladly seen to their removal my damn self." I lift a brow and purse my lips.

"They got you too, huh?" He chuckles, twirling the chisel in his hand.

"Only once. But once was enough for a lifetime. How about you?"

He looks back at the stones. "Enough that I should have done it eons ago," he grits out, bringing the chisel down once more. The stone splinters, and he picks up the pieces, tossing them into the pail with the others.

"Actual eons or are you being facetious?" I offer a genuine smile.

"Yes, actual eons, but also long enough that it should have been handled." He grunts as he strikes another stone.

"What, your magic castle couldn't have fixed it for you?" I slide down the wall, taking a seat as I watch him fuss with the stones.

"I am sure it could have, but I told myself that this was a task to be completed with my own hands. Besides, it seemed like a waste of power when I could get more enjoyment from their destruction." He pants as he pounds another stone apart.

"It's hot watching you toil and sweat. Pounding away at the stones and placing all your frustration behind each strike." I allow innuendo to seep into my tone. "You should do manual labor more often. Makes you seem almost... *human*."

I tilt my head, my eyes feasting on his glistening forearms. His veins pop to the surface as he flexes his arm. I scoff. "Now you're just showing off." I roll my eyes.

"I think the word you were looking for is *mortal*. And besides, you said it was hot. I am only making sure you get a show worth salivating over." A devilish smirk lifts the corner of his lips as he stares me down.

"Who said I was salivating?" I look away, breaking the hold he has on me.

"You did not have to *say* anything." Hades sets down the chisel and rocks back on his ankles before rolling to a crouched position. He stands, wiping his hands on his skirt, and then walks toward me. Sliding down the wall, he takes a seat beside me. Then, shaking his head, he showers me with sweat; the droplets bead on my face.

"Fucking gross. Really?" I let out an exasperated, "Ugh!" I rub my face, and he catches my hand mid-swipe.

"As if you have not had my sweat coating your flesh before." He licks his lips.

I know what he is implying, but that does not change the fact that he is a glistening, slimy mess. I pull my hand free. "And you smell," I counter.

"A good smell or a bad smell?" He lifts his arm and sniffs.

"Is there a difference?" I lean away.

"That depends," he says, exaggerating the "s." "For example, your smell is sweet and full." He sniffs. "Jasmine, lavender, and..."

"And what?" I practically gasp, my tone breathy. His gaze is so intense that my body heats, my throat working a swallow as my mouth waters.

"And all you. I would know your scent anywhere." He leans toward me, nuzzling his nose in the crook of my neck. "The way you smell fresh from the grotto." He rubs his nose up, trailing his tongue along the line of my throat. He nips. "Your arousal and need that permeate the air when I am close to you." He grazes his teeth along my jawline, and I shudder. "The longing that escapes your lips when you exhale." He trails his tongue along my bottom lip before drawing it into his mouth and sucking. He lets go.

"I think you have an overactive olfactory system," I mumble, lost in the feeling of him.

"The better to stalk you with." The charge in his eyes is electric, sparking that molten silver before being replaced by cobalt flames that flicker around his irises.

"As if I'm your prey or something?" My shoulders rise in surprise when his hand cups my face. "Something to be chased? To be caught?"

"You are here, are you not? That would suggest that my methods are satisfactory." He stares intently into my eyes, and I meet his gaze.

The war in his eyes subsides, and I hold my breath as I await his next words and his next move.

"I'm just a conquest then?" The words are strained as they escape my lips, but I do not move. He has me coiled in his grip, his body like a cobra ready to strike.

He places his other hand on the opposite side of my face, his thumb rubbing across my cheek. "No. Not a conquest." He kisses me softly and then leans back, studying me. He does not let go of my face.

"Then what?" I try to look away, but he grips my face tighter. I squeeze my eyes shut. I feel him drawing me to him, pulling me into his lap. He leans me back, cradling me, and I open my eyes.

As I look up, I see so much in those storm-cloud eyes: need, longing, hunger. He hesitates, his eyes softening, but then his body heats and he tightens his embrace, the inferno burning once more. "You are mine, Melody. Not by force, but by choice."

His lips crash onto mine, and his heat becomes my own. My hands shoot up and I fist his hair, the silky strands gripped tightly in my palms as I hold him to me.

I devour him, sucking his lip into my mouth. He moans, the sound strained, impatient, and I savor his flesh as my tongue dances across the surface of his pout.

He pulls back, panting, his heated gaze turning to anguish before my eyes, and I do not know what to think, to feel. *Is he rejecting me? Denying me? Denying himself?*

His arms slacken, and I roll out of them, bracing off the floor. I stand, confusion washing over me as I pull my robe closed. I take a step back.

Then, looking down at Hades, I see disappointment written on his features. At me? At himself? I cannot tell. "I... I should go," I stammer, reining in my emotions.

He clenches his fists at his sides, his legs outstretched as he looks away. "That would be wise," he growls.

"Oh? Okay. Well, goodnight then," I say, turning and padding down the hall as I mouth out, *what the actual fuck?*

Silence awaits me when I step into our room, but nothing can quiet the storm raging inside me. I am all conflicted emotions and unease, the swells and squalls battering my insides like a tsunami as I wonder what I have done wrong.

As I close the door behind me, my stomach churns, and I rush over to the basin where I release my anxiety into the bottom of the bowl. *Fucking great*, I think, wiping my face with a damp cloth. I then place it over the basin to hide my sick.

Now, not only am I confused, but I am sick to my stomach at the thought of being rejected by him. Not that I had any expectations for our evening, but being alone certainly was not how I saw it ending.

I sigh. For every one step forward, we keep taking two infuriatingly frustrating steps back. *I am never getting laid again.*

WASHED AWAY (HADES)

My hands are still clenched at my sides while I watch Melody with her shoulders drawn back and spine rigid as she walks away. She does not sparc me a glance over her shoulder as I hoped, and I know I am losing her.

With the fear of pushing her too hard or moving too fast coursing through me, I sit rooted in place as she turns the corner out of sight. I allow my head to fall back, and I bounce it off the wall. *I am just distancing myself, pushing back to give her space,* I think. But as her footsteps fade, I know that instead of giving her time to adjust, I only offered what she perceives as rejection. *Way to fucking go, Hades!*

As I sit chastising myself, I hear the distinct clicking of nails and heavy padding as Cerberus makes his way down the corridor. He stops at the bend in the hallway, two heads looking back and watching Melody behind him, while the other meets my look of consternation with one of disapproval.

I look away, dreading the eventual disappointment I will see in three sets of eyes. "Do not start," I say as his grumbles of agitation meet my ears, growing louder with each step in my direction. "You are supposed to be on my side."

Eventually, wiry scruff brushes along my face as one head butts against me. Then, puffs of air blow my hair off my nape when the other two heads chuff to gain my attention. I turn my head and come face-to-face with three scowling maws.

"I know," I growl. "Are you pissed at me too?"

Cerberus plops down beside me, and I reach up, running my hands through the raised hairs between his shoulders and down his back. He settles, rolling onto his side, and offers me the expanse of his belly.

"Okay, boy. At least you are easy to please," I say, rubbing my palm back and forth across his wide chest and then down to where his waist narrows at his muscled abdomen. "Big fucking baby. Any thoughts on what I should do about my Melody situation?"

Three tongues drape out of the corners of his mouths, and saliva pools on the floor as his breathing comes out in pants, blowing ash across the stones in front of him. "Nothing? You have got nothing? Well, it was worth a shot." I give him two more hard pats as I chuckle, and then push him away as I rise, walking over to where the pail sits waiting for me to continue my assault on the threshold.

Little remains of my destruction task, and then I will need to find something to repair the entryway, so I go back to chiseling the stones, the clanging from my earlier efforts turning to loud battering as I pound mercilessly.

Once I am done removing the uneven stones, I carry away the debris. I do not have the energy to scout stones for the entry, so I dust off my palms on my gown and head toward the grotto.

With the scent of the night-blooming jasmine lingering in the air, I strip off my soiled robes once inside the cavern and toss them in a basket along the wall. I then step into the pool, submerging myself, and walk over to the side with the shelf full of scented body washes.

Removing the cap from one, I lather up. She said I smell, and I can't have that, but I didn't grab my usual sandalwood. Instead, I am met with the faint odor of lavender, the floral notes filling my nose, and immediately I think of Melody. I picture her in our room, alone with just her thoughts.

I absentmindedly massage my body, the suds dripping down my abdomen, and sigh. *I fucked up.* But how do I make things right? How do I explain my response, when I was only trying to do right by her? She has already been through so much, and has much more to overcome, so how can I be selfish and allow myself to find comfort, when all she has found thus far is unrest?

Wanting to escape the thoughts tormenting me, I drift to the bottom of the pool and allow my limbs to float at my sides as water fills my ears. The silence and weightlessness are calming, so I close my eyes and just let go. I let go of my mistakes. Let go of my inadequacy. Let go of my shortcomings. I fucking let it all wash away like the soaps that cleansed my flesh as I sink to the bottom and hold my breath.

I am still holding my breath, and have been for quite some time, when the surface of the water is broken. My eyes open to see ripples breaking the tranquility as Melody's delicate feet take one step after the other until she too is wading in the pool.

Graceful arms swirl around as her feet lift to the waterline where she wiggles her toes, and like a shark I stealthily move toward her.

Without alerting her to my presence, I reach up and wrap my arms around her waist, pulling her beneath the surface. She panics, clawing at my arms that wrench around her middle, and I loosen my grip. Then, twisting, she breaks away, pushing her legs off of me.

I rise like a Leviathan, bringing my face and shoulders into view, and she splashes me as she gasps, sputtering while she catches her breath. "Fucking asshole!" she shouts, moving toward the steps. "You scared the ever-loving shit out of me!"

"My deepest apologies." I smirk, much to her chagrin. "I thought for sure you knew I was here." I move toward her slowly.

"How the fuck would I know that?" she counters. "Last time I saw you, you were lounging in the fucking hallway." She finds the steps and leans back on them.

"Lounging?" I raise my voice, taking another step toward her. My chest breaks the surface, and droplets of water trickle down my torso. Her eyes drop from my face to where my heart beats wildly, and I stop my advance. "What I was doing could hardly be considered lounging. And besides, last I knew, you went to bed to pout."

"To pout?" her irritation rings out. "I don't fucking pout!" She sits up, and her breasts bob up and down in the water like buoys, alerting me to the danger that is her rage.

"You most certainly do. And you most certainly were," I argue, my eyes falling to her ample bosom. My cock stirs as I take in her nakedness, and I remind him that now is still not the time. He has other plans.

My plans—burying myself deep inside of her until she cries out my name—would be the same as my cock's current ones if she weren't so standoffish. I stand, allowing her eyes to wander, taking me in as I maintain some distance.

"Well, if I was pouting, it was with good reason." She crosses her arms over her chest, pressing her breasts together and denying my eyes the feast of her rose-colored nipples they were thoroughly enjoying.

"Good reason? And what would that be exactly?" My tone is anything but understanding as I prod her.

With my eyes trained on her flushed skin, her pulse thumps

heartily along her neck, and I lift my heated gaze to meet her eyes filled with apprehension. I want to touch her, but she turns away, refusing to meet my stare, and pulls her knees to her chest as she sits atop the second step. Her shoulders curl forward, and she rests her chin on her bent legs, ignoring me as I move toward the steps.

Once I reach her, I run my hand down her spine, and she stiffens. "Tell me. What was your 'good reason'?" I soften my tone, and she turns her face to look over her shoulder at me.

With a child-like voice—quiet and hesitant—she responds, "It's nothing." Her eyes flutter closed as she gets lost in the feeling of my hands while I stroke up and down her back. It is meant to be soothing, but goosebumps rise across her shoulders and down her sides. She shivers, and I watch as every inch of flesh that is visible prickles.

My fingertips bump over her spine, reading her body like braille as they follow the water trickling down, but the message is lost on me. I lean in to kiss her shoulder. Then, rubbing my nose against hers, my lips are so close I could kiss her, but I don't. Instead, I purse my lips as I hold back a smile. She is so damn cute when she is flustered.

"And nothing is code for?" I finally continue, waiting for her to fill in the blank.

Annoyance surges forth when she says, "Nothing is exactly that —nothing." She shrugs her shoulders and attempts to pull away.

Not allowing her to withdraw from me again, although I was the first to do so, I wrap my arms around her guarded form. I pull her back against my chest, and again she tries to escape, but I twist her to face me. "Look at me," I say, gripping her arms tightly while still hoping I can break through her resolve.

Her lips straighten, her face hardens, and I think she is shutting down. *Not again. We are not doing this again!*

After an uncomfortable silence, she opens her eyes, and I say, "There she is." I smile, raising my hand and caressing her cheek. Her skin is so soft, the surface smooth and inviting as it heats beneath my touch.

She leans into me, and again my hope sprouts wings. *I can fix this*, I think. But first I have to get her talking, and then meet her halfway. So maybe I should be the one to take that first step? "I had a great and epic love once. Did you know?" I ask, looking down at her expectantly.

She meets my gaze for a brief moment, and then a pained look dresses her features before she looks away. "Everybody knows," she says. "The tales of *Hades and Persephone* are just as epic as the love you speak of." She scoffs.

My tone is calm when I say, "Don't be callous, Melody. It does not suit you. And you know damn well that I was *not* talking about Persephone." I rest my chin on her crown. "After everything you have seen—all the moments you witnessed through her memories —you know there was no love lost where Persephone and I were concerned."

"I mean..." She shifts in my embrace, turning to face me, and wraps her legs around my middle. Her features soften, and her voice is filled with unease as she looks up at me and asks, "If there wasn't love, then why did you do it?"

She studies me closely as I sweep the wet strands of hair pasted to her cheek back behind her ear and then answer, "Because I was a selfish asshole." My derision bursts free as I continue, "Our pairing wasn't *rooted in love* and able to survive the gusts and gales of the storms we faced because our foundation was strong. It should have been, but it was not. I ignored her wishes, deprived her of her will, and, ultimately, drove her to hate me with every fiber of her being."

"Is that why she did what she did, and why rage consumed her?" Melody asks, resting her head on my chest as I twine my fingers through her locks floating around her in the water. "I could feel it, you know? Seething and writhing beneath my flesh until she clawed free."

"I think that is part of it. Honestly, I will never truly understand her motivations, or what she hopes to accomplish now, but I have my suspicions. And I am not sure you saw enough of her memories for you to understand either, but the fact remains: she sought to be free of me, no matter the cost. Even if it meant her life. In some ways, I would say she succeeded, but I do not think we have seen the last of her, that is for sure. She is plotting *something*. But I am at a loss as to what that is, or whether there are others working toward the same end."

Melody suction cups herself to my chest, and I can feel her heart racing. "Will she come for me next?" she asks, her terror evident.

I want to lessen her fear, but I also do not want to lie to her. So instead I say, "That is a problem for a different day." I kiss her again. "For now, how about you tell me what happened in the hallway when you fled? From your point of view, of course," I offer—the first olive branch of what I am sure will be many. "I will refrain from interjecting, and when you are done, I will do my best to offer some clarity. Deal?"

She tries to draw back, but I do not let her. I just continue playing with her hair as I wait for her assessment of me. Because I know it is coming.

They say that the eyes are the window to the soul. If that is true, then after everything I've seen, my windows are cracked and my soul is the haunted house on which they are set. Lined with cobwebs and fissures, they don't sit flush within their frames. They are recessed, the trim exposed, and the insulation has long since disintegrated—chipped and peeling with gaps that allow the elements to seep in freely.

He said that he wanted to know what happened in the hallway from "my point of view." But how do I articulate any of it when I *still* don't have a fucking clue? I mean, things between us seemed to be moving in a direction I was all too willing to go—my body was primed and yearning for more, the sensations from his ministrations stoking the fire within. But then he slammed on the brakes, dousing the flames, and the instantaneous alteration to our forward momentum gave me whiplash.

As I sit in his lap, his fingers comb through my hair as it floats on the surface of the water, and I lean back to stare into his eyes, searching.

He asked me for my truth, for what I thought transpired in the moments before I fled. But I didn't flee. Not really. I had just, as gracefully as I could, removed myself from a situation where I was grasping for more and he put up a barrier, blocking my affections.

I choke down my anxiety that burns like bile as I work a swallow, and know once I begin to speak I will be unable to stop. I will verbal vomit everything that has been plaguing me, unburdening myself of every worry, and there will be no turning back. Every insecurity, every unanswered question, and every hesitation will be laid bare. It is a curtain that needs to be drawn, thoughts that need to be shared, but I dread his scrutiny.

Being self-conscious is not a feeling I am familiar with, and I have never held my tongue to spare the feelings of others. But this dynamic—our dynamic—is new territory indeed. I don't know which feeling to lead off with, or which train of thought to follow, because they so often run straight off the track, so I just say the first thing that comes to mind. "Why did Persephone say, 'I think I like you best this way'?"

Hades is taken aback by my question. His mouth falls open, and his brows furrow as embarrassment washes over him, painting his face and neck in strawberry blotches. He is searching for the right words, but the proverbial cat has gotten his tongue.

"For context, each time Persephone took a life, she would look down at her victim and, this is just the feeling I got, *taunt* them with those words," I say.

"I see."

There is a long, awkward silence as he stares at me wide-eyed. He slides me off his lap and onto the step beside him as one eye seems to twitch. His jaw clenches as he places his hands on his knees, and he bounces them anxiously while staring at his hands.

"So, in my defense... and I acknowledge it was not my *finest* moment," he prattles on, "but you see..." He shakes his head and answers through clenched teeth. "When Persephone first entered my realm, I was different." His shoulders roll forward, and now he seems almost... defeated. "Now, keep in mind that I have changed *a lot* since then. But yeah, she used those words to taunt, but it was not her victims. Not directly, anyway." He twists his fingers together as he wrings his hands. "They were a jab at me, because she assumed I was watching."

"Why would she do that?"

"Because those were the exact words I said to her as she cowered at my feet. I am not proud of it, Melody, but it is like I said, I was different then," he blurts out, opening his hands as his eyes plead with me for understanding.

"Okay. But why would she think you were watching?"

"The first time she went back to the mortal realm—during the six months she was at her mother's—she had an affair with a man... and then took his life. I saw everything through my peering stone and punished her once she returned," he rushes out.

"Wait, what?" I gasp. "I never saw any of that," I admit. "And you saw her ummm... saw everything?"

"I saw her, yes. I saw *them*. Together. Naked. Writhing. *Moaning*." He balls his fists at his sides as his lips curve into a sneer. His teeth are clenched so tightly I think they might crack. "And I was fucking furious because... how dare she offer to someone else what was *mine*," he seethes, "but then she killed him and—"

"Is that all she was to you—something to own?" I interrupt, crossing my arms in agitation. "It's no wonder she wanted to be free of you. Women are not property, Hades. We are not *things* to be collected. We aren't some bauble you can tuck away in your precious chest until you have use of us." My anger bubbles to the surface, but I don't strike him. It is childish really, but I splash water in his face, pulling him from the emotions overtaking him.

He shakes his head and just gapes at me; the water dripping

down his chin and plopping into the water. I can see his anger mounting, the silvery ether circling his irises. He squeezes his eyes shut and releases his balled fists. When he is finally calm, he replies, "I know you are not property, or a *thing*, Melody." He sighs. "I said I was different. But the kind of different I was… well, it was not the good kind. And I would like to think I am doing better with you."

It isn't a question, but still I reply, "How do you figure?" Before he can respond, I continue my rant. "I had two choices—a final death with the chance of an afterlife, or you. I chose *you*, and regardless of that choice, I still don't have you. Not really. Nor do I know you." I slide back onto the step, putting some distance between us so I can gather my thoughts, but there's no stopping as the words continue to spill out. "We sleep in the same bed, sure. We, *sometimes*, even eat our meals together. But the connection I *thought* we had… Like, where the hell did that go? One minute you want me, and the next it's like you think I'm just this delicate little bird whose wings you might crush if you hold her too tightly. For fuck's sake, Hades. I need some reassurance, some affection, some passion. But I also need to know, *to feel*, that I made the right choice. Especially since I made it without knowing exactly what I was agreeing to!" I finally take a breath, and panic sets in. *Shit!*

Hades can sense my unease and scoots toward me. I try to pull away, but he circles his arms around me, drawing me into him. He pulls me onto his lap, and I don't fight him, *because I couldn't even if I wanted to*, but I don't look at him either.

Frustration and a barrage of other powerful emotions come over me, and my body revolts, sending an errant tear streaming down my cheek. I casually wipe it away.

"I did not mean to upset you. I only wanted for us to talk." His voice is somber as he says, "I want nothing more than for you to know me. And I, you. Even if what you come to know does not paint me in the most favorable light." I turn to face him, laying my head on his chest. With my ear pressed against him, his next words come out as a deep rumble. "I am dark and moody. These are things I know about myself. Things I am desperately trying to change. And I will get it wrong nine times out of ten, but what I do not want to do is push you away. That was never my intention, and I truly am sorry if that is how you perceived it."

"Perception is reality," I argue, the words coming out like a whine, but I still don't lift my head from his chest.

He kisses the top of my head and then says, "We should exit the grotto and talk more over a meal, should we not? Your fingers and toes are nothing but wrinkles, and I could do with some food."

I shiver when he trails his fingertips down my arm, and nod my head in response. Then, I slide off of his lap, and exit the pool, grabbing my robe from where it sits on a stone seat along the back wall.

He joins me and grabs a towel off the small table. He wipes down his chest, bending to dry his legs, and all I can do is stare at his gorgeous body—full, round ass that meets with muscular tree trunks for legs before trailing down to chiseled calves that tense above his big ass feet. His olive skin glows, and the condensation in the air steams off of him when it touches his hot skin, sizzling like oil drizzled into a pan. How my skin does not blister when it contacts his is a mystery.

"Is there anything in particular you would like to eat?" He turns his body toward me as he wraps the decorative towel around him, securing it in a knot and then tucking it into the waist. I can see his cock bounce against the light linen fabric, with the Meandros pattern doing just as its namesake and meandering down the center and around the edges. He is stunning to behold.

"Honestly, I would like to try some traditional dishes. Something that you wouldn't find at most Greek restaurants. I am very food adventurous, so nothing is off the table."

Still naked with my robe draped over my arm, I grab a towel to wring the excess water from my hair. He stops me, taking the towel and rubbing it down the strands. He scrunches the ends and then wipes off the water beaded along my shoulders and collarbone.

I turn, and he drags the cloth down my spine before bringing it around to my front. He stands behind me, and I am stilled by the grandiosity of his presence. I hold my breath when he steps into me and his cock rubs against my lower back. Heat radiates from him, and my body shivers despite it.

"We can start with loukoumades and tiganites, which are sweet. And although I am sure you have had souvlaki, you have never had it like we make it here." He continues drying me off, and it takes everything in me not to arch into him when he circles my breasts.

Once he is certain I am dry, he slides my robe off of my arm and holds it out for me. I extend my arms out to my sides, and there is a sensuality to his movements as he guides the fabric over them and up to my shoulders.

He leans over me, draping his arms over my shoulders as he ties the sash at my waist. I turn my head and come face to face with him. He is so close, and my breath hitches in my throat as I croak out, "Thank you."

His eyes twinkle, finding humor in my discomfort, and then he steps back, allowing me to pass. He gestures for me to walk ahead of him, holding his arm out to the side, and I do. But as I reach the entrance to the grotto, the stone slides back and steam billows out into the hallway, taking my unease with it.

We slip on our sandals in silence and step out into the corridor, walking beside one another until we find ourselves outside the dining hall. He opens the door and I step inside, where all the torches along the walls are blazing and the table is set with dishes down the center.

"See. Magic," I say, wiggling my fingers in the air as if casting a spell. He smirks.

There are steaming piles of bread, and what looks like pancakes, while clay jars with ornate black designs depicting Cerberus and Minotaurs sit beside them. Then there are the silver trays, piled high with sliced meats, and containers of olives, dates, and figs, while other platters bear sliced fruits. The smell is amazing, and the aroma of the spices overpowers my senses when I take a big whiff.

An exaggerated moan escapes my lips, and before I can say anything, Hades steps past me and pulls back a chair, offering me the seat. I lower myself into the chair, and he pushes it in before taking a seat on my left. I push the sleeves of my robe back to my elbows, ready to dig in.

As large as the table is, he could have sat anywhere, seeing as the table accommodates twelve. And, hell, the head of the table seems to be set for him, with an ornate gilded chalice sitting beside a large golden plate, even so, he took the one beside me. I smile about that.

Reaching toward the center of the table, Hades lifts some meat, placing the slices on the plate before me. He then grabs some bread, cheese, and olives, positioning them around the edge of my platter.

I reach for a spoon, since there is not a single fork on the table, and he slaps my hand. I pull it back and shake it in my lap because it fucking stings a little, and hold back my curse that wants to fill the silence.

"You said traditional. Traditional is with your hands, little one. Knives for cutting and spoons for soup."

He smiles when I finally take my hand and tear off a piece of bread, using it to grab a slice of meat. Then, as I bring it toward my mouth, he lifts his hand and halts me.

"Do you want me to eat, or don't you?" I quip, leaning back in my chair and glowering at him as I hold my hand above my plate. The meat is soaking into the bread, and the drippings that have coated my fingers are now drizzling down my palm.

"You would be missing the best part," he says. He then grasps one of the clay jars and pours the golden yellow contents onto a small plate beside my larger one. It is olive oil, I can tell by the pungent odor, but it has been infused with what smells like... *lemon, garlic, and bay leaves, maybe.*

I dab the food in my hand onto the plate once, twice, and then bring it to my mouth. I take a bite, and flavor bursts on my tongue as juices fill my mouth and dribble off of my chin. I hold back a moan, and savor the oregano and hint of cinnamon I am getting from the meat, mixed with the lemon and garlicky goodness of the oil.

"Is it good?" he asks, his gaze hopeful. He looks so young with his eyes wide and lips parted expectantly, and I can't help but cover my mouth in embarrassment at how full it is.

"It's wonderful," I mumble around the mouthful of food, hoping I don't spit any out when I answer. I should have waited until I swallowed, but I couldn't handle him staring at me a moment longer, and wanted him to plate a serving for himself.

With my hand still hovering over my mouth, I motion at the table with the other. He gets I want him to help himself and places several slices of meat on his tray before reaching for the bread. Then, just like I had, he pinches the bread over the meat, and picks it up before dipping it in the infused olive oil on the plate between us.

He is more graceful than I was when he leans over his plate and takes a bite, but his fingers and wrist are just as coated as mine had been by the oil and meat drippings trailing down his hand.

I chuckle beside him, continuing to chew as a genuine smile lifts the corner of his lips. Both of our mouths are so full we can't speak to one another, but it doesn't matter, because when I lean into him, my shoulders shaking at how ridiculous we are, that small show of affection speaks louder than any words I could have shared.

CHAPTER 11
SMALL VICTORIES, BIG HARD-ON (HADES)

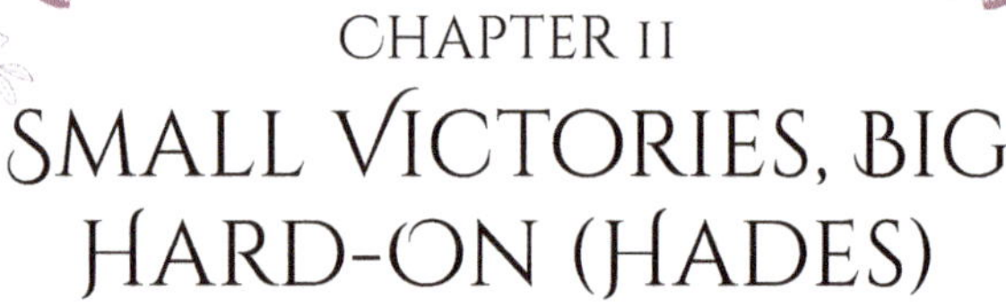

We spend hours in the dining hall, Melody and I, laughing and just enjoying one another's company as we take our fill. We drink red wine, lots of it, and sample the sweet treats, all while nibbling on sliced fruit between each bite of the different roasted meats. By the time we finish, it is very late, and we are both so full that we might have to be rolled out of the dining hall and down the corridor back to our room.

Cerberus entered the dining hall halfway through our meal, and has been enjoying having Melody at the table. Where I would normally make him wait until I was finished, she gained the beast's affections by tossing him scraps from the untouched platters in the center of the table between lulls in our conversation.

She figured if we had not touched it at that point, then we would not eat it, and it should not go to waste, now should it? He was 100 percent behind that logic.

I laugh at the scene before me—Melody sitting with her back straight in her chair while Cerberus, that monstrous beast, sits prettily before her, looking down with his mouth open and whining as he waits for his next morsel. It is ridiculous to see how he dwarfs her in size, only to whimper when she takes too long to toss him the next scrap. Then, when she does, he gorges himself on the bite before simpering. That is right. My three-headed dog, my hellhound, fucking simpers for that woman, and I cannot hold back the guffaw that rumbles from deep in my chest and bursts from my mouth.

"You have ruined him," I say to Melody. She scowls at me and then turns back to Cerberus, running her hand through the wiry hair on his chest. "Look at him! He's going to be so fat, you can forget him roaming the Wastelands between the scales and Elysium. Some guard dog you have turned out to be!" I scoff and the beast ignores me, but his eyes seem to twinkle in amusement as his tongues loll out of his mouths. "Damn traitor."

"Be nice to him," she admonishes, leaning forward and running her cheek across his chest. "You're a good boy, aren't you, baby?" she infantilizes.

"I think I might be sick," I tease.

"Ignore him, Cerberus. He's just jealous, isn't he?" she croons, and the baby talk is just too much. "Yes, he is. So jealous."

The beast's shoulders shake in his version of laughter as he side-eyes me. I roll mine and look away.

"Okay, that is enough for one day. Or the next week, judging from the size of his gut after that smorgasbord. Do you know how bad his farts are going to smell? He is sleeping outside the door, that is for damn sure."

Cerberus lets out a huff, and I am certain he's politicking with Melody to the contrary, but I hold my ground when she sends her pleading gaze in my direction. "Oh, no. Not you too. You can both give me those puppy-dog eyes all you want, but he is not sleeping in our room. I would like to get a wink tonight, and that will not happen with 'Sir Gaseous' in residence. Sorry, boy. It is the hallway or nothing. Your choice?"

Three heads grumble before they turn and walk out the door. He looks back at me only once, harrumphs, and then continues down the hall. His bellow of protest can be heard echoing down the hall as he walks on.

"Look what you did?" Melody points toward the door, disappointment written on her features. "You've broken his heart." She pouts.

"Broken his—you cannot be serious?" I argue. "Are you actually falling for that over-dramatized piece of theater?"

"It's not his fault," she whines.

"No. I agree. It is not *his* fault; it is *yours*."

"Mine?" her voice pitches up before she erupts into a bout of laughter. When her fit finally subsides, she says, "Okay. I'll own it. But if it's as bad as you say. Then yes, his ass is indeed sleeping in the hallway."

"I am glad we can finally agree on something." I offer her a smile, and she stares at me, her eyes transfixed on my mouth. I lick my lips, and goosebumps raise the tiny hairs of her arms, visible beyond the cuff of her robe she has slid back to her elbows. "Are we done here, or would you like something else?"

"I think we're done here," she says, lifting her glass to her lips and draining the contents.

A dribble of wine escapes the corner of her lips, and I reach over, wiping it away with my thumb. She startles from the contact, but I keep my hand there, cupping her chin in my palm. "Time for bed, little one. Shall I carry you, or are you fit to walk on your own?"

"I think I can manage," she says, nuzzling into my hand and kissing the palm. A jolt rushes through me and goes straight to my dick. She does not seem to notice and rises from her chair on shaky legs, stepping toward the door. When she realizes I have not moved from my seat, she stops in the doorway and asks suggestively, "Are you coming, or do I have to offer you *treats* as well to gain your favor?"

"No treats required," I say. "I would follow you without the offer, but I have been known to beg with the right incentive." I rise and meet her at the door, where I take her hand and let her lean into me. "How about we see what it takes for you to have me groveling at your feet, shall we?" I wrap my arm around her shoulder and we make our way down the hall, swaying a little.

It has been a long time since I have been under the influence of alcohol, and perhaps it is just her company that has me giddy, but I am all too keen on finding out where she plans on leading me now that both of our inhibitions are quieted by three jugs of wine.

An hour later in our room, with my big ass on all fours on the rug at the foot of the bed, wearing nothing but a collar with a leash attached to it she has gripped firmly in her hand while she stands naked before me, was not where I saw Melody leading me. And yet, here I am, butt-ass naked and kneeling before her as I wait to see what chaos she has planned now that she has me begging at her feet.

What incentives will she entice me with to continue participating in her role play? Where will she place her hands? Her feet? *Her mouth?* My cock jumps from where he hangs between my legs at the thought of all the things she can do with that pretty little mouth.

Oh, gods. She is going to be the death of me.

She acted so incredibly innocent when she took Cerberus' collar from where it hung next to the mantle above the hearth and asked me if it was his. My brows rose and lips turned up because I thought she couldn't possibly be so drunk she did not know the leash and corresponding collar belonged to him. Boy, was I dumb.

Then, when she slapped the leash across her palm and said, "Mine," asking me if I knew what it was to be *hers* in every way, in any way that she wanted me. Well, I should have known exactly what moment she had been mimicking. If I had, perhaps there would have been an ounce of fear that ran through me instead of an insatiable, pulsing need. But no, I did not put two and two together, forgetting completely about using those same words in a similar interaction with Persephone on the night of our wedding, and *rose* to the occasion for her.

However, the tables are now turned, and Melody is the one holding the leash and saying I am *hers* as she jerks me to and fro. To be honest, it is kind of a fucking turn-on, and I cannot wait to see what she will say, or even better, what she will do, next. She is a playful little minx, and we are just scratching the surface of her depravity, compliments of the wine.

If I had known all it would take to coax this version of her to the surface was several rounds of libations... I would have been cracking open one cask after the other a week ago. Because now, with a look of pure satisfaction on her upturned lips, she is a sight to behold, and I do not dare look away.

With a fire burning brightly in the hearth and sending warmth throughout the room, Melody stands before me with sweat trickling down her neck from the blaze as her dark areolas create a bullseye around each nipple. They stand erect, fascinating me as they beg for me to draw them into my mouth and scrape them with my teeth until she is *wild* and wanton.

Like the nymphs dancing unabashedly before the fire while guided by Pan's flute, I too want to give in to the instinctual— succumbing to Melody's sensual, untamed rhythm. It sings to the primal being within me. The one held at bay solely by the lust swirling in her eyes and sparked in the firelight.

Those eyes seem to flicker and flash an almost electric crimson as I drown in the abyss—pulled far beneath the surface where she will tear that final breath from my lungs. And like a siren with her kiss of death, she will drag me down.

But oh, what a way to die!

I gulp down the anticipation begging to break the surface of her treacherous depths.

Titans, she is so beautiful. Mesmerizing.

Melody takes my breath away as she lords over me with the room awash in that glowing hue. It pulses in time with the thrum of each heartbeat and refracts off of her luminous skin.

My eyes then stray to the nightstand where the heart stone strobes in unison, and I was right in my assumption that the two are linked; Melody and the stone.

It takes everything in me to tear my gaze from its glistening facets and back to her face, where parted lips and a twitching tongue trap me in her thrall once more. I am a servant to her whims as the collar rubs and scratches against me each time my throat works a swallow, and cannot tear my gaze from her full sensuous lips. She exhales as she twists the leash in her palm and pulls me haughtily toward her.

Allowing my body to follow the movement, I fall at her feet, willing to worship the very ground she walks upon. I am hungry for her, practically starved, and crave her touch more than I long to feel the sunlight on my face like I had when I was young, all those many years ago in the mortal realm. Because she is my bright star, burning brilliantly before me as my world goes supernova. And I relish the moment when all that destruction and chaos envelops and draws me toward her center, where we become nothing—scattered through the heavens once we have collapsed from the gravity that is her pull.

CHAPTER 12
TETHERED (MELODY)

I cannot begin to describe the feelings coursing through me as Hades supplicates at my feet. Heat rises from where his lips brush over my toes, kissing me, and buries itself deep within my bones before pooling at my center.

A groan yearns to escape my parted lips, and they curve into an "o" as he trails his tongue over each digit. Then, he pulls my big toe into his mouth and sucks, before stroking the underside of my foot with his tongue.

I knew he was talented from our earlier exploits—the one where he languidly paid homage to my pussy. But now, with him nipping the arch of my foot as he tears a moan from my lips, I am more off-kilter from his attention than I am from balancing on one leg.

The excitement sends a shiver up my spine, and I consider what words to offer as I fight off the giggles threatening to burst free. My control is like that of a fraying strand, pulled taut as the loose thread barely holds me together. Before I snap, and to take my mind off of the overwhelming sensations, I say, "There used to be *something* in the far corner, am I right?"

Hades halts his assault on my arch and pulls his mouth back, peering up at me from where he is sprawled out on the floor at my feet. *Foot.*

"There used to be. Why do you ask?" A brow lifts as one side of his mouth draws up in a smirk, and he lowers my foot to the fur rug.

Relief. Glorious relief greets me as I scrunch my toes into the pelt and feeling returns to my foot. I lift and lower said leg, shaking my toes out.

"No reason," I lie. "I just recall a flash of something in that back corner, and wondered why it's gone."

He leans back onto his haunches and comes to a kneeling position before me with his hands on his thighs. One snakes up, ruffling through the midnight strands curling at his nape, and then he looks over his shoulder toward the area I am referencing. "You mean over there?"

"And the other." He turns his gaze back to me, and I motion toward the front corner with a tilt of my head.

He chuckles. "I guess I did not figure you would be interested in those *somethings,* and had them removed."

"Huh." I hadn't meant for my response to come out as one of disappointment, but it did.

His eyes widen and sparkle with mischief as he stares me down. "Is that so? Well, I have to say, Melody, I never pictured you to be the type to be intrigued by that level of *play.*"

I lick my lips and then lean toward him as I say, "It's like I said, you don't even know me." Then, I lick the tip of his nose, and his eyes go molten.

Silver swirls, circling his irises, before being replaced by that fiery cobalt as he tilts his head. He closes his eyes and leans his head back, his jaw tensing as a whoosh sounds throughout the room.

When he opens his eyes, placed in the far back and front left corners of the room are none other than those *somethings* I asked him about moments before.

My gaze lands on the *chair*, I'm using that term lightly, and then slowly wanders to look over my shoulder to the front of the room.

"And your *toys*?" I continue my line of questioning. "I distinctly remember those as well." I turn my face back to him, biting my lip as flutters and waves fill my stomach.

Excitement and anxiety wash over me as his eyes train on my mouth. I don't take my eyes off him, watching as his pupils dilate, and another whoosh breaks the silence as his *toys* appear on the nightstand next to my ruby.

I hadn't bothered to look at the stone before, but now, as it rests beside all the thingamabobs, whozits, and whatzits galore, which I sing in my head, it pulses erratically, sending fractured crimson bursts of light bounding around the room.

The fractals wash over us and then settle when they are drawn back to the stone. I take a deep breath, and the pulsing subsides.

"I see." He offers nothing further as he rises from the rug and stands before me.

"Are the shackles new?" I ask, pushing the butterflies that rose from my stomach and lumped in my throat back down with a swallow.

"Not exactly," he says, stepping into me. My breasts brush against his abdomen, and my head barely reaches his collarbone. *No fair, you fucking giant!*

Snaking his hand up my body, he brushes over my nipple with his fingertips before circling my throat. He clasps his palm over the column of my neck but doesn't squeeze. He just holds me longingly as he searches my features for... *trepidation? Revulsion?* When he finds none, he says, "Now that I have given you everything you have asked for, what will you do with all of my... *toys*?"

It is not Hades the god who now stands before me, but more like a snarling beast, salivating as he waits to sample his next taste. And I'm not sure who is more anxious at that moment: him because of all the possibilities I've opened up, or me because I have no personal experience with how half of his *toys* are meant to be used.

Forcing back the hesitation creeping up my spine, just like Hades had with the tendrils of darkness in the hallway when it reached the door to the archives, I strengthen my resolve—reinforcing it just like he did with his wards. I swish it away with a wave of my hand, and play off the movement by reaching for him.

I take one hand and lift it above his head. I am too short to reach the top of the bedposts, even on my tiptoes, so I climb up onto the bed to fasten the shackle around his right wrist. Then, shuffling across the bed, I grab his other arm, and stretch him out before wrapping the opposite shackle around his left wrist.

Now, with both hands shackled and arms outstretched, he is in a very compromising position, and I get down from the bed to stand before him.

He is quite a sight—stretched out like the Vitruvian Man—with his impressive cock front and center. My mouth waters, and I long to feel his taste on my tongue. To savor him as I draw moans and whimpers from his lips. That is, if I can even fit my lips around his massive head. My eyes bulge as I circle him and consider his girth.

Shit! Lowering myself to my knees is no good, because even if I stretch my neck as far as it will go, I will only reach the top of his thighs. So, releasing a huff of frustration, I say, "Slight change of plans. I need to swap the shackles."

He doesn't follow my train of thought, and quirks a brow as he side-eyes me.

"Ugh! Just give me a minute, okay. I'm new at this," I grumble, climbing back up onto the bed and releasing one hand from where it is bound. I then move to the other, mirroring my movements, and tap on his shoulder to gain his attention.

He turns to face me, and my breasts are just above eye level as I stand before him. His lips purse as he holds back a chuckle.

"Don't even," I say, grabbing his arm and lifting it so I can once again secure him to the post. "This has gone beyond being sexy at this point, but I am trying here," I groan out as I tighten the shackle, my breasts jostling with every movement of my arms. I then scamper across the bed, struggling not to trip on the furs beneath me, and bind his other wrist to the opposite post.

I wipe my hands together once my task is complete and stand in the center of the bed with my hands on my hips. "There," I say with an air of satisfaction. "Now where was I?"

He doesn't allow the laugh building deep within his chest to rumble free, but I can see the corners of his eyes wrinkling as his lip quivers.

"Asshole," I curse, plopping my ass down onto the bed before flipping around.

I hang my head over the edge, because my thought process was that using the bed would put me at the right height to guide him into my mouth. But even with the advantage it gave me, I am still six inches shy of reaching him comfortably. I frown.

Not giving up, I scurry to the head of the bed and gather two pillows, fluffing them and placing them in front of him. He looks down at them, and then up at me, his lips widening when he understands what I am trying to accomplish. "Points for creativity," he teases.

"Shut it!" I bite back. "If I wanted lip from you, I would sit on your face." I stick my tongue out like the child my perpetual failure is turning me into and then flip onto my back.

Still, I am at the wrong angle, and frustration rises to the surface and rushes from my mouth as I batter the bed with my fists and yell out, "Fucking gods! It shouldn't be this hard just to suck a dick!"

There is no holding back his laughter now, and it bursts free as my anger turns my face several hues of red as I rise to my feet.

Through his cackles, he taunts, "Aww, little one. It was a good effort. But you do not have to—"

"No!" I yell, poking his chest with my finger.

He shakes his head from side to side, a wide grin pulling his cheeks tight as they lift toward his eyes. "If only there were another way?" His tone is anything but helpful as he mocks me.

I slide my finger up from his chest and dig it into his chin before drawing it back to eye level where I flip him off.

"So ladylike," he teases, his shoulders shaking as he blinds me with his toothy grin.

I can't stand looking at him any longer, so I turn away and force him to stare at my back. Then, I plop down onto the bed, crossing my arms as I wallow in my defeat.

"I was trying to be sexy. And if the disparity between our sizes weren't so great, then I would be writhing on the bed as you choke me with your cock right now. But no, it couldn't be that easy, could it?" I whine.

Several minutes of silence pass, and as I am hunched over with Hades at my back, twirling the strands of my hair between my fingers as I have all but given up on my hopes of getting busy with him, I go flying forward.

I do not react quickly enough, and taken by surprise, the force sends me sprawling onto my stomach before someone grabs my ankles and flips me onto my back.

The wind is knocked out of me when I land, and I struggle to release a gasp as my eyes go wide. I strain to focus on who is tossing me around like a rag doll, because it shouldn't be Hades, seeing as he was bound securely to the bed. But sure enough, there he stands in all his glory, a shit-eating grin stretching his lips while his massive cock swings between his legs.

A feral sound escapes through gritted teeth as Hades clamps his hands around my ankles and jerks me to the foot of the bed. My ass slides effortlessly, sending furs and pillows off the bed and onto the floor at his feet.

"I have had about enough of your damn tantrum!" he chastises, wrenching my legs apart with his hands that slide from my ankles up to my inner thighs. "I have been standing here patiently, tortured by the scent of your wanting, and refuse to wait a moment longer. You can hate me if you want to, and curse me until you are blue in the face, but I will have you, Melody. And a disparity in height *or size* will not fucking save you from what I am about to do to your body. You can moan, whimper, scream if you have to. Hell, I would fucking *love* to hear those sounds bursting free. But what I will not tolerate listening to for another god's damned minute is your *fucking complaining!*"

Still shaken up by how quickly he's turned the tables on me, I arch my back as I attempt to shift away from him. He doesn't let me flee, however, and grips the back of my thighs in his hands, pulling me flush against his face.

He buries himself between my legs, burrowing as he searches for my clit. He finds it, and effortlessly pulls it into his mouth where he sucks greedily. His need is at a fever pitch, and he devours me as my legs clench around his head.

I try to wriggle free—to wrench myself from his grip—but he is holding me in place with too great a force, and I am too weak to move him an inch, let alone the several I would need to escape the ferocity of his mouth.

Awash with electric sensations, sparking from where he batters my clit with his tongue to where his fingers fill me deep within my core, I burn uncontrollably. He does not let up, and there is no slower; no gentler. There is only *more. Deeper. Faster. Harder.*

He is feral—positively out of his mind and completely fucking out of control—and I cannot fathom just what the hell he's doing as my body ceases to function.

My head swims, and I am blinded by the starbursts exploding like it is the fucking Fourth of July, as the most exquisite fireworks display flashes before my eyes.

Hades has taken me past close, past the edge. Now he has me rounding second, not stopping at third, and within reach of home plate as his fingers, those unrelenting fingers, piston in and out until my walls are clenching around them. *He's done it! He's stolen home! That's the ballgame, folks, and the fans are in an uproar!*

My mind goes numb, and my entire body follows suit as I let loose every ounce of satisfaction he's been coaxing from me as I douse his cock, the end of the bed, and even the fucking pillows and furs he's resting his knees upon.

He's now drenched, I'm a sopping fucking mess, and my legs are quivering so fiercely while my insides don't know what the fuck just happened as they continue to quake around his slowing digits.

He pulls his fingers free, and what remains of his efforts gushes from my opening and cascades onto the bed, where they join the waterworks that preceded them.

A knowing smile adorns his lips and, with his eyes wild and chest still heaving from the exertion, he lathers my slick up and down my abdomen like lotion. He saturates my skin with my release before trailing it across my breasts, and then crawls up the bed, where he traps me beneath him.

Looming over me, he rasps in my ear, "Those are my fucking orgasms." Then, a growl that is rough and textured—coarse like sandpaper—rubs harshly over my skin as it rumbles free from his chest.

His lips crash onto mine, and he claims them, forcing them to submit as he pulls them into his mouth.

Once he pulls back from my lips, he reaches down, gripping me between my legs. "This is my pussy." *Crash. Devour. Claim.*

He pulls back again, this time smearing his drenched hand over my mouth and painting my lips with my own juices. "My mouth." *Crash. Devour. Claim.*

He spends longer devouring my lips this time, but eventually draws back so he can guide himself to my entrance. "And this is yours," he grinds out when he drives forward, slamming into me until he bottoms out.

The air whooshes out of me, and I moan when he finally draws back, rotating his hips in circles as he paints my insides with the head of his cock. The small circles allow him to touch all the places that have never been adequately tended to by those who lacked not just the skill but the perseverance to see the job done right. And, gods, does it feel *so* right when he pulls mostly out of me and uses his ridge—that notch—that curves itself and rubs right across my G-spot with each shallow pulse.

"Right there," I incoherently mumble as he pulses, holding that depth and maintaining a rhythm that has me drawing my legs to his sides and grasping behind my knees so I can bounce back and forth with each one.

When I am finally so sensitive, and at the point where I can't hold back another release any longer, he barrels into me, burying himself so deep I have no choice but to shatter around him. My walls clench with unyielding force, and he widens, straining as he follows me with an orgasm of his own.

My dam gives way to the surging waters, and it is pure and utter destruction. Nothing is spared, and my torrents carry away not just his release but mine as the deluge ends as a pool on the sheets.

We are coated, sticky, and I am about to recommend a bath, or perhaps a change of linens, when he says, "That is the scent our bed was missing. Now I should go right to sleep."

CHAPTER 13
TAKE A WALK (HADES)

With the scent of pure satisfaction permeating the room and filling my nostrils, compliments of the saturated sheets and moisture trapped in my beard, it happened exactly as I predicted: I fell right to sleep following my romp with Melody. I am a little embarrassed I could not manage a round two, seeing as she was so eager not only to have her way with me but for me to return all my playthings to our chamber. But I did deliver a stellar performance, and there will be plenty of time for me to indulge her when she is better rested.

I was hoping she would follow me into slumberland shortly after I drifted off. But if I did not know any better, I would say she had not slept a wink.

In a disheveled state, with dark circles and pronounced lines beneath her eyes, Melody is sitting upright on her side of the bed when I awake several hours later. Her knees are drawn into her chest, and she twirls a toy from the bedside table absentmindedly in her hands.

She had another nightmare and has been crying again, if the red rimming her eyes and dried tears that left trails down her cheeks are any indication.

I scoot up the bed into a seated position, and, motioning for her to come to me, she does, dropping the toy onto the bed before wrapping her arms around my abdomen. Then, she rests her head in the center of my chest, and I lean down to kiss the top of it. I rub my hand up and down her arm, and she nuzzles into me. "That bad, huh?"

She sniffles. "It wasn't great, by any means." Her words are muffled as she buries her head in the crook of the arm encircling my waist.

"I am sorry, little one. If there were something I could do, anything I could do, you know I would." I continue caressing and she lets out a sigh.

I wish I could cease her torment, or at the very least ease the suffering she has endured because of that *bitch*. I feel powerless to stop the nightmares from coming and robbing her of what should have been the most glorious sleep.

After all the energy she expended during our earlier carnal celebrations, Melody deserves peace, at a minimum when she slumbers if she cannot be afforded any during her waking hours. But alas, she has found it in neither, no matter how hard I have tried, and it is taking its toll. Her face is gaunt—sunken eyes, dullness and pallor— and she looks malnourished. It is not for lack of appetite, seeing as she has eaten everything I placed before her each time we found ourselves in the dining hall. No, her sickly state is in direct correlation, and attributed to the quality of her sleep. *Or lack thereof.*

It has been weeks since she arrived in the Underworld and, despite racking my brain and torturing myself, I am no closer to a solution to the nightmare situation than I was when I first realized what was happening to her. Because in those first few days, she claimed she could not remember what her nightmares were about when pressed. But then, on that fourth night, still rocked by everything she had seen, she pulled back the curtain and gave me some insight into exactly how much Persephone had fucked with her head, sharing each excruciating moment she had been subjected to.

She described to me, in great detail, might I add, Persephone's last hours in the mortal realm before that golden bitch showed up and sucked her soul into the Infinity Stone. I had been there for the tail end of it, but I was not aware of how desperate she had felt in those final moments, or how much she despised me.

Then, she gave me a play-by-play of all the fucked-up shit my ex- got her into while controlling her body, after she escaped the confines of the stone. I have to say, what that parasite unleashed upon the world... Well, she made some of my more sinister punishments in Tartarus look like child's play. Because I am sadistic to a fault, delivering punishments befitting the misdeeds of those I judge. But what Persephone has done—trapping the unsuspecting souls of her victims in the stone—was unwarranted, and even I find her actions repugnant. Perhaps that is only because I feel their souls were rightfully mine and she fucking stole them, or because she is doing her damndest to spite me despite all the time that has passed.

Now, lying with Melody in my arms, I want to take her mind off of all she has seen. I had offered a bit of my backstory when we were in the grotto and I spoke of my first love, but I never got the chance to share the tale. I want to tell her now, but do not know how to broach the subject without it seeming to come straight out of left field.

Looking over at the stone pulsing on the nightstand, I ask Melody to hand it to me. With no question as to why, she rolls off of me, grabs the stone, and places it in my hand before curving back into me.

I twist it in my palm, rolling it back and forth. Her eyes do not leave where the stone glows in my grasp. "The essence that resides within the stone, the one causing it to emit this light, is yours," I say.

"And here I thought it was just a pretty gem you gifted me."

"It is that too," I answer, holding it up and studying it, "but with you, it seems it is so much more than that. It is like the stone holds more than just your essence. Almost like there was a power inside of you that the stone drew into itself, if only in part. When I hold it, the power is faint but familiar. As if I have known a part of you before. And it is not a remnant or echo of Persephone, either. It is something else I have not quite been able to figure out yet."

"Have you done this before? Saved someone with the stone, I mean?"

"I have." I close my fist around the stone, feeling its warmth, and then offer it to her. She takes it and looks at it intently.

"Who did you save?" she asks.

"Remember when I said I had an epic love before?" She nods and looks from the stone up to my face, pulling the heart lovingly to her chest. I lower my gaze to meet hers. "It is a long story, and one I would very much like to share with you, but I feel that words alone will not do it justice. There is a way for me to share the experience with you, but it would require you to see the events through my eyes and walk the road in my shoes. It will be jarring—pulling you into the memory—and doing it in the manner I am proposing could be as disconcerting as the nightmares you have been having."

"How would it work, this memory sharing?" Her eyes widen and her body tenses as she awaits my reply.

"Well, the Mnemosyne, or Waters of Memory, has, as you would call it, magical properties."

She quirks a brow and the tension in her body eases. "Go on."

"Where the waters of Lethe force you to forget, the Mnemosyne allows you to remember. I could share that life, because it was as different a life than the one I now live, with you. I could share those memories, and perhaps then you would understand, if only a little, exactly what you have been thrust into the middle of. Though if I am being honest, I am not entirely sure that the past and what is happening now are related. But there is a good possibility that the reasoning behind it all overlaps."

"Overlaps? Overlaps how?" She shifts off of me and rises to a seated position.

I sigh and then continue. "Well, if I did not know any better, I would say that most of what has come to pass is an attempt to get revenge."

"Revenge? Why would Persephone want revenge? From what I have seen, the chaos was of her own making. At least for the most part."

"And you would not be wrong," I say, "but it is not Persephone who is out for revenge."

"Then who?" She crosses her arms over her chest, the strobing of the stone increasing in brightness with her agitation.

"Calm down, Melody. If you want to know, you have to be willing to do this my way. Are you open to taking this walk with me? You said you wanted to know me. Well, if that is true, then there is no better way to know me than this. You will know me so intimately that you will feel what I felt, see what I saw, and live through what I have done as if you had done it yourself. Like I said, it will be a lot, but I would not offer this if I did not think you could withstand it. And you will not be in any danger, I promise you."

"If you are certain I won't be in any danger..." She is hesitant, but I can tell she wants to do this. "When can we start?"

"Tomorrow," I say. "Spend the day with me, join me while I see to my responsibilities, and then we will go to the Mnemosyne and collect the waters before coming back to the keep. Then, once in our room, I will mix the waters and you will drink the mixture. You will walk through the memory with me while in a dream state. And, like

I said, you will be safe, but once in the dream there is no going back. You will not reawaken until you have seen the memory to its end. Do I have your permission to proceed?"

She nods her head.

"I need to hear you say it, Melody. I need to hear you say that you want to do this. That you are going into this with an open mind and of your own volition."

She hesitates for a moment, once again looking down at the stone and then up at me. "I give you permission to proceed. I want to do this, and I am entering into this agreement of my own free will."

AND SO IT BEGINS (MELODY)

Once we wake in the morning and take care of our personal needs, Hades and I make a quick stop—first to the grotto to bathe and then to the dining hall to eat —before heading back to our room to dress.

It has taken some getting used to—wearing flowing gossamer gowns with ornate golden stitching draped across my body and sandals on my feet—and even now, as Hades stands beside me, wrapping the fabric of his own dark gown up and over his shoulder before affixing the tails at his waist and fastening his pteruges, I can't believe any of this is real. Not these clothes with all their finery, not this place with all its wonders, and not this god who stands beside me with such a powerful aura it takes my breath away.

We walk out of the castle and down the steps with Cerberus at our back as we pass the statues bearing his likeness. I can hear him grumbling behind me, so I turn to see one of his heads baring its fangs as the other two sniff the base of the statue on our left.

"Stop being ridiculous, you big baby," Hades chides, not halting his descent. He reaches back for my hand, and I take his, following behind him as Cerberus lifts his leg and pisses on the statue's feet. "You would think after a mega-annum, he would have grown accustomed to their placement. But no, he still has to assert his dominance over those damn effigies every single time."

I chuckle beside Hades as I step off of the steps and into the courtyard before us, holding in my intrusive thought.

He turns to face me, raising a quizzical brow. "Do I even want to ask?"

"It's nothing," I say, trying to play it off. But once we reach the archway and he pulls open the gates, as we step through my laughter breaks free once more. I choke it down, but not before gaining his attention.

He stops, closing the gate behind us once Cerberus pads through. "Out with it," he sternly orders. "It is obviously more than your human mind can withstand, or you would not be cackling so much."

"I am not cackling," I argue.

"Then what has got you giggling like a toddler running away with something they ought not to have?"

"Do you really want to know?" I tease. "I mean, really, really?"

"If I did not *really* want to know, Melody, then I would not ask. Spill it!"

"Well, I was just imagining *you* having the same reaction to your own carvings in the archway here as Cerberus had to his statues at the base of the steps. And if I see pee staining the foundation stones... well, I am going to lose it."

"You are already losing it," he says matter-of-factly, "as is evident by your childish belief that *I*, of all beings, would need to stoop so low as to pee on something bearing my image, that I placed there in the first place. Pee on the archway, indeed."

Hades doesn't need to scowl down at me because his likeness is doing a good enough job of it from where it sits high atop his throne on the face of each pier. I turn and face away from the gate and take Hades' hand once more as we continue on. But I caught the slight upturn of his lips that proves he is a big fat liar. He sees the hilarity in my imagining, but there is no more grumbling from him, however, only the heavy thuds of his feet that sound with each step as we continue toward the scales.

I can only imagine how I appear as I stand beside Hades' throne not an hour later when the first soul receives its judgement. With my mouth open as wide as the creature expelling scarabs in *The Mummy*, my chin practically rests on my chest while two beings draped in chains with more heads and arms than I wish to count drag a man away toward the group bound for Tartarus. His heels drag, scoring a trail deep in the sand, and his head hangs low as he is escorted to the group milling in the distance.

Escorted. I scoff. I suppose that's a nicer way of saying what they actually did, which is haul him off. The man didn't fight their restraint or scream for mercy; he submitted to the decision and accepted his fate. But finding distaste in the actions of the guards serves no purpose, because I don't have a clue what it is the man did that would warrant such a fate. Even if I had, it is not my place to decide whether his afterlife should be one of peace or an eternity of penance. It is Hades' responsibility to make the ultimate decision, and heavy hangs the crown, as it were.

Once the line has been divided into two groups, one mass is led toward the Wastelands by skeletal guards atop horses black as pitch with tails trailing flames behind them, and the other group is chained together by the Hecatoncheires, as Hades informed me the beings with many arms and heads are called, lashing them toward Tartarus.

One horse remained, however, standing patiently at the base of the steps leading up to the throne, and Hades motions for me to descend. I step to the base, and wait for Hades, who, when he reaches the bottom, calls for Phlox, which apparently means *flame* and is the name of his horse.

The steed stomps its front hoof impatiently, and Hades takes the reins before calling me to him. I move to his side, and he lifts me up enough so I can slide my foot into the gargantuan horse's stirrup, slinging my leg over his broad back.

Once I am seated, Hades takes his mount, squishing me between his arms when he crowds behind me on the saddle. Then, he taps back with his heels and the horse lurches forward, sending me bouncing off his chest. "Careful," he says. "This road is bumpy, but others have found it enjoyable."

I stiffen in his arms. "I am quite familiar, thank you," I grit out. "Though I must admit, even though I have her memories, I could do without the reminder of the intimacies you shared."

"Now, Melody, is that an air of jealousy I detect?"

"I am not jealous," I state firmly, "but comparing me to her is not the way to gain my affections."

We are silent after that, taking up the rear and trotting behind the group bound for Tartarus.

Not more than what seems to be twenty minutes later, after watching a volcanic structure deep within Tartarus grow larger and erupt behind a great wall in the distance, we dismount before the gates. The wall reaches high to the ceiling, a gilded structure of intertwining bones and skulls, and the golden connective sludge, because that is what it appears like to me, bubbles and boils like heated tar.

It oozes between the skeletal remains, trapping what writhes together, and creates the barrier separating the Wastelands from the land of torment beyond.

The group awaiting entrance shifts anxiously as Hades and I step before the gates, where three snakes undulate in a serpentine motion.

Around the center locking mechanism of the gate, one head extends from the surface and faces Hades and me. He lifts his hand in greeting, and it runs its scaled head across his palm lovingly before turning to look at me.

Pierced by a slitted gaze, I stand unable to move as the snake's tongue flips out, tasting the air.

"Be nice, Anástasia," Hades grumbles beside me, taking my hand. "She will not hurt you," he says to me, lifting my hand toward her head ever so slowly. "She only wants to get to know you. If it makes you feel any better, Persephone was so terrified she refused to touch her."

"It's a she?" I ask, unable to stop the quiver in my voice. "And how is knowing Persephone was just as fearful, if not more so than I am, supposed to make me feel any better?" I squeak, closing my eyes when Anástasia flicks her tongue in front of my outstretched fingers. Then, I feel her cool scales as she brushes against my fingertips. "She's so cold," I utter softly when I finally get the courage to open my eyes and speak.

As I focus on the slitted eyes gazing intently at me, they seem to peer deep within, pulling whatever essence I have left to the surface. Then, out of the corner of my eye, I see movement, and as I shift my stare, two more heads come off the gate toward me.

"Hades?" I plead, the fear causing my voice to pitch up.

"Settle, Melody. They will taste your fear."

"Taste it? I'm sure they can fucking smell it permeating from me, because I am all but shitting myself." My voice warbles as my lip trembles. "Nice gigantic snake ladies," I soothe.

"Not ladies in the physical sense, but they are female, and the guardians of the gates. Only by appeasing them will they permit us entrance."

"And we do that, how?" I squeal again, squeezing my eyes shut as yet another head flicks its tongue in my direction. When I feel more scales, I open my eyes, and now two heads butt off of one another as they fight over who gets to touch me.

Hades extends his hand, gaining the interest of all the snakes, and turns his palm upward toward Anástasia. Her elongated fangs drip with an opalescent viscous fluid, and she pierces his flesh with them.

As Anástasia takes her fill, licking the ichor that beaded on his puncture wounds, those same silvery swirls, like the ones I have seen so many times in Hades' eyes, circle her vertical pupils. They flicker and flash with power, and when she finally releases him, he takes a drop of the venom from one fang and lathers it over the puncture wounds. They seal closed, leaving no sign of her assault.

Hades huffs beside me. "Huh." It is not a question, just his exasperation breaking the silence. "Have I done something wrong?" he asks the snake when the gates remain locked.

Anástasia nods her head as one of the other snakes slithers over her toward us. She opens her mouth, showing her fangs, and Hades offers his wrist once more.

The new snake shakes her head in opposition and then turns her attention to me. "Wha—" I stammer. "What does she want?"

"Not me, apparently. Though they have never required appeasement from another so..." He doesn't finish his sentence. And judging from the look on his face, he is just as perplexed as I am.

"They can't want me, can they? I mean, what could I possibly have that would appease—"

Hades grabs my hand, cutting off my babbling, and thrusts it toward the new snake. Her tongue flicks over me, almost touching the curve of my wrist, and then she sinks her teeth into me.

I cry out from the shock of being pierced by fangs, but it doesn't hurt, not really. I watch the snake's eyes as they swirl, but the color of the power that clouds her vertical pupils is crimson. It wisps and billows across the surface, making her eyes look empty.

Her eyes flash once, and when she releases, I do just as Hades had and swipe some venom off her fang to soothe the wound on my wrist. It seals.

Looking at Hades, I ask, "Well, now what?" Just then, before he answers, the snakes disappear into an outcropping of rocks, and the locking mechanism clanks when the bolt slides free.

He is about to grab hold of the grotesque handle—a gilded skull with the spine still attached—when Hades turns to face me. He motions toward the gate. "Would you like to do the honors?"

"Me?" I squeak. "Hard pass. Bones don't gross me out or anything, but touching them is not a habit I want to get into."

Hades chuckles, and as he is grabbing the handle, he smirks and says, "I distinctly remember you wanted the opportunity to handle my bone quite vigorously earlier." He wrenches the gate open, and I glare at him. Then, a gust of hot air blasts me in the face when I step beside him. He says, "After you," before placing his hand on my lower back.

I step past him and into the fiery beyond.

CHAPTER 15

OUT OF TARTARUS AND INTO ELYSIUM (HADES)

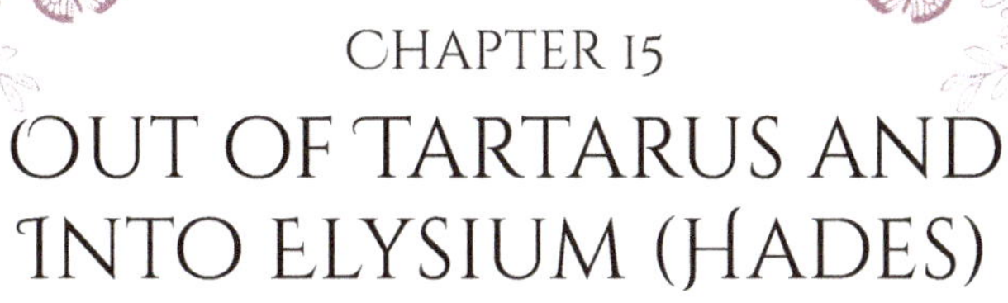

I cannot tear my eyes from Melody as she takes in everything that is Tartarus. The group of impenitents were pulled through the gates behind us and now stand wide eyed along with her as the wails and sorrows of those receiving their punishments greet us like some botched chorus. It is one where everyone is out of tune, and the ominous sound has the mass huddling together, grasping onto one another in fear as Melody presses into my side.

Heat from the fires raging everywhere makes all our bodies slick with sweat, and an errant bead slides down Melody's neck. I watch it with rapt fascination, and lick my lips when I remember just how good she tasted the night before.

Her flavor, which coated the tip of my tongue with every masterful swipe, was decadent like salted caramel, but there was also a hint of something *more*. Something that almost hummed from deep within her and sent electrical shocks sparking along the edges of my tastebuds. *Power*. God's power, to be exact.

Unsure of how God's power came to dwell within the essence of a mortal, it is time I get to know Melody better. She had said she wanted to know me, and we are on the cusp of taking the steps to do just that, but what was *her* life like before me? I need to know everything there is to know because, judging by the reaction of the guardians of the gates, I am not the only one who senses that *something more* within her. Not to mention how keen the Algea were to get their claws on her. There is something ancient, something that has been awakened since her death, but at this point, I know not what that is.

After an hour of walking through the depths of Tartarus and depositing my newest tenants, Melody looked on as I saw to the punishments of my most notorious condemned ones: Kairos, Hitler, and too many others to name.

She did not wince or look away when I doled out their punishments as I thought she would, and even stood at my back, tapping my shoulder to halt an errant play during my chess match with Adolf.

I will never forget the scene he caused—slamming his hands on the table before tossing the board to the ground. He cursed aloud, then stood and continued his tirade while flailing his arms about in a flamboyant fashion. It was rather unbecoming. Then, he straightened his top and tightened his belt, ending his adjustments by slicking his hair back.

Unfortunately for him, with the board toppled, that means the game is at its end and he will now be subjected to hours upon hours of excruciating pain instead of the several hours reprieve he often got during one of our normal matches.

As we walk away, Melody asks out of the corner of her mouth, "Was he speaking Spanish?"

"A dialect of it, why do you ask?"

"So much for the superiority of Germany, I guess." She clasps her hand over her mouth as if she thinks I will scold her.

"Don't be embarrassed, Melody. If anyone should be embarrassed…" I point over my shoulder, and she shakes her head.

"Still, I can't get over the Spanish. Did he learn it here?"

I am unable to hold back my laughter at her bewilderment, and as we walk on I explain. "Most people think he died by suicide, but the reality is he hid out in Argentina until the end of his days. Speaking German would have been a dead giveaway, so he learned not only to speak Castellano but Italian, seeing as there is a large Italian immigrant population in Buenos Aires and Córdoba."

"Well, that explains the tropical shirt and the khakis." Again she laughs, and I join in beside her. Once we stop laughing, she asks expectantly, "Where to next?"

"Now to Elysium. We will head back through the gates, and Phlox will take us across the meadows. It will be pretty at this time of day, and we should be done a little before sunset. That sight is the one I have been looking forward to showing you the most," I admit. "The way the gold seems to sparkle as it reflects through the reeds of the tall grasses is extraordinary."

"I can't wait," she says, placing her hand in mine and squeezing, "but seriously, that Kairos guy: is he ever going to get released? Because honestly, don't you think he has suffered enough, seeing as it wasn't really his fault, and all?"

"Tell me how you really feel?" I quip, squeezing her hand.

She drops mine. "I just told you how I really feel." Crossing her arms, she stares at me with a look that says, *I am not moving another inch until we discuss this*.

"My dearest Melody, would it please you if I allowed Kairos to pass into Elysium?"

"No, you'll have to do one better than that. Strike all those years of torment from his memory. You offered it to me because of the shit she put me through. Now do it for him." She points back behind us and then drops her arms to her sides.

"I suppose I could do that, if you wish it."

"Promise?" She pouts.

"How can I deny that face?" I say, reaching up and squeezing her cheeks until she bats my hand away. "I promise." I motion crossing my heart, and she reaches for my hand once I am done.

As we ride across the Wastelands, I finally gather the courage to broach the topic of Melody's past. I mention her roommate and the relationship they had, and she explains that when her mother died, Desire was the only connection, the only family, she had left in the world.

"What was your mother like?" I ask.

"My mother? It's hard to explain. She's hard to explain," she offers.

Something changes in her demeanor, and I am hesitant to press further, but I need to know, so I continue. "How so?"

"Well, she never spoke of my father. In fact, anytime I brought him up, she changed the subject." She leans back into me and looks off into the distance. "She would say that he wasn't a part of our lives, so he didn't deserve the effort to consider him. I always took her response as one from someone for whom the wounds were still fresh. But I did some digging after she passed, and it turns out my mother's aversion to the topic was not because she was a jilted lover."

I am taken by surprise when she laughs. It is unstable—distorted—and I prompt Phlox to stop to take in her state.

Through her laughter she says, "My mother, apparently, was not my mother, and her ex-husband, whom I never met but always assumed, was not my father." She sighs and then wistfully says, "So all those years of questions, and searching for something of myself in her features, and vice versa, were for nothing. Because, even though she was the only mother I'd ever known, she was not the one who gave birth to me."

"I'm sorry, Melody. That is a difficult realization to come to, especially once the one person who could answer any questions on the matter is already gone."

"You think?" she scoffs. "But I am not angry at her for not telling me." She shakes her head from side-to-side as if to brush off her frustration, and I prompt Phlox to walk on. Then she sniffs, and I realize she is crying. "Honestly, I get it, but there were so many opportunities for her to come clean. And it's not like I was going to go searching for this mystery woman," she says with a hint of derision, wiping away the errant tear.

"Still..." I pause, unsure what I can say that will ease the tension. "So you were adopted then?"

She nods her head.

"Were you able to find out *anything* about your birth mother?"

"Nope," she answers flatly. "It was a closed adoption. No notes."

We ride on in silence then, but it isn't until we crest a ridge and the meadows lie before us, that Melody finally lets out a sound. She gasps, and as I pull her tighter against my chest, I say, "Welcome to Asphodel Meadows."

Her mouth remains open as she takes in the swaying grasses and fields of wildflowers that grow as far as the eye can see. Then, in the distance, I point out the large oak that lies in the heart of Elysium.

"I've seen that tree," she admits.

"From one of her memories?"

"Yup."

"A good one?"

"Not exactly."

"Care to tell me about it?" I ask, trying not to sound too eager.

She slumps forward and shifts her hips, adjusting her seat before leaning into me again. "There was a woman standing there at the base of the tree," she says, pointing toward the oak. "She introduced herself as Erymanthe, I think," her voice wavers. She squints, staring off into the distance as if trying to zero in on the memory.

"She was obviously not the oracle Erymanthe," I say, my irritation seeping into my tone.

"No, not Erymanthe. Though I am not sure why the façade since you *obviously* felt her presence."

"Remember that too, do you?"

She nods again. "Let's just call it a vibe I got from your dealings with Persephone that day."

"What else do you recall about the interaction?" I press.

"Well, she's the one who told Persephone how to use the Infinity Stone, and how to unlock it. But as we both know, she did not relay everything."

"Persephone did seem taken aback when Aphrodite appeared at her end and trapped her within the stone."

"I got that feeling too, but there was more to it than that. Persephone said for her to *do it already*, as if she expected something to happen. But as it was happening... I mean, as I saw the memory of it happening, Persephone didn't know what was coming, only that the stone would be her way to freedom."

"I suppose Aphrodite was half right, because she was indeed free of me." I laugh, but it is forced through clenched teeth. "But I guess she found herself trapped in another way."

Melody cannot see the war waging inside me—the anger burning within. "It's not funny, Hades. I feel for her, if only because she was led astray. Manipulated. Everything else... well, fuck her," she grits out.

I wrap my arms around her, if only to offer the comfort they seem to bring her. She kisses the one she leans on.

"Enough about Persephone," she says, tilting her head to look up at me. "Tell me about Adonis." I stiffen, and she can feel my hold tighten around her. "If it's too difficult…"

"No. No, it is okay. I am very much looking forward to introducing you to him. But first we gather the waters from the Mnemosyne and then we stop by the temple. Once we are done with all that, then you can learn everything there is to know about my first love."

We stop briefly at the banks of the Mnemosyne to gather a vial of the waters, which is rather anticlimactic, and then depart Elysium just as the sun is cresting the hill. Sinking in the distance, it paints the sky with dominant reds and yellows, while the purples and blues seek to announce the emergence of the stars. As their twinkling high above becomes more pronounced, we gallop back toward the scales, following the bend of the river.

Once we reach the crossing, we slow, passing over the land bridge and making our way to the temple. The guards take Phlox' reins at the base of the steps, leading him back to the stables, while we ascend and announce our arrival.

CHAPTER 16

TEMPLE OF THE GATEKEEPER (MELODY)

Stepping through the entry columns and into the temple, which is constructed exactly how I imagined the temples of Ancient Greece to be—with a rectangular layout and a central sanctuary—we are greeted by a loud shrill shout. "No. No. No. You are doing it all wrong. Not only have we talked about this, but I have shown you!"

A woman answers forlornly, and I can hear her voice echoing in the distance, "I am sorry. I must have forgotten."

We walk along the left wall of the temple and step between two columns into the main chamber. Before us, a figure wearing an ornate chiton pulls a woman in a billowy gown up to a dais and points at an altar beside the marble throne.

Where the statue of a god or goddess would normally sit, the throne sits empty, and the figure, who I assume is Charon, moves and repositions an offering bowl, chalice, and a golden platter atop the altar. Incense burns all around us, sending smoke billowing upward where it gathers along the ceiling like cumulus clouds.

"Like this," an annoyed Charon says. "I swear, if you were not the only attendant I have had in eons, I would send you away." He places his hands on his hips and shakes his head in disbelief.

"And here I thought you were happy to have her," Hades announces beside me.

Charon startles, turns his attention toward us, and then a wide smile pulls his cheeks taut. "Well, well. Look what the hellhound dragged in." He throws his arms wide, sending the billowing sleeves of his himation behind him. "Come."

As I stand quietly beside Hades, taking in the scene, I jerk my hand forward when a wet something coats my palm. Looking behind me, I see Cerberus sitting pretty, tongues lolling as he awaits my attention. He dwarfs me, even while seated, and I step forward, raising my hand so I can scratch under his chins. One after the other, until each head has been acknowledged, I dig my fingers into Cerberus' scruff and his eyes close. "I see you chose to grace us with your presence," I coo.

Cerberus snorts, his central head shaking off my affections, and then he steps to my side. Now I am caged between two powerful beings, and the unease of being in a new place that caused a lump to form in my throat dissipates as I swallow it down.

"Nice to see you again," Charon offers, stepping off the dais and moving toward us. Once he reaches us, he stands before me and takes my hands. He is tall, not quite the height of Hades, but at least a head and a half taller than me. He spins me around as he says, "You are looking well, my dear. How are you feeling? Better, I hope?"

I look over and up at Hades. "Today has been a good day," I admit, offering him a smile before turning to face Charon once more.

"This sapphire is a very becoming color on you." He wiggles his eyebrows. "Care for a glass of wine, my dear? I have an amphora from Chios that is to die for." He chuckles, and I do my best not to roll my eyes at his pun.

"I would love a glass. Minus the death, of course." I raise a brow as I offer him a genuine smile.

Charon steps to my side and places a heavy hand on my shoulder as he ushers me toward the dais. Hades and Cerberus follow behind us, and I sneak a glance back to make sure they are still there. Not that I don't trust Charon, but there is just something about him, or something in this temple, that has the hairs on my arms raising.

Once we reach the altar, the woman Charon was grumbling at before, who disappeared to the back of the temple, arrives with what I assume is an amphora in her hands. She grips the two vertical handles of the black and terracotta container, and the image of one of Hades' horses rearing up on its hind legs is drawn on the side.

Ornate repeating patterns mark the base of the belly and neck of the jar, their bold lines and swirls drawing my eyes. The woman sets the jar down on the altar, and Charon lifts a small jeweled knife from where it was placed beside the platter. It is gold; the jewels are a deep cobalt, and with one continuous slice, he cuts the wax around the stopper. It sounds with a *pop* when he wiggles it loose.

When I step closer, I am greeted by the sweet scent of wine as it permeates the air. There are notes of honey and spice when Charon pours a generous amount into the chalice, and he offers it to me.

I savor the aroma before taking a small sip, and hold the wine in my mouth, sliding my tongue along the back of my teeth before I swallow. "It's so good," I almost moan. "I have never tasted anything like it."

"Nor shall you," Charon gloats. He follows his response with a huff as he steps aside and motions for Hades to join us.

· · ·

After several hours and three amphorae of wine later, my head swims as I walk on wobbly legs. The giggles have set in, and they are excessive; involuntary. So, with Lenore at my side, her hip bumping against mine as we step off of the dais and down the steps, I am anything but steady.

"Come, my lovely," she says once we reach the base, grasping my hands in hers while she walks backward in front of me. The world blurs when she spins us like a fucked-up version of *Ring Around the Rosie*, and our skirts wrap around our ankles as we spin faster and faster. We fall down, crumpling onto one another in a pile of sapphire and cream fabric.

Hades sits high atop the throne in the center of the dais, holding the chalice, and Charon leans back on his elbows with his legs extended on the marble bench to his right. They are watching us, smiles lifting the corners of their lips, and I can't help but stare at my god, my King of Death, my Hades as my chest heaves from the exertion.

His eyes meet mine, staring so intently it is like he is peering deep within and knows what I am thinking. He licks his lips, and the kaleidoscope of butterflies that has taken up residence in my stomach flutters around and bumps off of my ribcage imprisoning them. My heart is so full, and every minute, hour, day, spent with him has been the greatest of my life. Or death, as it were.

Once the giggling subsides, and once I have regained some semblance of control over my body, I sit up, pulling Lenore with me. Then, as if bitten by something, she jumps to her feet with a gasp. She wiggles her hand, grasping her wrist as she stares at me in awe.

"What is it?" I ask, my full attention on her.

"I... I had an idea," she stammers. "How would you like to learn a dance?"

I'm an okay dancer, but I highly doubt the type of dance she wants to teach me is anything like what I am used to. I hesitate, and she grabs my hands, pulling me to my feet.

Lenore jerks me forward, and I stumble into her. She grabs my shoulders and stares into my eyes. "Wait here."

Like a statue, I am rooted in place, and Lenore ascends the steps before crossing the dais. She stands before the altar and then lifts the ceremonial knife before descending the dais again, looking over to ensure that Hades and Charon are deep in conversation and paying her no mind.

Once she descends and reaches me, she takes my right hand and quickly slices across my palm. I gasp, and my eyes widen when she does the same to her own. With both of our right palms oozing, she drops the knife to the temple floor with a clang, and then crosses her wrists in front of her. Blood trickles down my fingers, and a drop lands on the marble floor where it sizzles.

"What the—"

I look to Lenore, and she nods, so I mimic her motions, crossing my wrists. Then, she takes my hands, and a zap of electricity heats my right palm before running up my arm. Now, it could be because I am beyond drunk, but if I didn't know any better, I would say that our hands glowed where our sliced palms met.

I try to pull away, but Lenore squeezes harder. "I will chant as we dance, and once you learn the ode, we will combine in harmony. Can you do that?" Her voice is soothing, and I am entranced by the tone that vibrates and dings like ringing handbells, echoing in my ears.

Nervous, my eyes scan the temple to where Charon and Hades are still visiting atop the dais. They are ignoring us, and Lenore squeezes my hand, bringing my attention back to her. Then, she begins to recite.

*Her daughter is the key. The seed who yearns to be sown
so that she can burst forth from the earth and yield a
crop of plenty. Her power will abound, and there will
be none to strike her down.*

I listen as she repeats one more time, and then we incant, our voices entwining in a melodic chorus. We go through the words once, twice, my head falling back and a smile dressing my lips as we spin faster and faster. The world seems to corona; the diffraction ringing around us and filling the chamber in an almost mauve-like glow.

"What are you doing?" Hades bellows, but I can't find him as everything swirls around us. "No!" I hear him yell.

Then, my ankles cross, and I trip, sending both Lenore and me hurtling toward the floor where we land in a pile of heaving flesh. My head pounds, and the butterflies in my chest swarm in a frenzy as they try to burst free. But instead of my ribs cracking to release them, my head falls back and my mouth goes wide, a burst of power escaping.

As I look upward, a rabble of erratic wing beats, trailing the mauve-colored light in a stream behind them, scatter in every direction as they attempt to escape the confines of the temple. I can hear a cacophony, alarm bells ringing in my head as roars sound in the distance.

My head lolls to the side, and I see Hades standing at the top of the steps of the dais, his arms extended high above him, as the word *no* comes out in a lower pitch. It is stretched, and everything that happens next seems to do so in slo-mo.

Heat fills the surrounding chamber as cobalt flames shoot from Hades' fingertips, shattering each fluttering wing like glass when they are scorched. The remnants hang in the air, floating as they send several shades of red and pink prismatic light filtering through the aftermath. They drift to the floor, and their light goes out as they accumulate in heaps on the cool marble of the temple.

My head is woozy, but I force myself into a seated position and look over at Lenore. She is passed out, but the young woman with golden ringlet curls who danced with me moments before is now old and withered, her once gilded strands a gleaming white with smatterings of silver that frame her face. She looks so peaceful as she sleeps, but the atmosphere in the temple is anything but.

Rage has charred the flesh from Hades' face and shoulders, his sloughed skin reforming over the gilded bones that peek through. I struggle to focus on him as he descends the steps, and stops at my side. I reach for him.

Turning back, he yells at Charon, "Get her out of here."

"I..." Charon is dumbfounded. "As you wish," he says, bounding down from the dais and calling for the guards, who drag Lenore to the back chamber of the temple.

I feel weightless as Hades lifts me effortlessly, holding me tightly against his chest while Charon looks on with fear. There was so much before. So much power. So much love filled me, but in an instant, now there is nothing. No butterflies and no... purpose.

"You will find out what in the Titans' name that was!" Hades shouts.

"Right away." Charon supplicates and then runs from the room to the back of the temple where the guards dragged Lenore.

The cacophony that sounded before—the roaring—has ceased, and what had been terror is nothing but worry as it crinkles between Hades' brows.

Two more guards run into the temple and yell to Hades that the Algea have been contained. He nods his head in affirmation and then looks down at me. "So much trouble for one so small," he says, running his fingers across my cheek. "I think that is enough excitement for one day. You should rest, and I should get you safely back to the keep."

I say nothing. I just burrow my head into his chest, allowing the warmth of his body to comfort me because I feel so hollow.

CHAPTER 17

GODDESS OF THE ROSE (HADES)

Back at the keep, I take Melody to our room and set her on her side of our bed. I brush my fingers across her forehead, swiping the errant strands off of her face, and lean down to place a soft kiss on her temple. Then, I look down at her nightstand, where her ruby no longer strobes with her essence, but glows brightly as if a trapped star resides within. I pick it up, and it singes my hand, so I drop it onto the bed.

Melody picks up the stone and holds it lovingly to her chest as she says, "Well, that was something."

I reach out to touch the stone, and she clasps it tighter. The torches on the wall flare, drawing my attention, and I pull my hand back.

"That would be an understatement," I grumble. "That was careless, Melody." I purse my lips in disapproval.

"Careless?" She sits upright, drawing her shoulders back. "How do you figure?"

"Just what did you think you were doing?"

"Me?" Her tone is accusatory. "As if I had any clue that would happen. What about you‽ You could have stopped whatever *that* was if you weren't so *enraptured* by whatever Charon was saying."

"So this is my fault‽" I huff in irritation. "Melody, I swore to protect you, but I cannot do that if you start performing rituals with some defunct priestess of Aphrodite, now can I‽"

"How was I supposed to know *who* or *what* she was‽ It's not like you told me. In fact, you barely share *anything* with me."

I pinch the bridge of my nose, hoping to ease the tension headache building. "I am about to share so much with you, you will be sick of me."

"And what if I am already *sick* of you?" she throws out casually, her tone unaffected.

"Are you? Sick of me? Have you changed your mind about me, *about us*? Say the words, Melody. Because if you have, I need to know now before we go any further."

"No, you promised!" she implores.

"I very well may have, but if you no longer wish to be here, then it would be wrong of me to impart you with that knowledge."

"Why‽"

"Because then I would have to wipe your memory before sending you back." I reach for the stone once more.

"Back?" she asks, pulling the stone away from me, and the torches spark violently. "Who said I wanted to go back? I thought I couldn't?" She tilts her head, assessing me, then looks down at the stone. The sparks subside, and the torches go back to their original state.

"You should not. *I* should not. That is against the very nature of my responsibility. Souls come in, but they do not go out. It has always been this way."

"It's happened before," she retorts.

"What, with Eurydice? Yes, but with great consequence. Are you willing to pay that price? I know I am not. Nor am I willing to subject you to that torment."

"You say that like living is a torment," she rebuts.

"For one that has crossed the river, it is."

She huffs and slouches down in the bed, banging her head on the pillow. She sinks further, but does not draw her eyes from the stone. "Let's just get on with it," she says forcefully.

"Are you certain?"

She nods.

I pull the waters of the Mnemosyne from my waist pouch and set it on the nightstand beside us. "To get you to the right memory, I need to start with some details." I call a sleeping draft from the chest in my archives, and it appears in my hand. I set it beside the waters. "As I speak, I want you to visualize the scene. I will do my best to describe it, but your mind will draw you in and keep you there. Understood?"

She nods again.

"I need to hear that you understand." My tone is harsh, but I do not mean to be, so I rub my hands up and down her thighs. "You will fall into a deep sleep and walk through my memories as if in a dream."

"I understand," she says. "I still want to do this." She removes one hand from the stone and lays it on mine, squeezing. "All of it."

I lift her hand to my lips and brush a kiss over the surface before I begin.

"One hundred years after the imprisonment of the Titans, in a time of transition for not only the mortal realm but for the gods residing within Olympus, I finally accepted an invitation to one of Aphrodite's infamous *gatherings*," I tell her. "She had been sending me invitations, year after year, since her affair with her brother Ares had been disclosed by her husband. In the most scandalous fashion, the affair and the birth of her children with Ares was brought to light for all the gods to see and mock her, but she felt no shame because her husband was never of her choosing—a common theme with marriages of the gods. My eventual marriage to Persephone notwithstanding."

I continue my story-like recollection while Melody sits listening with bated breath. "Hephaestus was the lame son of my sister Hera, who was forcibly married to Aphrodite by Zeus to quell the constant squabbling between the gods seeking her hand. And since the affair, her husband had spent as much time apart from her as he could. So, finding herself lonely, she started throwing lavish gatherings where gods and mortals alike would be in attendance. From what I had heard, they were quite the *affair* and full of lasciviousness—another common theme amongst the gods."

"So, gods be fucking," Melody not so eloquently says.

"Exactly," I offer. "Often held in the Garden of Hesperides, a location to spite Hephaestus' mother, Aphrodite would throw day's long events filled with inebriation and promiscuity. All the predatory gods would be in attendance, and mortals seeking divine favor would offer themselves up as the *entertainment*. It was not my idea of fun, but being burdened by death was not either, so I finally chose to attend."

"And how did that go?" she asks as I stand.

I mill about our room, mixing the waters of the Mnemosyne with the sleeping draft. "As good as one could expect," I say, pursing my lips as I look over my shoulder to where she now sits cross-legged on the bed. Her skirts are bunched up, exposing her long tanned legs, and the fabric billows around her, looking like a cloud of sapphire.

"So that's where you met Adonis?"

I nod my head. "The first of many," I say, downheartedly.

"I bet it was chaos," she says.

"I do not think there is a better way to describe it. It was absolute pandemonium. At least for me." I swish the concoction together, and then walk to the side table on the other side of the room and grab a glass.

Pouring the contents inside, I sniff the sulphur-smelling liquid before walking back to the bed. I set the glass on the nightstand, and then push Melody to the center of the bed, laying down next to her.

"Now what?" She lies back beside me.

"Now we wait, and I continue my tale." I clasp her hand in mine at our sides, while her other hand holds her ruby over her heart.

She rolls her eyes. "Okay," she draws out, her tone impatient.

"This will take long enough, little one. No need to rush it."

"Says the man who has been here forever."

"Thank the Titans that you do not know the half of it."

She kisses my shoulder. "I will at least know some of it after this." She nuzzles my arm, and I slide mine under and around her.

"Where was I? Oh, yes. The *party*."

Melody closes her eyes, and I continue. "One party was for Thargelia, and there were numerous others for Noumenia. The first one was in late-spring. It was a time when the sun drifted toward the horizon and the rose garden was in full bloom. The nymphs and Ladon were in an uproar because Aphrodite's guests, and by guests I mean other gods, kept luring them away from the golden apple tree. And by the time I arrived that evening, the tree was looking rather... *sparse*."

"No better way to piss off your mother-in-law than by destroying what she holds dear," Melody quips.

"You mean besides humiliating her son?"

"That too. Gods, I can just imagine Hera plotting her revenge." In a loud voice, one several octaves lower than her own, she announces, "God versus god cage match."

I chuckle and then say, "Yes. The Parthenon would have been

filled to the brim for that pairing, and Athena would have been beside herself."

"What were the gods like back then?" She opens her eyes and lifts them to mine.

I stare back, and scrunching my brows in consternation, I say, "Callous, vengeful beings. You think Medusa was a monster? She had nothing on the Olympians." My tone drops as I say, "And then there was me." The gravity of my statement causes me to wince.

She reaches up and brushes her fingertips across my brows, evening them out. "You're not a monster, Hades." She moves her hand to my cheek.

"Save that sentiment until after you see the memory. Then we will revisit your thoughts on the matter."

"Monstrosity is born of trauma and abuse. I'm guessing you were victims of both." Her thumb runs along my lips.

"And then some," I admit, reaching up and taking her hand, entwining our fingers together as I lower our arms to our sides.

"Don't place so much value in the opinions of others," she offers. It is a bold statement, but I do not discount her words. "Only trust what you know to be true in your heart."

"Well, this story has that in spades."

"Has what?" she asks.

"My heart. And that evening I ignored my better judgement and fell victim to the whims of that same heart. But we will get to that. You see, by that time I had already heard of Adonis. Rumors had been echoing for months about Aphrodite's obsession, and even in the Underworld you hear things. So, when I got the latest invite, I went to see what all the fuss was about. It is not like Aphrodite and I had ever been friendly by any stretch of the imagination, nor did she expect me to come. So, when I appeared, sneaking up on where she stood high on the hill overlooking the gardens, with a very pissed off dragon flying in the distance, she was less than enthused."

"A freaking dragon?" Melody's eyes go wide, and she shakes her head.

"Another guardian of the tree," I explain. "With so many gods in the garden, she could not differentiate one presence from the next, so I could have gone unnoticed. I had already done so for hours while I watched naked bodies touching, tasting, writhing..."

"Sucking and fucking. I get the picture," she adds.

"Precisely. The one smart thing the gods did, however, was not offer any of the apples to the *entertainment.*" I wiggle my brows.

"Why is that?"

"Because the apples offered eternal youth and beauty."

"Immortality," she breathes.

"Desecrating a garden is one thing, but turning hundreds immortal would have been the beginning of something much worse. But I am getting off topic."

"You were walking through the gardens..." she rambles, twirling her finger.

"Right. So after I saw her meandering through the throng, blowing kisses to her fanatics, and caressing arching backs as she passed, she positioned herself above it all on a makeshift dais in the center of what she called her *menagerie.* All her little gilded hummingbirds flitted about, never truly resting as they sampled this nectar and then that one. Gorging themselves until they burst time and time again."

"Gilded?" she enquires.

"She painted the mortals in gold. It made them feel honored—special. But there were handprints and smudge marks on every bare piece of flesh, and many of the mortals died when their bodies over-heated from the paint. Her gatherings led to an uptick of souls in my realm, and that is why I had to go see things for myself. I don't get involved in the affairs of the living, but seeing her misdeeds through the eyes of the dead... Well, let us just say I was heated."

"So it wasn't mere curiosity that had you there?"

"Not just curiosity, no. But I will not lie; I wanted to experience a little of the living that took place at her parties."

"You scoundrel," Melody teases.

"I may preside over the dead, little one, but even gods have needs."

She snakes her hand down my chest and over my gown, tapping her fingers on my cock. "By all means..." she coos, "tell me about your needs."

I lean down and press a kiss to her lips, feeling a spark when my skin brushes over hers. I pull back. "No time for that, dirty girl." Then I push her lingering hand on my aching length away. "Your libation is ready."

She frowns and rolls away from me, but then draws her legs in as she sits up. I stand and move to the nightstand, then grab the glass before plopping back down onto the edge of the bed next to her.

"Last chance to change your mind," I say, offering her the glass. She takes it and then hesitantly lifts it to her lips.

Her eyes are on me as she tips the glass back and takes a generous gulp. Then, I take the glass before her hand goes limp, and she falls back onto the bed. Her eyes flutter closed, and her body jolts once, twice, and she is out.

I set the glass down, pull the covers up and over her body, then kiss each eyelid before I set to task. Because whatever the fuck happened in the temple, I need to get to the bottom of it. And to do that, I would rather Melody not be a witness to how I go about my business.

I call Cerberus to my side and implore him to watch over her. Then, I leave the room, looking back only once at her still form before closing the door behind me.

CHAPTER 18

THE ACOLYTE (HADES)

I am enraged by the time I reach Charon's temple, stomping up the steps and cracking them as I call out his name with a growl. "Charon!"

Charon stumbles from atop the dais, throwing himself at my feet when I reach the center of the chamber. Keeping his head low, his forehead rests against the cool marble as he cowers. "If I had known—"

"If you had known what, Charon? If you had known she was once in the service of that hateful *bitch*, you would have stopped her?" I am so angry that I grab a fistful of his hair and wrench him to his feet. "But you did know. You *knew* because I *saw*, and she told us. Her words spoke the truth that neither of us wanted to see, yet you still took her into your service, and gave her access to immense power by doing so. You allowed her to serve that *bitch*… in my *realm!*" My booming voice shakes the walls of the temple, loosening the keystones and shifting the roof. A central column wobbles and cracks on one side, sending dust into the air, but luckily does not collapse the roof overhead.

"I could never have suspected there was an ulterior motive," he cries. "You know that."

I release Charon, and he falls to his knees, clasping his hands together and pleading.

"How do we fix this, Charon?" I turn away from him, taking a deep breath to cool my flames that want to be unleashed.

Shaking his pleading hands, he says, "I do not know."

"You do not know?" I scoff. "For the keeper of rites, you do not seem to know very much."

"Much has happened in the mortal realm, and she has hidden so much from us." His voice quivers, and rises in pitch as he continues. "There was no way I could have predicted she could access *her* power here, you know that."

"Get up, Charon. We will not be able to salvage this mess with you on your knees, and I need you."

"Thank you, Hades. Thank you." He takes my hands and kisses them. "Thank you," he cries.

"Stop sniveling and take me to that so-called *Acolyte*. If she thought the way I invaded her mind before was uncomfortable, then what I must do now will make her beg for an eternity in Tartarus. She will burn for this, Charon. I will char the flesh from her bones and grind what remains to dust before disposing of it in the waters of Acheron. Or perhaps Pyriphlegethon is more befitting of her deceit."

"Yes, the rivers. Either would suffice," he grovels.

"I do not want it to suffice. I want it to hurt," I say as he leads me toward the back of the chamber. "I want her to suffer. I want her pain to rival that of any before it. I want her cries to stir the Algea in such a way that Zeus himself can feel her torment where he slumbers on Olympus!" I slam my fist into the archway leading to Charon's quarters and crack the surrounding stones. They shatter beneath the force of my strike, sending shards hurtling into the air.

Charon dodges the remnants, and several strike my shoulder. I do not react to the contact, but as I look at where they hit me, several beads of ichor trickle down my arm.

"Here. Let me—"

"Leave it," I grumble, sending Charon cringing back from where he was about to wipe my arm with the sleeve of his robe.

"Of... of course," he stammers, "I was just trying—"

"I know what you were trying to do," I interrupt, and Charon wrings his hands in his sleeves before dropping his arms to his sides, "but I think you have done enough for one day."

He is silent after that, but eventually calls for the guards to open the door to his chamber when we step into the hallway. They do, and as we step inside, Lenore stands in the back of his chamber with the ceremonial knife to her neck.

"Stay back!" she shouts.

We halt, but she must know that slitting her throat will not stop me from exacting her punishment, so she looks about the room wildly, hoping there is something, anything that can save her from the fate I have in store for her.

Stepping toward her, I say coldly, "Whatever power you think you have in this situation, you do not."

"I don't care. This was never about me. It was always about her," Lenore rambles.

"And just what do you think it is you have accomplished here?" I ask.

"Accomplished?" She shakes her head, her face taking on a manic expression as she laughs aloud. "It was never about accomplishing anything. Only about atonement."

"Atonement?" Charon questions. "Atonement for what?" He looks up at me and then back to Lenore.

"For denying her what was rightfully hers. I had been forsaken. I had been exiled and denied my birthright, but now…" There is an evilness in her tone, something unhinged.

"But now?" I ask, stopping when she backs herself into a corner of the room.

"But now it begins. Her power will abound, and there will be none to strike her down. Her power will abound, and there will be none to strike her down. Her power will abound, and there will be none to strike her down!"

Charon moves toward Lenore, and she reaches onto a shelf and grabs a small vial, tossing it in her mouth and crunching down. Her teeth grind over the glass, and she swallows as Charon yells out, "No!"

Lenore slumps to the floor, her body jostling once, twice, and then she goes still as Charon continues to whimper *no* while froth bubbles out of the corner of her lips.

"What is it? What has she done, Charon?"

"She has tasted the waters of Lethe." He sighs, and then breaks out in hysteria as he tears at his hair. "That fucking bitch! Arrgghh!"

I try to be calm when I say, "So what you are saying is now we will never find out what the hell is going on, or what happened to Melody?"

Charon doesn't answer; he just walks out of the room as I watch the waters of Lethe wipe Lenore's slate clean, drowning any memory that remained in her head as it courses through her body.

"Fuck indeed," I say, turning and walking out the door. The guards look to me for guidance, so I command, "Burn the bitch in the river. She deserves nothing, no rites, and nothing she shall have."

The guards say nothing; they just nod before entering the room and dragging the body out.

I make my way to the temple's entrance, where Charon sits on the top step, hanging his head between his legs.

Calmed down, I sit beside him, and he leans into me. I look up at the night sky I fabricated above and wonder where Melody is at in my memories. Then I say, "Well, that could have gone better."

Charon's chuckle starts out as a snort and then transitions into full-bellied laughter. I join in and we shake our heads, because after eons together, we have seen some shit.

CHAPTER 19
Affair of the Heart (Hades' Memory)

The garden of Hesperides is lush and green, but the sun setting in the distance has the leaves of the *Tree of Immortality* looking almost transparent and all aglow as golden light filters through the boughs. Rustled by a gust of wind, the limbs of the apple tree shift, causing the remaining fruit to shimmy while the surrounding grove seems to bow down to the centrally located tree's majesty.

Ladon has once again wrapped himself around the tree, guarding Hera's fruit, and his many heads ungulate in a serpentine motion as he watches the nymphs dancing beneath the canopy.

I can feel the tree's power radiating out, and it washes over the groups of gods and gold-painted mortals as they gyrate and grind into one another. Moans fill the air, drowning out the rustling branches, and I cannot help but take in my fill of all the golden smudges and handprints decorating the flesh of the gods and mortals as they fuck faster, harder, louder.

Eros wanders amongst the masses, his delicate wings trailing behind him as his golden curls frame his face. He looks so young, so innocent and out of place in this setting. But the love... *No, not love.* The *lust* he spreads as he touches one mortal after the other is all about desire and passion.

The music transitions, the sound of the lyre and aulos halting for a moment, and then a horn blows long. As if signaled by the deep resonance of the horn, the pairings shift. Like a dance, they circle to the right, greeting their new partners with a deep kiss.

Little time is spent with introductions, if there are any, and soon lips, mouths, and fingers are exploring, invading, savoring. There is so much to see, but my eyes do not linger too long on any one couple and instead move to where Aphrodite sits draped in golden silk atop a dais. Her skirts flow over the edge, and one long tanned leg is exposed where a beautiful boy with lush golden curls and a chiseled chest lounges at her feet.

Wrapping his muscular arms around her leg, my gaze traverses from the prominent veins converging at his elbow down to where his wrist flexes as he grips her calf. An intricately patterned leather collar dresses his neck, and transparent fabric drapes over his lap, barely hiding his impressive erection as he digs his fingertips into her flesh.

His eyes scan the scene before him, and Aphrodite jerks on the leash attached to his collar when his gaze lingers too long on one group. He averts his eyes and looks up to where she scowls above him. Like a good little pet, he doesn't allow his attention to stray again.

Curious about what warranted his correction, I scan the groups and find exactly what held his fascination. A woman is splayed out on the ground, with golden smudged handprints painting her ample breasts and hips, while a man is nestled between her thighs with his face buried so deep in her pussy. He laves and sucks vigorously.

As he feasts, she raises her hips and fucks his face, chasing her pleasure while her back arches. Deep indents form where his hands grip her hips, holding her to him. And directly behind him, a god, possibly Anteros—the god of requited love and Aphrodite's son—presses his hips flush against his backside, sliding his cock in and out of the mortal man in languid strokes. Their movements are fluid, rhythmic, and almost in time with the tune being played. I cannot look away.

Why was Adonis so transfixed? I think. It could be nothing. It could be Eros' lust and desire clouding his judgement. Or maybe what Anteros is doing is something he wants in his own life. Something missing.

A warmth pools in my chest and my cock stirs to life as I imagine burying myself deep within Aphrodite's beautiful little pet. Would his back arch and hips raise in welcome? Would he bounce back onto my length? How would it feel as I slid in and out of his tight ass? Would sounds of pleasure escape his lips while his fingers dug into the soft earth as I rode him harder than one of my steeds?

Titans, how I want to break him! How I want to waltz up to Aphrodite and offer him my hand and have him accept it, all so I can take him while she watches. But I cannot do that here. So, I jerk my own leash—metaphorical as it is—and tear my gaze from his tantalizing form, offering myself for the next rotation.

When the horn sounds, I step into the circle, and gasps escape the lips of my new *playmates* when they realize who I am. The commotion draws Aphrodite's attention, and she nods to me. I return her acknowledgement, and her pet stares at me while I kiss my mortal partners.

My partners shiver at my touch, but I do not melt into them as they do into me, and keep my eyes open and trained on Adonis. Then, his mouth drops open, and I smirk when he gulps down his response. His throat bobs, and I imagine biting him there as I dig my teeth into the throat before me.

Aphrodite unexpectedly moves from her seat and slides the thin straps of her gown off her shoulder before dropping it and the shawl that had been draped around her to the ground. Then, she steps out of the fabric and places her hand on the top of Adonis' head. He turns his face upward, giving her his attention, but she does not look down at him. Instead, she trails her eyes around the grove, stopping when she meets mine. She smirks, and then takes a seat beside her pet before laying back so her head hangs over the dais.

Adonis knows what is required of him, and positions himself between Aphrodite's waiting thighs while she looks out over all the naked bodies. Now with her attention elsewhere, Adonis' eyes lock on mine as he leans down and places his mouth on her mound. She grabs his head with both of her hands, holding him there, and I position one of my partners on his hands and knees before me.

Grabbing a small jar, I coat my cock with the oil, lifting and dribbling some on the ass of my waiting playmate. Then, I run my hands up and down my shaft, almost getting lost in the feeling while Adonis stares at me from between Aphrodite's parted legs. He laps up her essence, nudging his nose against her clit, and his hardened cock hangs expectantly between his thighs.

With his ass in the air, Adonis is visibly wanting while he services the goddess. But Aphrodite has never been about the needs of her lovers. Everything is always about her. So, poor Adonis will experience no pleasure tonight unless she allows him to sink deep within her heat, but it is highly unlikely.

Knowing he will be left unsatisfied, I slowly slide the head of my dick into the ass of my new playmate—Damon, I think—a few inches at a time until he has taken most of my length. He is warm and inviting, but his ass is not the one I crave to plunge myself deep within. His hole is not the one I want to invade. But as Adonis watches me with a look of pure fascination, not stopping his assault on his goddess' clit, I thrust into Damon.

Damon moans into the pussy of the woman he had been feasting on, and the sensation has her writhing in ecstasy. Then, I place both my hands on his hips and pull him back into me, burrowing deep.

With Aphrodite's satisfaction dripping off of Adonis' chin, he leans back on his haunches and she rises, dropping his leash as she departs. Looking over his shoulder at her retreating form, Adonis stands, unwrapping his skirt and allowing me the sight I have been deprived of until this moment.

His engorged cock bounces away from him, insistent and hungry with its raised veins twisting up the velvety length. He takes it in his hand and watches me.

My arousal reaches a fever pitch with his eyes on me, and I slam into Damon with wild abandon as Adonis strokes faster and faster. His arm strains and his wrist twitches as he rotates his hand forcefully up and down, up and down.

Reaching between my legs, Damon cups my balls, squeezing them, but I do not take my eyes from the glistening tip of Adonis' cock. His shoulders tense and his eyes close as his head falls back, and with one more thrust into Damon, I groan loudly as Adonis and I cum in unison.

Pump after pump and jerking erratically, I spill into Damon's ass as rivulets of cum stream from Adonis' dick and paint his abdomen. Then, as my dick deflates, I slide out of Damon, who is panting loudly as my satisfaction drips down his thighs. He falls forward onto the woman leaning back on her elbows.

Still watching Adonis, I am in awe as he drags his fingers through his cum and brings some to his mouth. He rubs it across his lips, and flicks his tongue over them, savoring his own taste. Then, he gathers more and extends his fingers into the air, offering them to me.

Titans, I want to taste those fingers and those lips. I want to bare my teeth and growl, biting down and pulling his flesh into my mouth so I can taste everything that is him.

My dick gets hard again, but Damon thinks it is for him and chuckles, gaining my attention for the first time. I look down to where he grips the breast he is leaning against. "I could not possibly, dark one." Damon sighs. "I would if I could, but you are just so…" he trails off, not finishing his statement, but his sentiment has me grinning wide.

"Save yourself, young Damon. The night is still young, and that ass is too good not to take another run around the circle," I say, slowly rubbing the soft flesh of my now too-hard cock. "Perhaps another time."

"If I could be so lucky," he says lazily, twisting a nipple between his fingers and biting his lip. Then, Damon slaps the thigh of the woman he is leaning against, and rises, leaving the circle. He swishes his hips as he walks away, my lust trailing down his inner thighs, and I cannot help but watch his perky ass as his flesh stretches over the taut muscles.

I, too, walk away from the circle, grabbing my gown from the ground, but take no chances of drawing attention by looking back at Adonis. So, walking off into the darkness of the grove, the music dies off the farther into the trees I go, but I can still hear the faint tinkling in the distance.

As I am about to step out of the privacy of the trees, I am grabbed from behind. I react, spinning around, and grasp for purchase. Pinning someone against a tree, I grasp their neck and lean in. Then, when I meet an icy-blue stare, wide with shock, I realize I am face to face with none other than Aphrodite's little *pet*.

CHAPTER 20

ESSENCE OF THE DIVINE (HADES' MEMORY)

It was never meant to be anything, and our physical connection was never supposed to matter. Hell, Adonis was never supposed to matter. He was meant to be a conquest, and a way to get under Aphrodite's skin. But as surprising as it was, he did matter, and now he does, and things in my life, which was never really a life at all, would never be the same.

That first night in the grove, standing with our bodies pressed together in the darkness and staring into one another's eyes, something happened between Adonis and me. Our faces were so close and his skin was so warm beneath my grip as I wrapped my hand firmly around his throat, that the scent of the cum wafting off of his lips and accosting my senses was so overwhelming, there was no way I could resist. Did not want to resist.

With the temptation of his heady scent—masculine, powerful—overpowering every rational thought, I gave in, snaking my tongue out and tasting him. Aphrodite's wrath be damned. Then, my lips crashed into his, and he greeted me willingly, parting his lips and granting me entrance. I twirled his tongue with mine, sucking the tip gently and biting down, and his grateful moans rumbled free.

That sound. That wonderful, glorious, transcendent sound transported me into another plane of existence where Olympus, with all its turmoil and chaos, and the mortal realm, with all its strife, did not matter. Hell, in that moment, and with his arms wrapped around my back and squeezing me tightly against him while my heart stuttered in what I thought was a heartless chest, even the Underworld did not matter. Not my responsibilities. Not my duty. Not the fate of all spending their afterlife there. Only he mattered. And in his embrace, trapped in his arms, for the first time I felt like I mattered.

Adonis was not shy with his affections, and he did not restrain his needs. What he did that night, surrounded in darkness and deep within the grove, was a pivotal moment in what had been a rather drab existence. And I never again wanted my existence to be anything more than what it was with *him*.

When he lifted his skirt and tucked it into his waist, baring his beautiful cock to me, it took everything in my power not to drop to my knees and draw him into my mouth. I held myself back, biting his lip and growling when he brushed the back of his hand against my dick. And instead of grabbing him like I wanted to, I dug my fingers into his nape, my eyes drawn to the smudges of gold my hand left on his throat.

Releasing a tortured groan, Adonis tilted his head back and glared at me, his hunger burning as brightly in his eyes as mine did in response. I could feel it begging for release—my flames—scratching beneath my skin and sparking across every inch of exposed flesh, as heat enveloped us both.

"You are playing with *fire*," I grit out, tilting my hips and rubbing my length against his.

He whimpers, his arms hanging limply at his sides. "What if..."

he stammers, his previous confidence fading away before me. "What if I welcome the burn?" He takes hold of my hips, pulling them forward and chasing the friction. His eyelashes flutter, and then his eyes widen when I thrust back. "Oh!" he exclaims.

"Oh, is right," I rasp, tilting my head and licking the side of his neck. His throat bobs, and I bite down, the feeling taking me by surprise as it drug its insistent nails down my back. It surpasses anything I had imagined while watching him at Aphrodite's feet.

His skin is salty, and the sweat from his previous exertions coats his exterior, so I do my best not to think about what it is from—who it is from—and whose flavor, besides his own, coats his beautiful pout. *No, not going there.*

"I want..." Adonis' voice is breathy—labored—and he clutches my hips once more, banging his head back against the tree.

"What do you want?" I whisper into his ear, but he does not answer. "Do you want me?"

His answer is strained. "Yes."

I run the tip of my nose down to his chin, then up and around to his other ear. "Do you want to touch me?"

"Yes," he pants.

I take his hand and place it on my chest, running it down over the tight muscles of my abdomen, bumping over each one and stopping when I reach my cock. I turn his hand, placing mine atop it, and then squeeze his open palm over my straining erection.

"Do you want me to touch you?"

"Yes."

I release my hand, turning my palm toward him, and brush it lightly up and down. The light brushes turn to hungry gripping, and before I know it, both of our hands are wrapped around our cocks, sliding against one another, and we are shuttling them up and down as we burn.

The heat is overwhelming, the fumes suffocating, and the friction supplied by our fervor is so intense that I can feel my pleasure building and building as it threatens to burst forth in such an explosive fashion that my head swims.

I am dizzy, my vision clouded as I struggle to focus on the beautiful creature pressed tightly against me. And before I can beg him to slow down, to stop, Adonis' pleasure surges to the surface and coats not only our hands but my dick in his essence. He groans into my chest and then his back arches, thrusting his cock against mine, and I cannot hold back the pressure any longer. I burst everywhere.

Once our dicks deplete, we drop our hands and I grab my skirt, lifting it and wiping us clean. Then, after the evidence of our passions has been hidden in several yards of pale blue linen and the heaving of our chests has slowed, I place a quick kiss on his puffy lips, once needy and now bruised, before turning and walking away. I leave him there, his eyes burning a hole in my back, and offer nothing further as I crest the top of the hill.

Back in the Underworld, I am walking by Charon's temple on my way to the palace when he calls out optimistically, "Well... how did it go?"

With the crunch of loose gravel beneath my feet, I answer with a clipped, "Fine."

"Fine?" There is a long pause as I continue walking. "Just *fine*?" He follows me, but I wave him back. I make it several more paces when I faintly hear him yell after me, "Later, then?"

I do not answer, ignoring his incessant questions to avoid his judgement, and instead lift my hand in the air as I continue back to the keep. Then, when I reach the archway, my effigies, too, seem to judge me from where they sit high above with their brows drawn together in disapproval. I wave them off, just as I had with Charon, and walk through the gate, clenching my fists at my sides.

There is so much going on in my head, so much to ponder, but the silence I wanted to sit in with my thoughts is broken when a loud chuff greets me as I reach the stairs.

After pissing on the base of the statues—an act that has become almost ceremonial—Cerberus announces his presence with a whine and a nudge to my hand as I ascend the steps. I do not stop, looking over my shoulder at him as I continue on, but it takes everything in my power not to laugh when he tilts his heads.

"It is fine," I say. "I am fine."

He halts, whimpering, and the remorse I feel for causing those sounds of dejection to ring out has me calling him to me. "Come on, boy."

My hellhound trots up the remaining steps with his claws clicking their way up each one, and is at my side as I walk through the entry door. We walk down the dimly lit hallway together in silence, our steps echoing around us, but then I scratch under each chin before leaving him outside my room.

I want to be alone. Want to sit in the darkness and mull over everything that happened between me and the most beautiful boy I have ever seen. But to do so without the sounds of his infernal licking and scratching, my companion of many years must remain in the hallway.

He whines, scratching at the door, and it thumps several times from his assault before he plops down outside it. I can see his wiry fur peeking through the bottom where he has laid down in the hall, and then he howls, voicing his opposition.

"So dramatic," I tease. "One night alone will not kill you," I call out. Though considering where we are, and how many nights alone I have spent, that statement is rather callous of me. Because within this castle, where I have only Cerberus, endless amounts of time, and loneliness to keep me company, it is hard to feel anything but dead. I mean, I am the King of Death, so feeling dead is not a foreign concept for me, but still...

I should take a soak in the grotto. I should put on my robe, travel the length of the hallway, and take advantage of its soothing waters to wash away the evidence of my earlier rendezvous. But now that I am in my room with my solitude, I no longer have the wherewithal to do so.

Unwrapping my gown, I bunch it up and feel that unmistakable crunch from our satiation, and have every intention of tossing it in the basket with the rest of my soiled linens. I do not, and instead place it on the other side of the bed before crossing the room.

On a small table by the door, I have a pitcher of water waiting, and pour myself a glass, chugging it down to quench my thirst. I wipe my lips with the back of my hand, freezing when I smell... *him*. Then, turning my palm upward, I see the gold paint from gripping Damon's hips still on my fingertips, so I rub my hands together, washing it away in the basin.

Once my hands are as clean as I can get them without soap, I walk over to my soiled linens basket and grab a small cloth, wiping them dry. Then, I move to the left side of my bed, and pull back my covers before climbing in.

Sleep beckons me beneath its decadence, and I want to answer the call, but lying in bed and staring at the ceiling, I ignore that song despite how badly I need the rest. I toss and turn, flipping over and rotating my pillow for hours upon hours, all while wondering how many souls from Aphrodite's latest party will become my newest tenants. I finally give up trying to sleep.

It should not bother me—the deaths of her partygoers. The consequences of their actions are their own, and they will be judged accordingly, but it pisses me off that their threads were cut too soon.

Now, some would say it would not have happened if it were not the will of the Fates. That is naïve because the Fates' hands were not the ones responsible for snuffing out their light. It was Aphrodite, and every shit thing that seems to be happening as of late can be attributed to that golden bitch. Everything except Adonis.

"Adonis," I whisper into the darkness, his name tickling my lips. I pull the bottom one into my mouth and nibble the corner. The uttering of his name and the memory of not only his lips parted in ecstasy but his body pulled taut as a bowstring has me so hard it hurts.

I run one hand down my chest and take command of my cock, while bringing the other to my mouth. I bite down, muffling my groan with my fist, but stop when I realize I washed away the remnants of *him*.

I want *him*—the feel of his body, the scent of his skin and his arousal. And need him, a realization that is not just hard but also torturous to admit. But he is not mine to possess; he is *hers*, and it is highly unlikely she will let loose his leash and free him to fall into the waiting arms of someone like me. I grimace.

It should not be so affecting—the thought that he is *hers* and can only be mine in secret—but it is. The idea that the only way I will see him again is if I attend another one of her events, watching as she uses him to get off while I stare on, has me reeling. Does he even like it—being used in that manner? Does he enjoy being collared and led around, forced to see to her needs with no hope of quenching his own?

Well, now I am not only rock hard but angry, and jerk my cock as I chase my release. Shuttling my hand up and down my length, my glistening anticipation beading on my tip, I writhe, every muscle tensing as my back arches off of the bed.

I am so close, but my body seems to be denying me, and the pain that wells up in my abdomen has me yelling out in frustration,

"Come on, damn you! Come on!" I urge my cock on, looking down at where it remains strangled in my grip.

I release myself, then roll over onto my stomach, finding my face buried in the gown I laid on the other side of the bed earlier. Breathing in deeply, I take in the scent of him, me, *us*... and my body goes rigid.

Then, picking up the gown, I scramble to my knees, bracing one hand on the back wall as I hold the fabric over my nose. *He*... is here. *He*... is with me. His essence, my essence, *our* essence, is so sublimely divine as it fills my nostrils that it has a glorious, pulsing need coursing throughout my entire being, and I know I can do it now.

Wrapping the gown around my neck, I nuzzle into the linen, and then take hold of my dick once more. There is an urgency, a yearning that burns deep in the recesses of my darkened soul that is screaming to break free. So, with our scent coursing through my veins and fire licking over the back of my hand, I pump.

Up and down, harder and faster, I yank and pull, closing my eyes and envisioning every sculpted inch of his body that reacted so exquisitely as I tasted him with my tongue. But that vision alone is not enough, and I want more. So, I imagine him before me, on his knees and bracing himself with both palms pressed into the wall as I pull his hips back into me.

Still gripping, my movements are erratic as I fuck my fist. I am intoxicated by our scent, and the vision of him taking my cock so beautifully while he bounces back into my every forward thrust has me building, then cresting, and finally bursting.

Rope after rope, my cum paints the headboard and wall with my release, and I pant loudly as the flames licking up and down my arms subside. Once bright cobalt, an inferno that sloughed my skin from my bones and allowed my gilded skeleton to peek through, the fire is now light as it dwindles to nothing. It prickles as it dances over me, just small electrical shocks that remind me of the same feeling that greeted me when his fingertips rambled down my stomach.

My skin reforms, and once back to... well, myself, or as much of myself as I can feel now that I have experienced him, I fall back onto the bed, bringing the gown with me. I drift off and into the most blissful sleep.

CHAPTER 21
DEATH OR DISHONOR
(HADES' MEMORY)

Month after month, I found myself drawn to Aphrodite's Noumenia celebrations with the promise of seeing Adonis once more, and each has been better than the one that preceded it. Like the Thargelia celebration, I joined the circle, and kept my eyes on Adonis the whole time while I took my pleasure in the holes of so many others.

Damon has been a most gracious partner, offering himself to me, and much like Adonis had that first night, and every night I have been in attendance since, he watched as my body moved in rhythm with the music. I would rotate my hips, pump in and out of one muscular rump after another, all while staring deep into Adonis' eyes as he pleasured himself high atop the dais. I did not partake of the women, because I knew that was not what he wanted to see.

Tonight, after four months, and with his lips pulled back into a snarl as he services Aphrodite, I watch as Adonis brings her to the edge with his hands, his fingers, and his mouth, but never his dick. Then, as expected, she rises and departs to clean herself in the fountains, while he is left wanting with his leash on the dais at his feet. Again.

With Aphrodite gone, Adonis stares intently into my eyes, taking his cock in his hand, and we pump. In and out, I thrust and grind into Damon, while Adonis jerks his dick. He is angry, which has me bemused, and with a smirk lifting the corner of my lips, I pound harder and harder as he looks on.

Frustrated, he loosens his cock, lowers his skirts and steps from the dais, storming off to where I know I will eventually find him waiting at the edge of the trees. But I cannot just leave the circle and Damon unsatisfied. It would raise suspicion. So, I reach forward and beneath him, jerking him wildly until he spills his need onto the ground. Then, I slap his ass and thank him once more, rising and exiting the group for the darkness and the boy... no, *man,* I really want to satisfy.

Once shrouded in darkness, I move to the tree where Adonis and I first met, my eyes scanning the grove all around it, but he is nowhere to be found. It is odd because this is where we always meet. Where we have since feasted on one another's lips, lowered to our knees to satiate our need, or he has fallen into my arms as he cried about how awful it is we cannot be together.

I would run my fingers through the curls framing his face beneath this tree and, because I am not heartless and understand his wishes, explain that I did not see how it could ever be so.

His tears on the matter almost broke me, and every time he would tell me he understood, gladly accepting whatever moments we had with one another.

Running my hands along the bark, I know that this tree will always hold the fondest of memories. But now, our tree of memories stands in solitude, and the keeper of my heart is absent.

Still looking for Adonis, I hear snorting and rustling in the distance. It is, from what I assume, a large boar spooked from the hunt earlier that day in preparation for the next day's ritual sacrifice. I move toward the sound, but as I transition from the darkness into the clearing, expecting to see a beast for offering, my eyes instead fall on the body of a man. His skirts are so saturated in blood from a gaping wound in his abdomen there is no way he will survive.

The man is not gilded as all the other mortals on the island are, and as I step to where he lies writhing on the ground, pressing his hands over his abdomen, familiar golden curls come into view. I fall to my knees beside him. "No. No. No!" I shout, taking his beautiful face in my quivering hands. "Just hold on," I whimper. "You will be okay. It will all be okay," I soothe, pressing my lips to his forehead.

I stare down into his face, and he lifts one coated hand to me, brushing his fingertips across my cheek and smearing his blood along my jawline. It is warm, sticky, and despite the pressure he has applied thus far, with his intestines trailing down his side, I know there is no hope.

"Hades." Hearing my name escaping those lips, so loving and in a way I do not deserve, is torture, and I urge him to be still.

I take his hand from my face and move his intestines onto his stomach, placing them and his hand on his abdomen. Then, pulling his head into my lap, I continue comforting him. "Hang on. Someone will come, I promise. Someone will come," I cry out.

"They have," he says, his voice emitting a calmness it has no right to.

"No. Not me. I am not here for you. I mean, I am, but not in that way," I explain, my voice cracking.

The rising and falling of his chest slows, the movements minuscule, and holding his stomach as blood pools beneath him, he breathes out, "It is okay, Hades. Now I can have you."

"Not like this," I whimper, my lip quivering as I try to force tears to fall so he knows how much this hurts. They do not fall, but the smell of sulphur rises from the ground beside his head, and I know it will not be long. I can feel the pull of my responsibility calling me back to the Underworld, so I yell out, "Aphrodite!"

With my call to the goddess, she appears, wrapping her scarf around her shoulders as she steps toward me. "Seriously, Hades. Could it not—" Her words halt on her lips. "What... what have you done?" she accuses.

"I found him this way." I look up into the seething eyes of the golden goddess.

"Of course you did," she spat. "You just could not allow me to be happy, could you?" She does not fall to her knees to comfort him as I expected, and instead stands glowering over us, her eyes burning with so much hate I can feel her power prickling over my skin.

"Enough!" I yell. "Can you not see he is in pain?"

"Oh, I see," she scoffs, "but any pain he feels in his final moments shall fall on your conscience, not mine."

"Your cruelty knows no bounds, Aphrodite!"

"My cruelty? Well, that is rich coming from you," she attests. "He is *mine*, Hades, and you just could not stand it, could you? You had to *steal* him for yourself."

"Steal him? I would not wish this end on anyone, especially not *him*," I counter.

"You think I do not know what you have been doing? That I am clueless as to how you have been sneaking around and taking pleasure from one who does not belong to you?"

"Belong..." I cannot bring myself to finish that statement, and rise to my feet, lording over her. "Adonis does not belong to anyone! He is a person who has the right to autonomy. Not that I would ever expect you to grasp the concept of choice." I am so angry I cannot keep my hatred of her absent from my tone.

"Choice?" she contends. "As if those who come to you have a

choice. At least the choice I offer pertains only to living with love or beauty or without it. What do you offer? Only torment."

I hate that this is her assessment of me. How she and everyone else forget all the good I do for those who cross the river and enter my realm. "The afterlife I offer to those who are deemed worthy is far from torment."

In a voice that can barely be considered a whisper, Adonis utters, "Stop fighting." He coughs, and blood pools in the corner of his lips.

I look to him, but I know I cannot stay. I am being summoned back to my realm, and there is nothing I can do to stop it. "I am sorry," I say, brushing my fingers across his eyes. He closes them, and looking up to Aphrodite, I plead, "Stay with him. Please, Aphrodite. If not for me, then for whatever affection you might have for him. I beg of you."

"You will beg, Hades." She glowers at me. "If it is the last thing I do, I will see you pay for this."

Then, against my control, the ground opens up, and I am pulled back to the Underworld where the masses line up beside the river to receive my judgement. And I, as always, will sit and do my duty as Hades, King of Death, ruler of the Underworld, whether or not I like it.

I could not attend Adonis' rite. My presence would have been unwelcome even if I had been able to attend. So, I saw it from my throne room. Through my peering stone, I watched as Aphrodite spouted false declarations of love while garnering attention from the attendees. Then, as the coins were placed over his eyes, I knew I should shed a tear of sadness for his mortal life as he burned, but did not.

I will see him once he arrives for judgement, I think. That realization offered me a sliver of comfort, even if only for a couple of days until he will step up to the scales. Because that is the moment I am most worried about.

I needed to get out of my realm, needed to see Aphrodite once again to explain that his death was out of my control and hope she will forgive me. If not, then who knows how far she will take this feud, or to what lengths she will go for something that neither she nor I could have predicted.

On Olympus, I see Aphrodite walking toward her temple, and offer her my sympathies. And what did the golden bitch do? She curses me and spits in my face, putting on a show for all the onlookers, and then they glare at me as I walk up the hill to wait for her in her quarters.

I will try again, and perhaps be received better when there are not so many to witness, I think. But who am I kidding? It is more likely that she will whine to Zeus and have me thrown off of the mount and banished back to my realm once and for all than accept that what happened to Adonis was not of my making. I wait for her regardless.

When she arrives, stepping through the gold satin draped entryway to see me sitting at her table, she huffs her disapproval. "What now, Hades? Have you not done enough to humiliate me? Why have you not tucked your tail and gone back to that *cesspool* you call a realm?"

She saunters over to her offering table, where she grabs a handful of grapes, and then pops several in her mouth before lifting a chalice and downing it.

"We need to talk, Aphrodite." I stand before her, but still she ignores me, milling about the room before taking a seat. I do the same.

"Do we?" She does not even try to hide her indifference, and inspects her nails. Thrumming them on the table, she taps her hand twice before crossing her legs. "You wanted him, and now you have him. What more is there to talk about?" She leans back in her chair, glaring at me.

"Are you not the least bit concerned about how he will fare when he steps on the scales?" I ask, irritated, leaning my elbows on the table and clasping my hands atop it.

"Should I be?" She flips her golden locks behind her.

Titans, how can someone so beautiful of face be so rotten to the core, I think.

"Are you so unmoved that you cannot spend one minute of your *precious* time on what will happen to him down there?" I scowl.

"What happens to him now is up to you. Unless..." She lets the silence linger, knowing I will ask for clarification.

"Unless, what?" I lean back, my eyes never leaving hers.

"I am so glad you asked." She is excited, and springs to her feet and crosses the room to her offering table once more.

I think she is just going to continue being a bitch, and get herself another glass of wine without offering me any, but no. Instead, she lifts the lid of a small chest, picks something up, and walks back to the table.

"Here." Plopping something onto the table, she keeps her hand over it, obscuring it from my view.

"And, that is?"

"You say you are *sorry*." She fake pouts. "That there was 'nothing you could do'," she mocks. Lifting her hand, she shows me what is beneath it: a glittering ruby in the shape of a heart. "Well now there is, and if you are truly *sorry*, then you... can make... it up... to me," she sings, her voice melodic as she emphasizes the word groups with a tap of her finger on the top of the stone—four, to be exact.

"How do you propose I do that?" I raise a brow.

She waltzes back to the other table, this time grabbing two chalices of wine, and comes back and offers one to me. Then she lifts the glass in salutation, I return it, and she throws it back in one gulp.

I sniff the glass, not sure I can trust the contents, but smell nothing off, so I, too, take a swig. There are notes of honeysuckle and pomegranate, *her favorite*, and it tingles the back of my throat as I swallow it down.

Picking up the stone, I twist it between my fingertips. "What is it I am expected to do with this?" I ask, holding the stone up to the light. The facets send prismatic pinks dancing across the table, and I can feel it is powerful, but have no clue how this... *thing* is supposed to help Adonis.

"It is one of the Nostos Stones, *silly*," she says, her light-hearted tone meant to be coy, even though it is clear she thinks I am stupid for not knowing. "There are six," she says, walking around the table. "Each one has a unique property or power because of the remnants of the Titans' powers held within. Like this stone, all the stones were mined from Mount Othrys, and lost during the Titanomachy."

Her smile is stretched wide, and her eyes are twinkling with so much malevolence that I am not sure I can trust a word out of her mouth. But still I ask, "And this one does, what?"

She moves to take it, but I pull it to my chest. Shrugging her shoulders, Aphrodite turns and goes back to her seat. Once she is seated, she says, "I call it the Anastasis Stone."

Getting agitated, I raise my voice when I state, "Telling me its name tells me shit about what it does, Aphrodite."

"Ugh!" she groans aloud. "Anastasis, as in *rebirth*. It counteracts the effect of crossing."

"Elaborate, Aphrodite," I order. "My patience grows thin, and at any moment I could be summoned—"

"Okay, okay. Calm yourself. You know, the other gods might like you better if you ever pulled those crossed bidents out of your—"

"Enough!" I shout, standing. "If you will not tell me the purpose of the stone, then this visit is over."

I move to set down the stone and have just lifted my fingers when she calls out, "It can bring him back!"

Nostos Stones

Apeiron Stone
"Infinity Stone"

Anastasis Stone
"Renascence Ruby"

Basileios Stone
"Kingmaker Emerald"

Epirroí Stone
"Subjugation Stone"

Eos Stone
"Aurora Sapphire"

Kruptós Stone
"Mustēria Stone"

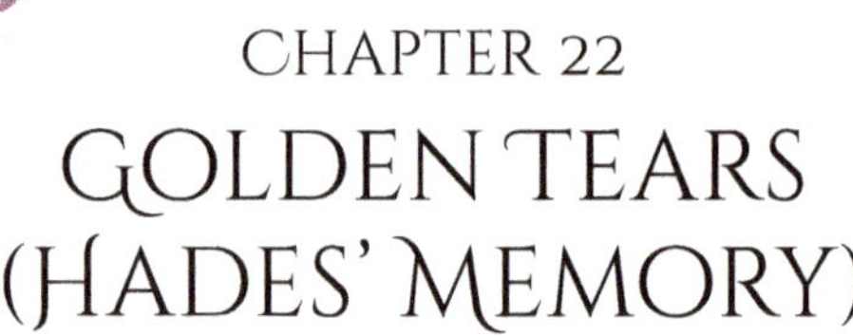

CHAPTER 22
GOLDEN TEARS
(HADES' MEMORY)

"I am sorry, but what did you say?" I ask, my tone anything but friendly. "Bring him back how?" I want to keep the anger that is building within my chest from bursting forth at her proposition, but fail, and my flames flicker at my fingertips, illuminating the stone. "No, do not tell me, because what you claim *that* stone can do is not only impossible, but against the very nature of death itself."

"You are only saying that because you and you alone are meant to preside over death. But with this stone…" She points to my hand. "One could forgo the effects of crossing the river and have a second chance."

"A second chance? How?" I study the stone, and as I do, she reaches out and snatches it from my hand.

"Unlock the power trapped within, releasing it, and in doing so trap the soul instead. Once the soul is housed within the stone, the power of the Titans will allow the mortal to choose to return to the land of the living." She holds the stone up to the light. "In essence, rite of passage and ferry ride be damned, the mortal can return."

I stand, raising my voice when I say, "The Titans are locked away in Tartarus, and you propose releasing their power when none but them can control it? Have you lost your senses?"

"Relax, Hades. You would not be releasing their power completely. Merely a remnant resides in the stone. A fraction, if you will. There is hardly enough to do any real damage," she says flippantly. "Besides, it is not like the soul is trapped for eternity. The mortal can die. And when they do, it is off to the afterlife or wherever you choose to send them, and their soul is finally yours, ripe for the picking."

"You think my only concern is claiming the power associated with their soul? I am not so power hungry that I could not forfeit one if, and that is a huge *if*, I thought there would be no consequences to wielding such a power."

"Forfeit, consequences... you say those words without the reverence they deserve. This is not about me or you, Hades. It is about him. And you would not be here if you did not care, or worry about what may come to pass. What I offer is the chance to take all that worry and turn it into hope. Hope for a future with him, perhaps for us both. Would you give him back to me if it meant you could have him in turn? Or would you deny us both?"

Aphrodite tries to remain indifferent, but I can see the way her shoulders have curled forward and her eyes are pleading. She wants this, needs it, but the why behind her emotional blackmail, because that is exactly what *this* is, eludes me.

Curious, I ask her to tell me everything, and she places the stone back in my hand, walking over to refill our chalices.

With a nonchalance the gravity of our conversation does not warrant, she walks back and plops down, offering me the chalice and motioning for the stone back. I give it to her and she turns it in her hands as she explains that if the soul has decided to live, and is holding the stone in their hand before they step onto the river's edge after exiting the ferry, instead of being claimed by the Underworld, their soul is absorbed into the stone.

I ponder her words, sipping the wine from the elaborately decorated chalice in my hands. It is gold, and my fingers bump over every ridge of the intricate swirls and scrolls on the surface.

The aftertaste of honey lingers in mouth, just as strong as the urgency Aphrodite is trying so hard to hide. It washes over me, and I know there has to be more than she is letting on, so I clear my throat. "And what of the *remnant*? Once the mortal dies, what happens to it?"

"It returns to the stone," she says.

"And then?"

"And then it waits for the next soul to take its place, releasing it once more." She lifts her hand holding the stone and flourishes her fingers, trying to act like what she has relayed is no big deal, but it is.

"So..." I trail off, my mind jumping from one possibility to the next about what that released power could mean to her, because it is obvious it has nothing to do with Adonis and everything to do with the *remnant* itself. "Let us back things up a bit."

She grips the stone tightly and lays her hand on the table between us, her irritation washing off of her.

"The mortal holds the stone and steps off of the ferry, at which time the remnant is released and their soul is sucked in. Do I understand the process correctly?"

"Could not have explained it better myself." She grins, opening her hand.

"Then, with their essence in the stone, the remnant goes where, does what?"

"Nothing," she claims, her palm still open and waiting.

"Nothing," I parrot her, but the word does not sit right with me, and my tone is one of derision. "That makes absolutely no sense, Aphrodite. The Titans were power-hungry busybodies. There is no way their power, even a sliver, after remaining dormant for so long, will not try to do something. Whether it be death, destruction, chaos, or creation... something must come with the power. There would be ripples. But you are saying you are unaware of such a cost?"

"To my knowledge, nothing will happen, Hades." She takes another sip, keeping her eyes trained on me. Mine trails down to the stone glistening in her hand.

"Well, if nothing will happen, then why did you not give him the stone? Why do I have to be the one to do it?"

Her palm closes tightly around the stone, and then a trail of ichor streams down the side of her hand. "And just how do you propose I do that? Shall I walk into the labyrinth, somehow find him and hand him the stone before he reaches the gates?" She pauses, and now I gulp down another swig of my wine while I consider her answer. "What if another takes it from him? What if he refuses to accept its importance and discards it somewhere along the way? Or what if he does not trust me and instead tosses the stone into the river? He would arrive on the other side, hands empty, and neither of us could help him at that point."

Neither of us could help him at that point. The thought rambles back and forth in my mind, dragging its feet and kicking rocks in the desolate space that has become my brain in this moment. Because I can think of nothing else but saving him.

"If I do this, Aphrodite, what are your terms? There has to be a catch—some expectation?" I shake my head, still hesitant. "What would we each get from this situation that would be worth releasing a Titan's power in my realm? Or into the world, for that matter? Seeing as I would have no way to keep it from doing whatever it is meant to do once free, which you claim you have no knowledge of."

She is somewhat sassy when she says, "Well, I guess that is a *you* problem, is it not. Seeing as you are the only one able to offer him the stone now. But the time lessens the longer you wait." She stands and walks toward me, placing her hand on my shoulder. I look up, and tears are welling in her eyes as she offers me the stone.

One golden tear streams down her cheek, and with her lip quivering, she says, "For all you know, at this very moment, while you sit here arguing with me, Adonis is stumbling through the labyrinth, two coins in hand, ready to pay Charon his tribute and cross the river empty-handed."

I brush her hand off my shoulder and ignore the stone in her outstretched hand. "Do not be so melodramatic. I would know—" My words are cut off by the scent of sulphur rising into the air.

She smells it too and thrusts the ichor-coated stone into my hand. "Go. Give him the stone before he crosses, and save him," she pleads, more tears spilling off of her chin.

With the stone in my hand, I stand. And before I can take one step, the ground opens up, and I am pulled into it, once again summoned to sit on the throne and weigh the masses.

Stumbling through the labyrinth, I can hear the mumbling of all the confused souls up ahead, and know I must find him. I call out, "Adonis!" My voice echoes, bouncing off of the walls and spilling out into the next cavern. No answer. I call again, "Adonis!" Again it goes unanswered.

Now with a sense of urgency, I bound into the darkness, pushing through one mass grouped together, and then another, and another, until I reach the open cavern. I call for him, and this time in the distance I hear a faint *Hades*. It is to my ears but a whisper, but just that one word, cried from his lips, is everything, and my heart swells.

In a chest that was once hollow, a warmth radiates out, filling the cold chamber with the love burning inside me. *I love him*, I think, my knees going wobbly with the realization. Despite spending eons with none by my side except Cerberus, I cannot imagine another day going by where I do not get to wrap my arms around him.

So I run. I run into the next tunnel, run toward the gates. I run with a love in my heart that burns, swells, and bursts from my chest. My love illuminates the darkness as I bounce off of one wandering soul to the next until the only one I wish to set my eyes upon is there.

"Adonis." It comes out like a plea—hushed but urgent. Then he is rushing into my welcoming embrace where I pull him into me and crash my lips onto his so fiercely that I know I would accept whatever consequence that comes from keeping him. Whatever the price may be, I will pay it because... *I love this man* and never want to be parted from him again.

Standing at the edge of the river, after watching several ferries full of souls cross, I pull the stone from my robes and place it in Adonis' hands. I close mine around them.

He looks down. "What is this?"

I kiss his forehead, then lean back, trapping him in my gaze as I say, "You said 'now you can be mine', and with this you can."

"I do not understand." He shakes his head in confusion. "How—"

"Just trust me," I say. "Do you trust me?"

"Yes, but—"

"No buts. There is no time for hesitation or questions. I need to know only, *do you trust me*?" My words come out more harshly than I intend them to be, so I continue. "*If* you trust me, and *if* you wish to remain by my side, living a life in my arms, accept the stone and cross the river."

He nods his head, and I remove my hands from his and motion toward the ferry. We step aboard, where Charon gives me a questioning glare, but I ignore him. We cross, and once on the other side, with the stone in one hand and my hand in his other, Adonis steps from the ferry.

When he steps onto the bank, sinking into mud up to his ankles, the sound of thunder claps overhead and a fractured light escapes from the stone. It surges forth, bouncing off the false ceiling above, then ricochets back and forth off of every cavern wall before disappearing in one last burst of light over Adonis.

Once the light dissipates and I am satisfied it worked, we walk to my throne and stand at the base of the steps, while Charon ushers the rest of the souls to the line. They join it, their eyes darting wildly, but mine keep trailing back to the beautiful man at my side.

I squeeze his hand in mine, and he tears his eyes from where he was watching the line form, dragging them slowly up my body and to my face. I offer him a smile, and he returns it, but his eyes—those big, bright, beautiful azure eyes that once were full of life—now hold so much worry behind them, my smile fades.

"What is wrong?" I ask. "I thought this was what you wanted?"

"It is, do not get me wrong, but what of the others?" His eyes trail back to the line. Mine follow.

"What of them?" I say callously.

His eyes shoot to me, and he scowls. "Is my life *so precious* that I alone may live when so many others have met their end, forever to reside here?" He motions all around us.

"That is the nature of death," I say matter-of-factly. "They each will be weighed, and then will enter an eternity befitting the life they have lived."

"What about the life I have lived? Are my sins not so great that I may be spared judgement?" His eyes are no longer filled with worry, but with an emotion I am all too familiar with: guilt.

"You have chosen me. Chosen to live. There is no guilt to be had in such a choice. Any of them would do the same if offered." I brush the back of my hand across his cheek soothingly, and he closes his eyes. Then, he reaches up and takes my hand, opening it and kissing my palm. He nuzzles into it.

"I want you, Hades. Chose you. But you have no right to rob me of the guilt I feel for doing so." He pulls back. "And I will stay with you and find happiness. But know that not a single moment will pass where I do not feel the guilt for such a choice."

I am angry, and grit out, "Would you rather I kill you now, releasing your soul for judgement so you can stand in line with all the others?"

He is hurt, and his features morph into one of anguish. "That is not what I said!" He closes his eyes, places one hand on his hip and pinches the bridge of his nose with the other. "You know what, forget it."

"The words have been spoken, and I am somehow supposed to forget them?" I scoff. "I thought you would be grateful?"

"I am grateful, Hades!" He works a swallow, and then steps back, turning away from me. "Perhaps I am just tired," he says forlornly.

I step to him, curve around his back and rest my head on his shoulder. "There is much for me to do here. You should go to my palace and rest. And when I am finished, I will join you and we can further address your concerns. Cerberus will guide you."

Motioning to Cerberus, he steps forward with speculative eyes, looking to me, Adonis, and then back again. I pat his heads and point to the castle in the distance. "Go and take him with you. I will join you both later."

He chuffs and nudges Adonis forward, who steps hesitantly, looking back at me only once as he walks away with a bristling Cerberus trailing behind him.

"Great," I say. "Now I have two who are pissed at me."

Stepping up onto the dais, I take my seat and usher the first soul forward. They step to the scales, hesitating, and the guards push them onto it with my bident. Then, I once again fulfill my duty by presiding over their judgment.

Several hours later, with one group sent to Tartarus and the other walking across the meadow before me into Elysium, Aphrodite appears at my side.

"Is it done? Did you unlock the stone?" Her need for an answer is too insistent, her tone too hopeful, so I know her request of me had nothing to do with Adonis.

I do not answer her. I just sit atop my steed in silence, watching the sun drifting toward the horizon while her agitation grows beside me.

When she can take it no longer, she accuses, "You did not, did you?"

"What makes you say that?" I smirk, her discomfort satisfying.

"Damn you, Hades, we had a deal!" She huffs, crossing her arms. She searches the silhouettes in the distance, looking for one she recognizes.

Getting off of my horse, I grasp her shoulder and say, "You gave me the stone, but the choice was still mine. And I guess when it came right down to it, I was not willing to risk the consequences of releasing the power trapped inside."

"Choice? There was no choice to make. When I gave you the stone and you took it, I assumed that was you agreeing you would use it as discussed!"

"No need to shout, golden one. He is at peace, and we should both be happy with the knowledge of such."

She brushes my hand off of her shoulder, turning on me so

quickly I am not sure what to expect. "You've taken him from me!" she bellows. "My plans, my future, all of it *gone* because of your infatuation!" She flails her arms as her pacing creates tread marks in the lush grass of the meadows.

"Infatuation? What infatuation? I could not give him back to you even if I wanted to. The risk was too great. And your future? Your *progeny* are safe and sound." I fist the skirts of my gown, wrenching the fabric in anger.

Aphrodite's tears stream down her cheeks, trailing down and beading in golden droplets at her scowling lips. "Liar!" she accuses. "It was within your power. You could have given him back to me. You could have forgone *one* soul if you wanted to!" Her body shakes, and she draws her shawl tighter around her as if pulling it snugly can wrap her in comfort.

"I make no exceptions, Aphrodite! If I did it for you, I would have to do it for others. I will not forsake my vow or my responsibility, nor chance the aftermath that would surely manifest once that power was released. I could not give him back to you, *would not*, and that is that!" I declare.

"I want to see him," she insists.

"You have forgotten your place, Aphrodite. This is my domain, and I will not jeopardize *his* peace for the likes of *you*," I counter.

"But I love him!"

"That was not love; that was possession. You loved the *idea* of him, and the novelty of his presence. But what you *had* was far from love. Did you even ask what *he* wanted? Did you consider *his* wishes? Or did you merely enjoy the attention from having him by your side?"

"I do not expect the likes of *you* to understand," she snarls.

"Understand or not, I will not waver. I will not do this for you, and as such, I think it is time that you leave."

"Not without the stone." She turns, reaching her hand out.

"I think it best I keep it and you leave. Who knows what you might *try*, what you might *do* if I allow you to have it."

"Leave⁈ And go where? Do what, Hades?"

"I heard your husband misses his wife. Perhaps you could see to his needs for once instead of your own," I offer with a hint of disdain.

"Fuck you, Hades. This is not over. If you think I can just forget him, *will* forget him, you are sorely mistaken," she cries, "and the stone is mine! You have no right to keep it!"

"Mistaken or not, and ownership be damned, our business here is done. The stone is now *mine*, and you are no longer welcome in my realm."

"Until when?" She sniffles.

I am unmoved, and my tone is without feeling when I say, "I would say until you have forgotten him, but seeing as you declared that an *impossibility...*" I pause, considering my next words. Then I proclaim, "Aphrodite, Goddess of the Golden Robes, I, Hades, do hereby banish you from my realm from now until forever."

"You can't do this!" she declares, fighting against the whistling wind that swirls as the power of the Underworld tries to eject her.

"Stay, if you can. But know this: the longer you stay, the weaker you will become. The choice is yours, Goddess of Love and Beauty. Will you deny the mortal realm of your power and influence, or will you stay here and diminish yourself, all on the off chance you might lay eyes on him once more?"

"I will have my vengeance, Hades. I will take everything you hold dear and tear it from your cold, heartless hands, and you will be powerless to stop me!"

"Fine," I challenge. "So, I guess I should expect to see you once all the power of the undead has been drained from my realm, and no other gods are willing to protect this place from the likes of *you*." I sneer, shooing her away with a swish of my hand, and she is torn into the sky as the power of the Underworld does my bidding, banishing her from my realm in a burst of golden light.

Back at the palace, I sprint through the hall and tear open the door to my room. Adonis is waiting inside, sitting on the edge of the bed with his head in his hands, wrenching his fingers through his golden curls.

When I enter, he stands and his hands drop to his sides. "That sound—the burst of power—was her, was it not? Is she gone?" he asks.

"I've sent her away. You are safe here," I insist.

Adonis runs to me, and I throw my arms around him, pulling him tight against my chest and kissing the top of his head. Whispering into his hair, I promise, "You shall fear her no longer."

His reply is muffled against my chest. "For how long?"

"For good," I answer. "You will never be hers, and I will always protect you."

Lifting his head, Adonis' eyes lock with mine. Then, I take his face in my hands and lean in for a kiss. It is hot from our breaths coming out in pants, and wet from his tears, with an insistence and hunger that consumes us both as we melt into one another.

Pulling apart, I take his hands in mine before grabbing the stone on the nightstand. It is cold, lifeless, but he is here, so I lead him from the room and out into the hallway. "Come."

"Where are we going?" he asks as I pull him behind me.

"There is just one matter we have yet to attend," I say.

"But I thought it was done?"

"She is gone, yes. But I would be a fool if I thought she would never return and attempt to find you in Elysium, regardless of the effects to her power."

"Then it is not over. Not yet." Adonis stops, dropping my hand.

"Almost, my love. There is one way to ensure she can never seek you out. One final change and you are mine. Only mine." I step to his side.

"I want to be yours, Hades." He gulps loudly. "But I do not know how much more I can withstand." He shakes his head, distressed. He chokes out, "I…"

I pull him to me and wrap one arm around his shoulders as we continue down the hall. "I know," I say, knowing my words are far from comforting.

When we enter my archives, shoving open the door and then passing over the threshold, I guide him to the back of the room. Then, dropping his hand, I bend down and open a chest hidden in the darkness.

When I touch the chest, the torches spark, burning brighter and illuminating the space, and I place the stone inside. Then, I open a second chest, picking something else up.

Adonis peers about, turning in a circle as he takes it all in. And then his eyes land back on me and what I hold up. "What is that?"

"The only way I know to keep you safe," I offer. "With this draft, I will take away everything she valued about you, leaving us to be together without fear of her return." I am confident in my decision, and offer him a comforting smile so he will be too.

He takes the vial, loosens the stopper with a *pop,* and a trail of smoke rises into the air.

"Hurry," I say, "before the air takes hold."

He places the vial at his lips and then throws the contents back, my eyes trained on his throat as I watch him swallow it down.

Titans, that neck is gorgeous, I think. Then, I step toward him, wanting to scrape my teeth down it. But as I lower my head, he begins to transform before my eyes.

Tufts of wiry hair split his flesh open and burst free, first along that beautiful neck, and then down his sculpted abdomen. The skin there ripples, separating as muscles that bulge more than his current ones form, covered by tawny flesh. No, not flesh, *a hide*.

I jerk away from him, my eyes widening as his body twists and contorts, growing in size and tearing out of his linens until a horned, beast-like *thing* stands naked before me. It is a man/minotaur, with the head of a bull bearing two marble-like horns on each side of his abnormally large head, and bunches of hair running down and around his neck and ending at the nape.

The hair is tufted, much like Cerberus', and the skin of his chest and abdomen is now, not so much hairy, but hide-like—velvety and smooth. Then, where his muscular thighs once were, haunches trail down and end in large human feet.

The minotaur towers over me as I cower back against the wall. And, in what can only be considered an utterance of disgust than the question it should have been, I call out, "Adonis?"

He steps toward me with his arms outstretched and, in a voice deeper than it has ever been, says, "My love," and I lose it.

I scamper back away from him, quickly rising to my feet. He advances, and with every step in my direction, I circle around him.

He turns, following my every move and gauging my reaction. "What is it? What's wrong?" the gruff voice asks.

Finally realizing his voice is not his own, he pulls his hands to his mouth. Well, what used to be a mouth but is now a muzzle. He gasps, crying out each time he moves his hand over another unfamiliar feature—first his snout with enlarged nostrils, then his wide eyes, and lastly the two massive horns.

"I am a monster!" he shrieks, lowering his hands. They remain human, but are now larger, and covered with tawny hide-like flesh. "What have you done to me?" he asks, stepping toward me.

I have circled around and am close to the door when he tries to rush toward me. On unfamiliar legs, he stumbles, landing outstretched on the floor where one horn impacts the threshold. He lands with a crack, and a stone wobbles loose beneath him.

When he attempts to stand, he slides, his feet unable to gain purchase, and lands on the stone once more. It lifts slightly from its placement, and finally I move toward him.

With him sobbing, I offer him my hand, allowing him to brace his massive weight on me while he gains his footing and settles his emotions. He is only slightly shorter than me now, but everything else about him is so powerful, so magnificent. Still, the puffs of air escaping his nostrils with each burst of panic has me sneering in disgust.

"I am sorry," I say, pulling away and leaving him standing at the threshold while I back up.

"You have made me ugly," he cries. "You have turned me into something that not just Aphrodite, but even you cannot love." Then, he turns and runs from the room, one foot catching and lifting the stone as he almost trips out of the door, and escapes into the hallway.

PART TWO

"Come to me now: loose me from hard
care and all my heart longs
to accomplish, accomplish. You
be my ally."
SAPPHO

Gasping and gasping, the movements of my mouth much like a fish out of water, I flail, grasping at my neck before two large hands pin my arms at my sides. "It is okay, Melody. Breathe. Breathe," he soothes. "You are just coming out of it."

I am disoriented, with a fog billowing around inside my head and making me nauseous. "I think I am going to be sick," I say, turning my head off of the side of the bed so I can retch onto the floor and not all over Hades. Or the duvet. Or the bed. *Or me.*

When I am done, and the contents of my stomach paint the floor in a greenish slime, I wipe the corner of my mouth with the back of my hand and slump back into my pillow. It is soaked with sweat, and my damp hair sticks not only to my face but the sides of my neck.

Hades wipes back the coated strands, brushing a kiss across my forehead before he stands and walks over to the linen basket. Grabbing a towel, he says, "If you are feeling up to it, I could carry you to the grotto and wash away your body's reaction to the walk."

"The walk?" I force out.

"Yes. Do you not remember?" he asks.

"Remember?" I shake my head *no* involuntarily, my tongue feeling too heavy to speak.

Panic dresses his features, and he rushes to my side. "What is your name?"

I try to sit up, but wince when pain shoots down my spine. Hades sits on the edge of our bed and assists me when I try again. There is so much pain, and my head, my neck, my body, my *everything* hurts, but still I answer, "Melody."

"Good," he coos. "Yes, you are Melody, and I am?"

I look at him as if he has a penis growing out of his forehead. "Hades," I grumble.

"That is right. I am Hades." He pulls me to his chest in his excitement, and I cry out. "Oh, sorry," he says, loosening his hold. "I was worried you—"

"You were worried you gave me some fucking *disgusting* concoction that allowed me to see things *beyond* my wildest imagination and now I have no *memory*?" I scoff. "Whatever confidence I had that you knew what you were doing... gone," I say, my tone filled with less irritation than it should be.

"Okay, so you remember who you are and who I am. What else do you remember?" he asks, hopeful.

"As in, do I remember that, there I was minding my own damn business, living a slightly unfulfilling life, when *your* ex- decided to play invasion of the body snatchers and fuck up said life with, what I can now assume was, one of the Nostos Stones?" My tone is beyond condescending. Luckily for me, he takes no offense and guffaws so loudly the bed shakes.

"Oh, thank the Titans. I was getting worried there for a minute," he says, struggling to get the words out through his laughter.

"You think!" I say, not as a question but simply a nicer way to deliver the *fuck you* I want to slap him with to wipe that look off of his *smug ass face*!

"With the way you are looking at me now, I would say it is time to revisit the aforementioned sentiments about me being a *monster*. Care to amend your previous response?" All the hilarity pulling his lips up into a smile before, are now overshadowed by the darkness that has taken its place—the shadow of that red devil perching on his shoulder and telling him just how monstrous I should find him —making the room go cold.

I shiver. Not from the lack of warmth radiating from his body but from the icy stare he has on me. I choose my next words carefully. "No amendments." My answer is clipped, but accurate. "No realization that I have been seeing you through rose-colored glasses, or a change of heart," I insist, reaching for his hand and pulling it into my lap. "I still want whatever this is we have. *Love,* whatever this is. What about you, are you having a change of heart I should know about?"

He is silent for a moment, and instead of answering my question, he leans down and places a soft kiss on my lips. I return his affections, but our kiss is not as hungry as before. Still, there is a lingering tingle as he draws back, the same I felt once we came back from Charon's temple.

"Now for a soak," he says, standing and lifting me up, cradling me in his arms as he makes his way toward the door.

"Wait!" I call out. "Robe or you'll be carrying me back naked."

"You say that as if that is not how I would prefer to have you in my arms."

"Preferring me to be naked or not, grab the damn *robe*," I scold.

He rolls his eyes and then steps to the cabinet. I push it open with my foot, and he turns, reaching inside and grabbing one. He drapes it over my head and I pull it off of my face, smiling up at him.

"There she is," he says, returning my smile. Then he heads back to the door and we leave the room. Next stop, the grotto.

As we are walking down the hallway and past his archives, I make him stop, staring down at where new stones are placed. They are different—cleaner—and their recent placement is obvious considering how they differ from the other stones lining the hallway.

"So much makes sense now: Erymanthe, a.k.a. Aphrodite's interference with Persephone, your comments to her about loving Adonis after his death during dinner, your irritation at the stones. All of it," I offer.

"What about those instances makes sense?" he asks.

"Oh, no you don't," I say. "We are not getting into *any* of that standing here in the hallway. Grotto," I command, pointing down the corridor.

We move on, his steps sounding with a flop from his sandals, and then we are there. The stone slides back, the smell of jasmine spills from the room, and the torches illuminate within the cavern, lighting the space.

He steps inside, following along the left wall beside the pool, and then we reach the steps. He sets me down, offering to take my soiled gown. I give it to him, and he tosses it in the air. It appears on the other side of the room where it falls into the soiled linens basket by the entryway.

"There's that magic again," I quip, making my way to the steps.

I enter the pool, one foot following the next and disturbing the water with ripples that spread throughout it. Hades disrobes and does the same. Soon we are both wading in the center of the pool, moving our arms back and forth as our feet kick along the surface.

Steam lifts off of the water, billowing upward where it lingers amongst the night-blooming jasmine hanging from the ceiling. The temperature of the water is positively sublime, loosening my muscles that ache, and I moan. Then Hades swims up behind me, pulling me back against his body and moving us toward the side of the pool.

With one arm around my waist, he pulls me around him, pushing me up onto the lounge chair by the shelf of soaps. He deposits me there while he treads beside me.

I reach for the soap, and he stops me, pulling the bottle from the ledge and pouring some into his palm. He smells it, then drops his hand in the water and washes it off with a sneer. He then tosses the jar across the room, where it shatters against the wall.

"Do I even want to know?" I ask, my eyes still wide as I lean back away from him, unsure of what just transpired.

"It was hers," he growls.

"Oh," I say, reaching for another bottle and pulling out the stopper. I sniff, and it is lavender this time, so I hand it to him.

With a generous amount poured into his palm, he hands the bottle back to me, and I take it, getting ready to pour some of my own when he says, "Wrong answer."

I falter, placing the stopper back in the bottle and setting it back on the ledge as I screw my features. He grins, and once I place my hands in my lap, looking at him expectantly, he leans me back on the chair.

My back curves into the seat as I settle in, and Hades wades to my feet where he takes one and rubs. With his pointer finger bent, he runs it up my arch, and I jerk my leg back, giggling. "No tickling," I say, splashing the water.

He lifts a brow and takes hold of my foot again, this time rubbing until I groan.

"Gods, that feels *so good*," I moan.

"Keep making that sound and you will have the cleanest feet in all the Underworld."

I do my best to hold in my moans after that, and Hades washes my body, one leg after the other, until he is trailing his fingers up my abdomen and across my breasts. I lift my left arm and he cleans it, washing from my armpit to the fingertips before asking for the next. I give it to him, and he repeats his cleansing ritual, stopping when he gets to my right palm.

Staring intently at my hand, he trails one finger down the middle. Where the slash from the ceremonial dagger once was red and irritated, there is now a faint pink line bisecting my hand. I hadn't looked at it since waking, so I am just as taken aback as he is at its current state.

"How long was I asleep?" I ask, pulling my hand back for closer inspection. "This looks like only a scratch."

"Mm-hmm," he mumbles, not voicing the question pooling in his eyes. They are narrowed, confused, and not the least bit comforting.

"Is that all you have to offer?" I squeak. "Just some Neanderthal-esque grunt that tells me jack shit about how long I was asleep, or what is currently tormenting that mind of yours?"

He closes his eyes, his face pained. "Three days."

"Three days? There is no way I should have healed in just—"

"Yes, I know. That is why I cannot think of anything else to say about it right now." He sighs.

"I am not the first to use the stone. Surely Adonis was injured once?"

"He was." His answer is clipped.

"And?" I am on the verge of panic waiting for him to elaborate. "How long did it take to heal his injury?" My hands are now pulled into my chest, shaking as I dig in my fingernails. I leave crescent indentations on the top of my right hand, and Hades pulls them away from me, kissing them.

Once I am calm, he answers, "Weeks."

"Weeks?" My voice pitches up in my agitated state. "He was a mortal. Well, kinda. But if another mortal that used the stone healed in weeks as expected, then why have I completely healed in a matter of days?"

"If I could answer that question, Melody, I would have given you more than just a grunt. But I cannot, and I have no clue why your healing is *unusually rapid*."

"Unusually rapid?" I am silent while he stares at me with a look on his face I can't quite discern. I shake my head in disbelief. "Three days can be considered a little more than unusually rapid, Hades. One might consider it—"

"Superhuman. Yes, I too have come to that conclusion. But among the Olympians we have another term for something *this* unusual."

"And that is?"

He doesn't answer right away, pulling my hands until I am in the water. I tread beside him, and he wraps his arms around me, nuzzling his nose up my ear where he whispers, "Demigod."

I try to jerk out of his hold, but he presses me to his chest. "I am no fucking demigod, Hades. Now let me go!" Continuing to struggle against him, he doesn't loosen his hold on me. Instead, he kicks his legs and moves us back toward the stairs.

Once we are there, with the scent of lavender lingering on my skin and mingling with the fear coming off of me in waves, he sits and pulls me into his lap, cradling me in his arms as he breathes me in. I stop fighting.

Over and over, he draws in my scent, his nostrils flaring at the crook of my neck. Then, with his fingernail, he slashes the soft skin above my breast, and I gasp, watching as my blood beads along the angry red line.

He sniffs again, his jaw clenching against my arm, and then he takes his hand and swipes over the mark, washing away the blood. I look down, and we both see that the angry red line is now pink—healed.

I jerk out of his hold and scramble up the steps, not believing what I just witnessed. "That's—"

"Impossible? Yes, it should be. And yet, the proof is there. Now not only on the palm of your hand but above your beautiful breast," he snarls. "Just what are you playing at, Melody? Did she send you? Did she?" he shouts, stalking toward me as if I am his prey and he is ready to pounce.

"No—no one sent me," I stammer, my voice rising with my fear as I back into the wall. "I am just who you think I am. I'm Melody, the mortal who Persephone killed, and you saved once I entered your realm," I cry, following the bend in the cavern toward the opening several feet away. He seems far from convinced.

"Oh, but you are far from mortal, my dear Melody. It was always there but I ignored every sign: the Algea, the scent of your blood, the guardians at the gate, the electricity in our contact. I thought I knew who and *what* you were, but boy was I wrong." His lips curl up in a sneer and he takes his first step out of the pool

He is disgusted, I realize. He is looking at me as if I have betrayed him. With fear coursing through me, as I continue backing toward the exit, I have only one thought. *Run!*

CHAPTER 24
SANDS IN THE HOURGLASS (HADES)

Betrayal may be a dish best served cold, but as I step out of the pool and into the cool air of the cavern, Melody's betrayal has me so heated my flames are not just licking over the surface of my skin, they are scratching, gnawing, and tearing open my foolish heart. It bleeds out not just ichor, but all the destructive passion I have felt for her and kept simmering beneath the surface. And I wanted to spare her the burn of my wrath, saving her from my ferocity. But as that bright cobalt inferno covers my entirety, there is nothing that can save her from me now. Because I am determined to see her suffer, and suffer she shall.

I am barely to the entryway of the grotto, preparing to exit, when the sound of wet feet slapping down on stone as she flees is drowned out by the slamming of a door. *Surely she cannot think that a closed door will stop me, or that there is anywhere in my keep she can hide?* But as I round the corner, with the torches in the hallway extinguishing as I pull all of my power from within the castle and into myself... Well, Titan's forgive me, because Melody has a date with the King of Death and he will have her begging for mercy the likes of which the Underworld has never seen.

With the torches snuffed out, my flames illuminate the darkness, casting the hallway in a sapphire glow. There is no rush, and I am in no hurry to see to her punishment, so I walk casually, keeping my ears trained on the silence so I can hear any... little... sound she makes.

The door to the archives stands open, so she considered that room, maybe even entered it but strayed from the thought because, of course, she did. And the dining hall door, too, stands ajar. But alas, she would not have gone in there. Or the throne room. Or *our* room. I crack my neck at that thought and continue on.

So where or where has my little Melody gone?

Standing in front of Persephone's door, I consider, *she could not possibly have gone into her room?* No, not after everything she has learned, after what she has seen. There is no quicker way to send me straight over the edge than to seek refuge in the one place I *despise* setting foot. And yet, there is no other room she could be in, given not only the time she had to escape, and the slamming of the door whose sound was not so distant, but that she knew, *or thought*, I would not dare enter.

Too bad she is sadly mistaken, and her mistake will cost her. But will my mistakes regarding Melody cost me more? Will they cost me everything? Will Aphrodite finally get her wish and best me once and for all, actually accomplishing what she said she would all those millennia ago—take everything I hold dear and tear it from my cold, heartless hands, as I am powerless to stop her?

No. Not today. Not in this lifetime or the next. There is no way she has accumulated the power she would need to conduct such a feat because I have *seen* to it! *Or have I?*

I cannot think like this. I need to remain focused and rational. I need to maintain my composure, seek out that little pretender, and get to the bottom of just what the hell it is Aphrodite has sent her to do. But to do that, first I have to be willing to step foot in that room. And when I do, I need to be ready. I need to be ready to combat an unknown force, with untapped power, drawn from an unhinged goddess who would revel in my destruction. Despite knowing that, I open the door and step inside.

With the door open and the threshold crossed, I feel Melody's fear. I can sense it billowing out from under the bed, and know that is where she is lurking.

Tricky little minx, hiding where she thinks I am too big to follow. Has she learned nothing during her time in this place? Does she not know that with a *mere* thought I could destroy that bed and leave her scrambling? Of course she does. So I do as I envision it in my mind and split the bed in half, right down the middle, and have the pieces falling apart in opposite directions to reveal a very terrified, but still *very naked*, demigod.

Her fear has power pulsing around her like a protective barrier, crimson and flickering. But what little sliver of essence she has is no match for a *true god* and son of a Titan. I mean, if she is in fact a demigod, which all evidence supports, she would have to be how many generations removed? It really does not fucking matter because, power or not, this bitch has nothing on me.

I go to move toward her but stop myself. *Wait, how can I go from loving her with every ounce of my being one minute and calling her mine, to wanting to eviscerate her in the next?* This is not right. I shake my head in disgust—at the situation and at myself. This is not who I am. Who I have become. I have worked so *hard* to be better, to *do* better, and all it took was an inkling of betrayal and that golden bitch has me careening right over the edge and back into my old ways.

Maybe that was part of Aphrodite's plan all along. Maybe now all the dots have been lined up, and an "x" is marking the damn spot for her to waltz right in here and claim the treasure she feels she deserves. The Acolyte had said she would drain the power from my realm and strike down all the false gods. But to do that, she would first have to weaken *me*. And what better way to weaken me than to make me kill my own love? My last love.

I had not told her I loved her. Maybe if I had, Melody would not be curled into herself, shivering, with her hands over her face for protection.

Now, despite my rage, all I want to do is let down my guard and sweep her up in my arms and hold her. Protect her. I promised I would. Hell, I wrapped her in my warmth and called her *mine*. Yet all it took was one ounce of skepticism, and I am ready to destroy her? I cannot do it, and that lingering question holds me at bay.

"Did she send you?" My question is more like a plea than a command for answers, and my flames retreat into myself as my skin reforms.

Melody is looking up at me between her fingers, and once I am more *myself* and have released my power back into the keep, she lowers her hands from in front of her face, but they are still drawn over her chest where she is clutching something.

"I will ask you one more time, Melody, did she send you?" My voice is calm, even, and I do not let my anger seep into my tone. "Are you working for her?" My voice cracks.

After several minutes of complete silence, she still has not answered either of my questions, so I step toward her and crouch down to seem less imposing. She meets my heated stare and relaxes, shifting to a seated position with her arms crossed over her breasts.

"I will not hurt you, Melody, but I need to know," I insist.

"She did not," she offers, her voice barely above a whisper.

I relax my tense shoulders and am about to take a seat when I realize she would be more comfortable in this situation if neither of us were naked. So, I stand to pick her up, step forward, and she scoots back away from me.

"You have nothing to fear from me. I just want to get us dressed so we can talk."

"Talk?" she asks, her voice unsure—doubtful. "Wasn't it just ten minutes ago that you wanted to end me?"

"A lapse in judgement, and an egregious one, so I truly am sorry," I say, trying my best to sound apologetic. I obviously fail because she looks at me like I am an absolute crazy person, but takes my offered hand.

Still clutching something over her chest, I pick her up once she is standing and take her to our room so we can both dress before we continue. Then, once we are clothed—her in a crimson gown and me in dark grey linen—she sits on the edge of the bed twirling something in her fingers.

I tuck the loose ends of my fabric in the waist of my skirt, and sit on the bed next to her. Her eyes remain on her hands and what she is fiddling with.

She lifts what she is holding and says, "I found this in her room, underneath the bed. I knew it was there, or... I had seen her put it there once, but forgot." She offers it to me, and I take it.

"Do you know what this is, what it does?"

She nods. "For a minute there I thought I might have to use it." She smiles weakly.

"With what purpose in mind?" I ask.

"To get you to stop, to see reason, and to pause a moment and think over everything you know about me so that you could come to the conclusion that should be evident by now—I am not here to hurt you."

"Easier said than done," I admit.

"Don't I know it." She chuckles, and just that sound fills my heart back up to brimming when it felt so empty before.

"All this time Persephone had this stone and not once did she use it," I say, holding it up. "I wonder why that is?"

Melody shrugs her shoulders and then leans into me. "I will say one thing though: history has shit on how crazy you can actually be. Like, seriously, Hades. You were nothing but a gold skeleton for a minute there. It reminded me of Halloween in Fayetteville. The houses around campus would have so many lined up on their front lawns. They weren't gilded, though. Just your normal run-of-the-mill skellys. Twelve-foot monstrosities."

I laugh and then place the stone in her hand, closing mine over top of it. "Here. Keep it so that if I ever get 'crazy' again, you have some protection."

"I'd love to say I have nothing to fear, but today proved the opposite." She looks up at me, and a tear trails down her cheek, her lip quivering as she tries to hold back her emotions.

I wrap my arms around her shoulders, and she loses it. "I am sorry. I know the words alone are not enough, and I should have never let things get that bad, but I just..." I cannot finish the sentence, because what I was going to say is my worst nightmare.

"You just struggle to trust others, and assume that everyone is out to get you. Yeah, that part was obvious," she says through her sobs. She takes several deep breaths and then composes herself. Wiping away her tears, she says, "Though one good thing did come of this."

"How do you figure?"

"Well, if you hadn't gone all psycho and destroyed the bed, this stone may have been lost forever." She holds it up, and the now flickering torches illuminate the stone. "And for someone with an archive meant to protect precious items and powerful remnants, you keep crappy inventory." She laughs, and I join her when that infectious sound melts my ice-cold heart.

"Speaking of remnants: now that you know what the Infinity

Stone is and what it can do, why do you think Persephone has taken it and Aphrodite wants it? I have been racking my brain trying to figure both out."

"Oh, well, that's an easy one. Persephone wants the power the trapped souls provide so she can keep on living free as a bird and causing chaos, and Aphrodite wants to fill it to the brim so she can truly access the remnant. One fulfills the other, and that is why Aphrodite has yet to interfere," she says matter-of-factly.

"And just how did you come to that conclusion?"

"I don't know; maybe it was Aphrodite's constant opposition to your statements that the remnant being released was a bad idea. Or that there are *six* stones containing power. The Infinity Stone, this one, and all the others I'm assuming you already have. One remnant, no harm done. But all six..."

"I do have the rest. I sought them all out and decided the only way to safeguard them was to keep them here. But yeah, still do not follow," I say.

"Aphrodite has this magic number of fifteen she touted to Perse-phone. She told her that once the stone was unlocked, and fifteen souls were housed within, she could be free of you forever. But I think her words had a double meaning."

"Double meaning, how?"

"She is using Persephone's desperate wish to be free of you to do her bidding by having her fill up the stone. Once the stone is full, she will no longer have use of Persephone. So it's bye-bye to one pain in our ass and hello to an even bigger one."

I smile, and as she looks at me I can tell she has no clue why I am smiling. "You said *our*." I kiss her forehead.

She pulls out of my arms and punches me in the shoulder. "Of course I said *our*, you idiot. If they are coming for you, then they are coming for me. Package deal, remember? You offered me a place here, and now this is my home. No one threatens my home and gets away with it." Her face is so stern and serious that I cannot help but laugh.

"Okay, so next question: how do we protect *our* home from those who wish to destroy it?"

She stands and tries to look tough, but then she deflates. "Beats the fuck out of me. I'm just a demigod, Hades. Don't expect too much out of me."

"You said *demigod*," I tease, drawing a hand to my mouth as I feign shock at her admission. Then, I pull her into me and kiss the top of her head. "Well, demigod, we better do an inventory to see if anything else is missing from my archives, because we have *our* home to protect." And with that, we walk back to my archives.

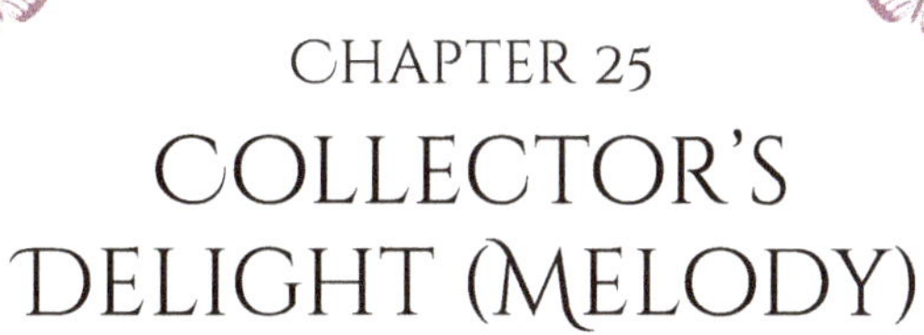

CHAPTER 25
COLLECTOR'S DELIGHT (MELODY)

Seated leaning against the back wall, I watch as Hades pulls one item after another from the first two of the three chests as I write each item down. There are potions for transfiguration and drafts for healing in the first chest, while the second is full of artifacts—some from Ancient Greece, while others are more modern.

Hades lifts a pocket watch from the second chest, handing it to me, and I ask what it is. He says, "That watch belonged to Jack the Ripper."

"No shit!"

"So, no one knows this, but he had OCD. He would rotate the crown five times and then flip open the front cover and close it five times while he stalked his victims." He mimics the motions of winding the watch with his hands, and then finishes by circling his finger by his ear while mouthing *cuckoo*.

"Really?" I chuckle, astounded as I look down at the silver timepiece in my hands. The crown is bronze and shell shaped while the front cover is etched with ornate scrollwork and patterned leaves. Then, when I flip it over, the pattern repeats on the back, but in the center there is a shield where the initials *C.F.F.* are stamped.

After cataloging the watch, Hades lifts the top tray from the chest, setting it down before me. Then, he pulls out a curved sword with an odd handle and offers it to me. I take it. "And this is?"

"That sword was used by Genghis Khan." He smiles. "It is one of my favorite pieces."

I run my hand over the handle, which is about six inches long, and bump my fingers over the pronounced rings. "Is this a piece of an antler or a bone of some sort?" I hand it back.

"Horn," he says, too busy playing with the sword to look in my direction. "Mongolian Saiga."

"Huh," I say. "I can't imagine it would be that comfortable or practical to grip."

"It was not. That is why it was usually wrapped in cloth."

"You learn something new every day," I muse.

Hades continues slicing the air with the sword, battling some imaginary foe, while I look through the tray in front of me.

Then I pick up a small pouch, loosening the drawstring. I turn over the bag, spilling the contents into my hand, and drop it immediately. Scooting away, I say, "What in the gods' names is that?" My lips turn up in disgust.

Hades sets the sword back in the chest and then leans over to pick up the small, wrinkled piece of something. It is about the size of a date, and weathered like a piece of jerky. He laughs as he motions for the bag. Then, putting the item back inside, he says, "That is the missing piece of Evander Holyfield's ear."

"Why would you keep that?" I shriek.

"It was one of the very few times I went to the mortal realm that century, and I was actually in Las Vegas for the fight because I wanted to see it in person instead of through my peering stone.

During the commotion, I scooped up this little piece of history, and away I went." He motions his fingers walking away.

"You know that's gross, right? Like, there is something really creepy about taking that as a keepsake. And how would you introduce that into regular conversation? Would you be like, this is Jack the Ripper's watch, and Genghis Khan's sword, but this... ooh, look at this one. This is Evander's ear?" she mocks.

"To be honest, you are the first person to see my collection, so... it is a non-issue at this point."

"Still." I avert my gaze, looking at the tray but not wanting to touch another item for fear of what I might find.

Seeing my disinterest in the second chest, Hades asks, "How about we move on to the third chest?"

"That sounds like a fabulous idea. Unless of course one of the gems was shit out by a Titan, then I would prefer a pair of gloves before handling any of them," I propose.

"Mined from the mountains as far as I know, so no gloves needed," he says.

The third chest, which houses nothing but jewelry, precious gems, and stones, is sitting open in the corner. Hades closes the lid, picks it up, and then drops it in front of me. Before lifting the lid, he asks, "Would you prefer one tray at a time, or for me to set them all out?"

"Bring them all out and we can go from the bottom tray and then put it back, and so on and so on."

"As you wish," he says, arranging each tray in an arc on the floor at our feet. Then he picks up a cloth from the far left tray, unfolds the wrapping and displays a chunky gold necklace with two entwining snakes that have red gems for eyes. "This is the Necklace of Harmonia. It is cursed, so do not touch it."

"And you have it, why?"

"To ensure no one else is plagued by this wretched thing. It was a gift from Hephaestus. And like many of the items crafted by him, the wearer did not fare well. See, Harmonia was a daughter of Aphrodite and her brother Ares. So, because he could not punish his wife Aphrodite directly, he did so through this."

"Poor Harmonia," I say.

"You have met her, you know?"

"I have?" I am confused by this revelation, because I don't recall meeting a single goddess since being in the Underworld.

"Once she and Cadmus were turned into snakes, I brought her here to be one of the guardians of the gate."

"You have one of Aphrodite's daughters guarding the gates to Tartarus? Do you think that's wise?" I ask.

"She can do no harm in her current state," he insists, "and she is loyal to me."

I write the name of the necklace in the catalog, listing it as *dangerous-do not touch*, and he places it back in the chest before lifting the next item.

"The Aurora Sapphire," he says, holding it up to the light. It is so small in his hand, but the teardrop-shaped stone could fit in my palm. "So, Memnon, son of Eos, used it to blind his enemies in the literal or figurative sense. His divine armor, which he wore during all his battles, was made by Hephaestus. I absconded with the stone right before his last battle—the one which led to his death at the hands of Achilles."

"I am sensing a theme here. Aphrodite knew of the stones and had the Renascence Ruby, and—"

"And the Infinity Stone," he says.

"Okay, and the Infinity Stone. And those with the stones had either a close connection with Hephaestus or were descendants of Aphrodite somehow."

"Yes."

"Which tray were those in?" I ask, holding open the ledger.

"Top tray," he says. "Here and here," he points to two open spaces in the top tray to my right.

I add the numbers of the items to the basic drawings of the trays I rendered to show which item was placed where. "What about the open space in tray three?"

He picks up the Subjugation Stone sitting beside me and places it in the empty space.

"Okay, so the Subjugation Stone is in placement four of the top tray. Got it. And the story behind it?"

"Peítho was a daughter of Aphrodite. Obviously, she was passing down the power of the stones to her progeny to ensure she always knew where they were. I stole this one shortly after getting the ruby and then the Infinity Stone."

"That leaves three spaces open in the bottom tray, none in the second tray, and... which, by the way, we haven't catalogued a single item from that tray," I say.

"The second tray's contents are all non-magical, as you would say. No special properties. They were just pretty, so I took them."

"You little thief," I prod.

"Like a crow, I too like shiny things."

"And what about that empty space?" I ask, pointing to the last empty space in the top tray.

"That is for the Kingmaker Emerald. So Cadmus, the first king of Thebes and grandson of Poseidon, was married to Harmonia. Her bride gift from the gods was her necklace," he says, pointing to the wrapped item in the bottom tray.

"Is that emerald the one from the center of Persephone's crown?"

"The very same," he says, going into the bottom of the chest and lifting the crown. He offers it to me.

I take it, turning it over in my hands. Then, I place it on my head. "How do I look?" It slips down and around my neck.

"Very regal," he says, chuckling. "Though you do not seem to have the same aversion to it as she did."

"That's because I didn't fuck the guy these hands belonged to," I say, motioning to the crown around my neck. "Again, creepy, just like the ear. But at least I get the reasoning behind this."

"So, are you going to request a crown as well?"

"One, we aren't married, and two, I am the farthest thing from a queen there could ever be," I say, handing him back the crown.

"Both of which are an easy fix." He is unaffected in his delivery. "And you are a demigod, so it is not too much of a stretch to see yourself as a queen. Besides the gods slumbering on Olympus, you are the closest thing to our version of royalty in this day and age."

"Yeah, well, tell that to Persephone and Aphrodite, both of whom only see me as some pawn to play in whatever game it is they are trying to win."

"That remains to be seen," he says, taking a seat beside me.

I look over the ledger. "What about the one space in the bottom tray?" I point to my drawing, and he scoots forward, lifting an item from the place I mentioned and handing it to me.

"The Mustēria Stone. This is how I found you in the mortal realm. Hermes, a close friend of Aphrodite who was often seen at her side, was not only the messenger of the gods but the mediator between the seen and unseen. He would guide the souls of the dead to the Underworld, and was often represented by an owl. So it came as no surprise that when I unlocked the stone, an owl appeared."

"That is something I would like to see," I proclaim.

He takes the stone and places it back in the chest. "Another time, perhaps. Now I am needed at the scales." He looks toward the door.

"How does that work exactly?"

"How does what work?" he asks, offering me his hand once he is standing.

"The call to the scales."

"Oh, that. Well, if I am in the mortal realm, I am involuntarily brought back to the Underworld. Quite violently, might I add. And if I am in residence, then I can feel the pull. It is like how your stomach feels when you are on a ride that the bottom drops out."

"You mean a rollercoaster?"

"Yes, a rollercoaster. There is a rush, a feeling of weightlessness, and then a twisting and churning in my stomach as it rises to my throat. It is rather uncomfortable."

"I bet," I say, taking his arm as we walk down the hall.

"One thing before we go," he says, and I turn my face up to look at him. He takes both of my hands in his. "If we could not mention what happened earlier in the grotto, and then our revelations that preceded it."

"Why is that?"

"Something just is not adding up, and I would prefer Charon not be aware of your demigod status as of yet. He has never been a fan of demigods, and he likes you at the moment. I would hate to change his view of you," he says.

I nod in understanding, though I don't understand at all. Charon not liking demigods is an odd reason to hide such a revelation, if he could offer some insight into how or why Persephone could control me in the first place.

CHAPTER 26

REVELATIONS (HADES)

There is not much excitement to be had in the weighing of souls nowadays, and even less indication it serves a greater purpose as it once did. Still, despite how boring it is as they step forward in line, ascend the scales, and are divided into groups, the responsibility falls to me, and has for a very long time. But on days like today, when I would rather be doing something, hell, anything else, the hours spent feel far from rewarding. And why is that? Because the quality of souls entering my realm has significantly diminished.

Mortals are not out in the world fighting monsters, making historical breakthroughs, or preventing atrocities on the global scale. They are pioneering for profit and living in mediocrity or ruling unjustly for the betterment of one instead of politicking for the quality of life for the many. As such, my cup does not runneth over from the power I attain by accepting them into my realm. To explain it in a way that makes sense in this day and age: the quality of souls I acquire is barely enough to make a dent in the deficit of power it takes to run this place, and some days I wonder how much longer I can keep the lights on, so to speak.

Then, as I sit massaging my temples while Melody shifts restlessly beside me, a soul steps onto the scales and I glean their life—its end more specifically—and the excitement I had been complaining was absent, shows up in a way I never expected. There, in the last moments before their eyes closed for the last time, I see a middle-aged woman straddling a man and holding an all too familiar dagger high above her head.

"Wait!" I call out, halting the guards who are ushering the woman standing before the scales to the group bound for Elysium. "You were in the United States? In Arkansas?"

She nods her head, clasping her hands anxiously in front of her. "My husband and I were visiting family for Thanksgiving," she says.

I look at the two groups waiting with the guards. "Which one is he?" Waiting for her to point him out, I scan the faces of all the men.

She does the same and then says forlornly, "I don't see him here." Stepping down from the dais, I cross the distance and stand at her side. "The last thing I remember, we went out for drinks at this really cool speakeasy my brother told us about. There was a woman. She was beautiful, charming, and a little forward, but we've always liked them that way," she admits.

"Liked who 'that way'?"

"The women we invited to… play with us," she answers hesitantly.

My eyebrows shoot up before I can stop them, but I fix my face so she does not shut down. I want her to offer the information freely. I do not want to have to tear it from her mind. "Where did you meet? The woman, not your husband. What was the name of the speakeasy?" I prod.

"I don't remember the name," she says, and I do not hide my

disappointment. "I guess we won't be making it to Thanksgiving this year." She sighs and starts to turn, but stops. "Oh, but it was tropical, if that helps?"

"Yes, you have been most helpful," I say, smiling. I motion for the guards to take her, and they lead her group away toward Elysium while the other group heads toward Tartarus. Then I turn to look back at where Melody still stands beside the throne. "Any chance you know of a tropical speakeasy in Arkansas?"

Melody lets out a stifled laugh. "Yeah, actually I do," she says, descending the dais one step at a time. "One of my friends from art school, Janessa, told me about it."

"Art school?"

Once she stands beside me, she says, "It is new, and so is the art gallery where she is having one of her pieces on exhibit soon. I think she said the local artists are in the first week of December. It is not December yet, is it?" she asks, and I shake my head *no*. "Well, the studio matters because that is how you get into the speakeasy. The entrance is through a hidden door in the gallery. Kind of like Alice stepping through the looking glass and into a magical world. But this magical world is all amber mood lighting, themed drinks, and tiki heads. I had never been, but Janessa showed me pictures, and I was looking forward to not only seeing it in person but all of us making a night of it after viewing her exhibit."

"And who all was included in the 'all of us'? Any chance there was a married couple—a man and a woman—in your group?" I take her hand and we begin our trek back to the keep.

"Charity and Marcus. Super cute couple who got married last year. I had some classes with Charity. But unlike me, she is actually using her art degree, where I just pretended to be an artist from time to time." She laughs.

I squeeze her hand. "Stop," I say, wanting her to quit the self-deprecation. "You are smart, funny, and beyond capable." I turn her to face me and stare into her eyes.

"How would you know?" She scoffs, looking away. "You have never seen any of my work."

"I am sure your work is just as amazing as you are," I praise, placing my hand under her chin and lifting her face.

She blushes and then says, "Back to Charity and Marcus. Why a couple?"

We walk again, and I drop my hand from hers so I can rub her back. "Because from what I have seen, Persephone has found herself a new hunting ground. If that woman's husband was the magical number fifteen you told me about, then shit is about to hit the fan wherever she is, and I do not want to be playing catch-up when it does," I explain.

She stops. "So what do we do now?"

I pull her into me, and she lays her head against my chest. I kiss the top of her head, breathing in her lavender scent before I say, "Now we have a few days to plan before we casually replace sweet Charity and her dear Marcus for the exhibit and dinner afterwards. A couple of the transfiguration potions you inventoried earlier should help. And if I know Persephone, this new host presents her with an opportunity too good to pass up."

She looks up expectantly. "And the parasite keeps killing until she reaches the magical quota and the freedom she was promised." She grimaces.

"Should we expect anything less?" We continue on, and eventually step through the archway.

"No, I suppose not," she says, "but going after couples is risky, and if she has collected the fifteen and nothing happened, there will be an escalation of her efforts."

"But if the fifteen fulfilled part of Aphrodite's plan, then we can expect she will make an appearance any time now to claim the stone."

Melody is quiet, her forehead scrunched as she is deep in thought. When we reach the base of the steps, she asks, "What then?"

I pick her up, cradling her in my arms as we ascend, but keep my thoughts to myself. I need to think things through, because what will I do if not only Persephone but Aphrodite are present when we are in the mortal realm? The parasite is one thing, because her host is mortal as far as we know and has no protection besides that fucking blade she seems to keep around. But Aphrodite? If she is in her true form and has been feeding off of the reverence of her *order*, as Lenore called them, then her power may very well exceed my own, and that is a whole other can of worms.

Once we reach the archives, I set Melody down and finally answer her question. "If we have to contend with them both, then we need to be protected. I hate to say this, but I may have to do exactly what I warned Aphrodite against and unlock the Nostos Stones. Your heart stone will remain here, locked away and safe, and Persephone already has the unlocked Infinity Stone, but if I unlock the Subjugation Stone, the Aurora Sapphire, and the Mustēria Stone, that might be enough of the Titan's power to give us a fighting chance."

"But I thought you said without the Titans there was no way to control the power of the stones?" She steps into the room and moves toward the chest while I consider her question.

"True. But we do not know that which we have yet to ask."

She frowns as she squats down and throws open the chest. "Could you be any more fucking cryptic?" From the top tray, she takes out the Mustēria Stone, and then lifts the top and middle trays, setting them on the floor so she can grab the Subjugation

Stone and Aurora Sapphire from the bottom tray. With all the stones at her feet, she replaces the trays and closes the chest.

Placing the stones in her right palm, she hands them up to me one at a time, and then stands, brushing her hands off on her gown. "I do not want to share where my mind has taken me until I am certain," I say, jiggling the stones in my hand. They clink together. "Until then, just trust that I am doing what I think is best. If the power cannot be controlled, we will have to find another way, but I assume I am on the right track."

"You know what they say about the word *assume*?" She bumps her hip against me and smiles.

"Yeah, yeah. Do not be so smug. We will be found victorious."

"Is that so?" She wraps her arms around my waist. "And if we're not?"

"Listen here, negative Nancy, I will bet everything I hold dear that things will turn out just as they should, and then we can get back to this." I lean down and place a kiss on her lips, and she opens her mouth, granting me entrance. I massage her tongue with mine.

When she pulls away, she asks, "But until then?"

"Until then, you and Cerberus get yourselves something to eat, and I will speak to the keeper of secrets. And before you ask, no, I will not tell you who that is. It is not an official title and just something I have been calling them for a very long time."

She throws me a skeptical glance before pulling away and walking ahead of me down the hall. When she reaches the dining hall where Cerberus lounges outside the door, she states, "Are you sure you aren't the keeper of secrets?" Then, she pets my hellhound, opens the door and follows him inside.

I do not dignify her question with a response, and instead continue down the hall and out of the front door. Because I have a date with a Titanide, after all, and if I know Rhea, her assistance will not come without a cost.

I just hope I can afford whatever concessions the Titanide will seek for sharing secrets of such magnitude. Because they would not have imbued the stones with their power, however minute, unless they had grand plans for them. The only question is, have those plans already been revealed to Aphrodite, and will my unlocking the stones play right into them, unleashing something the force of which this world has never seen?

CHAPTER 27

TREAD LIGHTLY (HADES)

Standing before the gates of Tartarus, the three sisters as I call them, slither over one another before Anástasia comes to the forefront, leaving Harmonia and the other one sulking in the background. Anástasia opens her mouth and I say, "Not this time, my lovely. I need an audience with Rhea." I point toward the outcropping of rocks, and Anástasia moves toward it. "Just Rhea," I clarify, my tone every bit the command my words did not specify.

Anástasia all but rolls her eyes at me, and Harmonia hisses loudly before they both move aside. Then, Rhea slithers over the other two, disappearing into the large hole in the wall beside the gate. I follow behind her.

Once deep inside the sisters' tunnel, the torches scattered sporadically along the walls flicker to life, illuminating the rotunda beyond in a pale blue light. And it is within the oval-shaped chamber at the end of that tunnel where Rhea begins molting.

Surrounded by skins piled high from the many years of changing each time the sisters entered their dwelling, Rhea's serpentine body twists and turns, transmutating before me as I watch with rapt fascination. I have never sought an audience with any of the sisters, knowing how long this process takes and the toll on their bodies, and have only made them do so once a day to deliver Tartarus' new impenitents.

As I watch, Rhea's eyes become cloudy, her scales take on a grayish hue, and then she rubs her snout along the rough wall to split the skin. She secretes an oil to aid in the process, and its scent is faint and musky, like wet soil, but nothing as pungent as if she were threatened. Because she knows I mean her no harm, seeing as I placed her here to keep her safe in the first place. And because of all the Titanides I could have saved, I chose to save her.

Still trying to wriggle free of her skin, Rhea turns back into the tunnel, using the sides to peel off the old skin so she can emerge. But it is only when the husk of her former self sits hollow near the tunnel's entrance that a very naked Titanide steps out of the shadows and into the light.

Brushing damp golden locks away from her face and panting heavily, Rhea says sweetly, "Hello, dear. Long time no see. At least through these eyes." She chuckles, and the sound is a little more malevolent than I expected, so I draw power into myself.

The torches flare, then flicker, and my hands glow blue with the power I have called upon, filling the tunnel with my cobalt heat.

"Now, Hades," she chastises, "is that any way to greet me after all this time?" She feigns offense, turning her head and scoffing, but I am not stupid.

I do not lower my guard or relinquish control of the situation, because to do so would be a mistake. So with flames dancing across my skin up to my elbows, just as sweetly as she had, I say, "Nice to see you again, *Mother*. I would offer you a hug but, well, you know..." I wiggle my fingers, alluding to my flames.

"Yes, yes." She waves me off. "Always a penchant for the dramatic," she teases. "Tell me, *my lovely*..." she trails off, using my words to taunt as she takes a step toward me. "How do you fare these days? Good, I hope. No troubles to speak of?" she all but sings. The smile that dresses her lips is positively wicked.

"What do you know of it?" I glower.

"Who, me?" She places her hand on her chest. "Well, whatever do you mean, dear?" Her affront is just as fake as her earlier offense, and it takes everything in me not to rage forward and strangle her.

"Come off it. You know why I am here."

"Do I?" She taps her finger on her lips as her eyes wander to the roof of the tunnel. "No, I cannot say that I do." She smirks, her eyes making her look just as deadly—as venomous—as when she was a snake.

"Well, if you know nothing, then perhaps I should go," I say, motioning toward the entrance with my head. She huffs loudly and slinks by me as I turn to keep my eyes trained on her retreating form.

Once she is in the back of the rotunda, she digs through piles of skins, muttering words I cannot make out. Then, she retrieves a tattered gown, once gold but now more of a dingy brown, and twists the fabric around her waist before draping the excess over one shoulder. With the remaining piece, she tosses it over the other shoulder, covering her breasts, and then finishes her movements by tucking the tail of the gown beneath her armpit. She takes a seat on a large boulder. "There," she says, crossing her legs and flipping her hair behind her. "That is much better now, is it not?"

"If you say so," I offer, decreasing my flames but not releasing my power. "Listen, I know you know something. If not why I am here, then the questions I seek answers to."

"Me? What could I possibly know that would have any benefit to you?" Her leg crossing over her knee sways back and forth as she leans back on her hands.

"The stones, Mother. I am here about the stones." I pinch the bridge of my nose. After all these years, her voice still grates on my every nerve.

"And which stones might those be?" She tilts her head.

"The Nostos Stones!"

"Nostos Stones, Nostos Stones. Hmm. I cannot say I have ever heard of them. What do they do?" she questions with feigned ignorance.

"Perhaps you know them by another name, but you know the stones of which I speak. You have to," I insist.

"Do I? I just, you know, it has been so *long*, and living as a snake is so confusing I—"

"What do you want?" My jaw clenches, and I hold back my anger because I need answers.

"Need? Oh, Hades, you have been so generous protecting me as you have by sparing me the same fate as the others, I could not possibly ask—"

"Just ask!" I interrupt, fisting my hands at my sides.

"If you insist?" She smiles. "Now that you mention it, this cave is just so cluttered and stuffy," she says, flipping her fingers to the piles of molted skin. "I mean honestly, Hades, these conditions are just dreadful." She pouts. "If only there were a way to..." She motions around the cave.

"Spruce things up?"

"That is it." She stands, turning as if she is taking an inventory of her surroundings. "A little sprucing up is just what we need in here. Clean out the piles once in a while and bring in some furnishings, maybe some gowns and such. Because sleeping on the ground is just so dreadful, and this fabric..." She lifts the skirt of her gown. "Well, it is beneath me, honestly. And if you truly loved me, you would—"

"You are dead, Mother!" I shout, stomping my foot. "You are dead and spend most of your day as a snake, so why would you need furniture and finery?"

"There is no need to shout, dear, I am right here. Seriously, is that anyway to speak to your *mother*? The same mother who sacrificed so much for you?" She starts to cry, hiding her face in her hands as she forces out the tears she could not spare to shed when our father swallowed us whole.

"Spare me the theatrics. I refuse to fall for your emotional blackmail. And sacrificed for me? You sacrificed not just me but each of my siblings except your precious *Zeus*," I sneer.

She continues to cry, pulling her hands from her face so I can see her massive tears streaming down her face. The droplets trail down her cheeks, dripping off her chin and landing on her gown. "After everything I have done, all the ways I served you, how I continue to serve you, and this is the thanks I get?" she wails.

I cannot take any more of her charade, or the show of emotion, so giving in I say begrudgingly, "Perhaps I could do something about the state of your *accommodations*."

With over the top excitement she says, "Oh, could you? I mean, I would hate to be bothersome, and I know you are just *so* busy, what with the remnants wandering around aimlessly and all."

"You said you did not know why I was here and... You know what, forget it." I pace back and forth, running my hand over my face while I think. Counting on my fingers, I relay her requests: "Regular cleanings, furnishings, gowns. Those are three concessions I would be beyond happy to make and—"

"And do not forget preferential feedings," she says, holding up a finger.

"Preferential feedings? You said nothing about preferential feedings." I am no longer trying to keep the frustration out of my tone because she has skipped past irritating and slithered right into infuriating.

"Anástasia feeds daily," she says petulantly, crossing her arms over her chest. "Every time you go in, she feeds." Erratic now, she strides before me, flailing her hands. "The guards go in during your absence, and what happens? She feeds. Day after day she siphons power, feeding on your ichor or their essence, and what do I get?"

"More grating the longer your lips are moving?" I say mostly to myself.

"I get nothing, Hades. It is not like Anástasia is bound to share what she takes. Oh, no. And Harmonia. Ugh. Even she has had the opportunity to feed. I mean, sure, it was from that little *demigod* pet of yours, but still..." she rambles.

I lift a finger. "Preferential feedings once a month," I offer.

"A week," she pleads.

"Every other week," I counter.

"Done," she accepts. "Once from you and once from your demigod."

"No." I shake my head. "I said nothing about Melody. Deal is off."

"You and the *demigod*." She stops moving, turning to face me. "Because if you do not, I might find it hard in my weakened state to remember what information you need from me," she threatens.

"Only if she agrees," I falter, "and if she refuses—"

"Yeah, yeah. If she refuses, I will take what I can get. But she will not refuse, because that simpering little demigod will do whatever you ask," she hisses, "and you *will* ask her, Hades. Or you, and your realm, hell, all the realms, will cease to be as they are now."

"What is that supposed to mean?" I take a step back, calling on my flames once more. My ichor rings loud in my ears, my heart thumping hard in my chest.

She forces air over her lips and through her teeth. It whooshes out as she exhales and turns abruptly into maniacal laughter. Then, out of nowhere, she just stops, her chest heaving as her eyes go wild. "It means that if I do not tell you how to control them, and soon, the remnants—the three that have so carelessly been released—will scratch, and claw, and bite, and seethe their way into everything, unleashing a power so great that neither you, the Olympians, your precious demigod, or the Titans combined cannot stop them. And then..."

"And then?" The ringing in my ears becomes almost deafening, and painful the longer she remains silent. "And then what, Mother?" I urge. "Rhea?"

She plops back down onto the boulder, crosses one leg over the other, and leans back on her hands once more like she has not a care in the world as she says, "And then *nothing*. Everything and everyone who has ever been will cease to exist, as life and power of every form is snuffed out in one colossal explosion." She mouths the word *boom*. "Why? Because that was our failsafe," she gloats.

There is no holding back my anger as I lord over my mother, sitting there with her shit-eating grin. The flames that were merely a flicker as they licked over my flesh, now rage, burning so hot they incinerate everything within the rotunda and the tunnel combined.

The molted snakeskin? Gone. Our clothing? Gone. The moisture that lingered in the air within the confines of the space? Evaporated. And now, without a speck of flesh remaining between us, both my mother's and my gilded bones glow red from the inferno as I lose my temper. And the cave walls? They crack from the heat, the sound so loud we cover our ears to spare us from the assault.

Reaching for me, my mother struggles to call out, "Hades, stop."

"No!" I bellow, curling into myself, before flopping onto my back. "I will not... let you... do this," I force out through clenched teeth.

But if I do not stop, then what she has threatened will indeed come to pass, and I cannot have that either. So, thinking of Melody, I summon every ounce of restraint I can muster, and calm, calling my heat and my flames back into myself.

The force of controlling such power takes my breath away, and lying on the floor of the tunnel, gasping and coughing, I struggle to remain conscious. My head lolls to the side, and pain radiates throughout my chest from my singed airway. It is so severe that my back arches off of the ground, and I writhe in agony as I stare over at my mother.

She is there, but just barely, staring at me with lifeless orbs as her melted skeleton bubbles like molten gold.

What have I done? I think as my bones cool and my skin attempts to reform. I have doomed us all. Because my mother already said she was weakened—starved—and with no power to draw on, it will take days for her to reform. We just do not have that kind of time.

So, even though bells of warning are ringing in my ears, I go against my better judgement and offer my mother my wrist.

Taking my wrist, she bites down, gulping greedily as my ichor flows out of me and into her. She is draining me, but I have to let her. I have to allow her just enough to see this through, because I will not be the one responsible for the destruction of everything. I cannot be.

The responsibility for the dead was already thrust upon me against my will, but I would rather die the final death than willingly let Melody die for my selfishness. Because *I* gave her a second chance. *I* asked her to stay. And every shit thing that has happened to her in the last month, up to and including her death, has been *my* fault, in one way or another. So, I owe it to her now to see that she continues on, even if I do not.

With my life force waning, I plead with my mother, "Please... see she lives." My head swims as starbursts fill my vision. "Stop her, and stop this," I pant. "Promise me." Those are the last words I force out as my life, my power, is sucked from me and into Rhea. Because Rhea was the one who started it all—the birth of the Olympians and the Titanomachy—she is the last Titanide, but above all, she is my mother. I did not shed a tear upon her death, but perhaps she will shed a tear for mine.

CHAPTER 28
GUT FEELING (MELODY)

For the first time since arriving in the Underworld, my sleep was *not* interrupted by the nightmares that had been plaguing me since my death. There were no twisted features or tortured eyes, and no maniacal laughter or sadistic taunts. Plus, I didn't feel like I was choking to death on blood spewing from my lips as a beautiful woman, and supposed oracle, turned into an angry goddess, so a win is a win.

Instead, I am startled awake when a bristling Cerberus tears the covers off me with his teeth. Jerking his heads from side-to-side as he grunts and growls, Cerberus' sound is so ferocious that it makes the hairs rise all over my body while the room seems to vibrate around me.

Irritated by the intrusion on my finally restful slumber, I come to my senses and try to wrestle the covers back over my legs, but stop when the torches flare wildly along the walls. They fill the room with an intolerable heat, and because I can't believe what I am seeing, I rub my eyelids.

Once my eyes are clear, I scan the room, only to have them fall on a hound who is all but pleading at the foot of the bed. He whimpers loudly, jumping back, and there is a terror in his eyes that has the irritation that was washing over me immediately subsiding.

Since it is obvious he will not allow me to go back to sleep, and because there is no ignoring his frantic movements as he pads anxiously, I decide to see what has got him all in an uproar.

Frustrated, I twist my body and throw my legs off the side of the bed, sighing as I attempt to stand. I need to grab my robe from off the chair on the other side of the room before traipsing about the castle, so I move, only making it two steps when I sway.

I stutter-step, wincing when the mark on my leg burns, drawing my gaze to where it is raised and glowing on my calf. Hades' print seems to pulse, and the outline of his hand blinks like a warning light. It is erratic, and time seems to stand still as I focus only on its insistent plea.

On wobbly legs, and with a head that pounds less from the glass of wine I had with my meal and more from the pressure building from the stifling heat, I stumble my way across the room. And as I do, I realize the stones beneath my feet are just as heated as not just the air around me but also the mark emblazoned on my flesh. I mouth a stunned *what the fuck?*

My equilibrium is thrown off when the floor seems to go topsy-turvy, but finally I make my way to the chair, bracing myself on the back. Then, pulling labored breaths through parted lips, I pull on my robe, and once the sash is tied at my waist, Cerberus grabs my sleeve, pulling me toward the door.

Just when I think I will make it to the door, I get all woozy and my stomach lurches, stopping my grasping for the handle mid-reach. My face flushes what I imagine is a bright crimson as heat rises from my neck to my cheeks. With another tug on my sleeve from my insistent companion, I then upchuck my meal into the basin beside me.

Cerberus releases my sleeve, his nervousness pulling my gaze to where he stills beside me, and I wipe my mouth with the back of my hand while doing my best to gain my footing. Even as off-kilter as I am, nothing prepares me for when I look into the basin and see remnants of gold flecks mingled amongst the chunks of food.

Ichor gilds the chewed-up pieces of meat, the sight turning my stomach again, and I place my hand over my mouth when the tart taste of sickness still lingering on my tongue leads to more nausea.

Swaying, Cerberus moves to my side to steady me, and I place my hand on the scruff of his neck. I am confused by my body's response to all the stimuli, but seeing as the last time I got sick and lost the contents of my stomach in this very basin was when Hades and I were fighting and both upset, I know something is very wrong now. Not with me, but with *him*. Especially since his essence, *his ichor*, was just expelled from within me.

Hades has yet to return from his visit with the *keeper of secrets*, and has been gone long enough for me not only to eat a full meal, but to drag my tired ass to bed.

More warning bells ring out as power radiates around me, and the sweltering heat has my body going rigid with fear. I grip Cerberus' fur firmly in my hand, while wrapping my other around the handle, and finally open the door to pure pandemonium.

In the hallway, every torch burns brighter than I have ever seen while the sound of the inferno rushes loudly down the passageway. With the state of all that lies before me—Cerberus' panic, the flaring torches, the sweltering heat that has power ebbing erratically—now I know things are not just wrong; they are downright catastrophic and I need to find Hades. But how do I do that? How do I find him and this mysterious *keeper of secrets* when he left me no clue where he was going?

A sense of panic settles in my bones and makes my spine straighten, but soon the urgency of the beast beside me pulls me from my stupor. With his muffled whines getting louder by the minute, his closest head takes my hand in its maw and tugs me forward, while the others howl in a manner I have never heard from him before. The sound echoes all around us, and I know exactly what needs to be done.

Remembering everything we inventoried earlier in the archives, I think back on how Hades said he found me in the mortal realm. He said he used the Mustēria Stone, and that he called it to action, releasing the hidden knowledge within. But that would require me to unlock another stone, and without knowing how to control the remnants, I am hesitant to do so.

So, knowing I need some answers, or at least a place to start my search, control of the remnants or not, I bound down the hall straight for the archives.

Then, once at the door we left ajar earlier, I slide to a halt, pushing it the rest of the way open before barreling into the room with Cerberus behind me. I reach the chest and throw open the lid, where the Subjugation Stone rattles in the top tray, emitting a light that washes the room in a kaleidoscope of colors.

Picking up the Subjugation Stone, it settles, but still the other trays in the chest shake insistently. So, I lift the top two trays out of the chest, setting them on the floor, and when I do, the Aurora Sapphire and the Mustēria Stone illuminate where they are nestled in the bottom tray, sending beacons of light into the air and onto the ceiling.

The blinding light from the sapphire combines with the dark onyx of the Mustēria Stone, projecting an image of Hades and a woman draped in rags in a cave somewhere.

Like a black and white film playing before me, I can see he is angry, but can't make out what they are saying. I know this must be his aforementioned *keeper of secrets*, and can tell the interaction is anything but friendly. Especially since the pain radiating from his handprint on my calf coincides with each time the power at his fingertips flares.

There is no time to waste, so, certain unlocking the stones is my only option, I pick up the remaining two, halting their projections. I then place the sapphire in my pocket with the Subjugation Stone while keeping the Mustēria Stone in my hand. Because if what I have seen is any indication, I am going to need every bit of power I can summon at my disposal to calm him down and get him out of there; if not unharmed, then hopefully at least alive.

I have not entered the throne room before because the occasion to do so never presented itself, but I had seen it from one of Persephone's memories. So, stepping into the space now, although it is mostly foreign, I know exactly where I must go, even if I can only surmise what must be done.

Cerberus follows me into the room, his nails scratching as he slides to a halt, and then we ascend the several steps to the dais. Hades' peering stone sits beside his throne, and I take a seat in the high-backed, tufted chair, while Cerberus paces back and forth in front of me.

I lift the onyx stone into the air, and it catches the light from the torches, glinting off the gold veins cutting across it haphazardly. Then, summoning the courage to follow through with my plan, I mutter to myself, "Here goes nothing," before closing my eyes and awakening the stone with one word: *Kruptós*.

I had told Hades I wanted to see the owl that emerged when the stone awakened for myself, but nothing prepared me for what happened when it did.

Pushed back into the cushioned throne by the force of the power that was released, Cerberus yelps and I squeeze my eyes shut as the room is filled with a blinding light. It flares across my closed eyelids, my cheeks shaking from the percussion, and once it subsides, I open my eyes. But instead of the onyx and gold *being* he described, all I see are tail feathers of the largest owl imaginable, whose outline glows as if illuminated by a black light.

The creature soars through the doorway and out into the hall, its powerful wingbeats cutting through the air with a loud *whoosh* as they brush along the wall. It turns toward the archives, leaving a trail of rose-colored light following in its wake. Then, with Cerberus and I gaping from the door, it swoops back in front of us, so low that the last thing I see is glowing eyes as I fall to the floor to avoid a collision.

Looking up from where I lay sprawled out on the stone floor, I watch as Cerberus jumps over me, bounding down the corridor after our winged visitor. I rise to my feet, wiping my hands off on my robe as I take to a sprint, and follow the loud growls of the hellhound out of the palace and down the steps.

Cerberus does not stop to pee on the base of his statues however, and instead jumps off the bottom step and into the air where he attempts to grab hold of the owl mid-flap. He misses, and the creature looks down to where my scruffy companion tumbles to a stop, then turns its head, making a beeline from the palace to the archway.

The owl swoops through the gate and turns, the trailing light following behind him and leaving a path for us to follow straight to the gates of Tartarus.

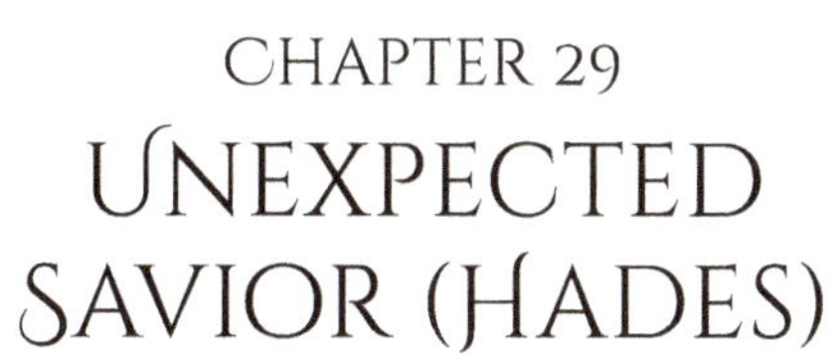

CHAPTER 29
UNEXPECTED SAVIOR (HADES)

Lying in a pool of melted bone, I open my eyes to see a silhouette at the mouth of the cave. I am not sure how long I have been unconscious, and my vision is blurry as I strain to focus on the forward-moving figure. But with a trail of light preceding their advance, and a powerful crimson aura that seems to glow around and beyond them with each step, I cannot look away.

Distorted voices echo throughout the tunnel, and when I move my head, I see another blurred figure, possibly my mother, moving toward the one with the aura. I blink several times to clear my vision, and now when I focus, the two forms seem to face off, their voices rising as an argument erupts.

Flailing arms and hostile postures join the raucous shouting, while the figure I identified as my mother turns her back on the other. The new figure is a woman, I can tell from their shape, but she is much smaller than Rhea, so it could not be Harmonia or Anástasia.

Then who has come to intervene? Who has come to check in on this chaos and is currently going toe-to-toe with the last Titanide?

Rolling over onto my stomach, I drag my form toward the two warring parties. My skin has reformed over my lower half somehow, but the top remains exposed bones, now blackened from my flames. The two women turn to face me, and I can now make out Rhea pointing to me and then back at the other woman.

The other woman steps forward, raising one hand in the air as her lips move, and a blinding light flashes wildly, sending my mother flying back into the wall of the tunnel with a *crack* before slumping to the ground. She stalks toward my mother, squatting down as Rhea cowers back.

Holding her hands out, the woman seems to threaten my mother, and as I watch intently, I see Rhea go rigid. Then, she scoots back and leans against the tunnel wall, submitting as the other woman stands before her. But she is not just any woman; *she* is Melody. And my Melody lords over my mother with one hand outstretched as her crimson aura strobes, washing over Rhea.

Their voices are no more than whispers and incoherent mumbling as they reach my ears, so I do not know what is being said, but whatever it is, Melody seems very pleased with herself. Turning to face me, Melody makes her way to my side while my mother remains as if in a trance, leaning back with her hands in her lap.

Melody squats down and looks at me, shaking her head in disapproval. "I can't seem to leave you alone for a minute, now can I?" she teases. Then she tells me to wait here, as if I had the strength to go anywhere, and returns to Rhea.

Melody is speaking again and seems to ask questions, but when Rhea fails to answer them, crossing her arms over her chest, Melody raises her fisted hand and speaks a word I cannot make out. Rhea finally answers, but I can see her reluctance twisting her features. This goes on for several minutes while I watch awash with confusion.

How did she find me and what are they saying? Even better question, why is Rhea being so damned forthcoming with Melody when she was all riddles and minced words with me before? Melody has the upper hand, and my mother seems to have lost all control, but for the life of me, I do not know how.

With as much power as I can muster, I move to a seated position, but everything hurts: my head, my eyes, my chest that remains exposed with my heart pumping wildly within. I lost too much of my ichor to Rhea to reform completely, but at least with Melody's arrival, and now with her control over my mother, I am less fearful that I will meet my end in this Titan-forsaken cave.

The whooshing sound that filled my ears from my ichor thumping loudly subsides, and now I can make out not only what Melody is asking, but what Rhea's responses are. "How do we control the remnants?" Melody asks.

Rhea bites her lip, trying to avoid answering, but Melody holds up her hand again, sending that crimson aura far beyond her and into my mother. "They need a conduit. An item of power created by the gods and repurposed to house the stones. Then and only then can you channel their power and halt their siphoning ability."

"Siphoning ability?" Melody steps towards Rhea, and she hisses.

"Yes. They are siphoning even now. Unlocking the stones releases the remnants and allows them to draw power, trapping it until the force can be contained no longer."

"And what happens when they reach capacity?" Melody asks, squatting down and meeting my mother's heated stare.

Rhea laughs, leaning her head back against the wall. "Then everything happens. Too much power, uncontrolled, needs to go somewhere. And when it does, it will tear the very fabric the realms were made with apart."

"But why?" Melody's face is fearful as she clasps her hand over her heart.

"Because myself and the four other Titanides, plus two Titans tethered a remnant of our powers within each stone. So, the powers of creation, destruction, order, the sun, the moon, and memory will all combine and combust in one massive pulse of power. Seeing as I am the last, I alone cannot offer my assistance. I do not have the strength, nor the will to see it done."

"But if we find a conduit?"

Rhea purses her lips, and they quiver as she tries to hold in the reply Melody is forcing from her with the Subjugation Stone in her hand. I can make it out now, the iridescence peeking between her fingers as she holds it out, and Rhea is helpless to deny her.

"Only a conduit can detain the five remnants that have been released now, allowing them to be controlled. And perhaps then you could do something about your little Aphrodite problem with those five, but six would be better. Titans, all six would make you unstoppable. But are you willing to wield such power?" She narrows her eyes on Melody.

Melody wavers, turning to look at me. I nod in her direction, and she returns to her line of questioning. "Say we have something suitable to be the conduit, how then do we control the stones?"

I am taken aback by her question. *Has my precious, sweet Melody thought of a way to command the power of which my mother speaks?*

"If there is such an item at your disposal, merely affixing the stones to *said* item will not contain the remnants. The power would need to be wielded. The remnants have already amassed so much that only releasing the excess would allow you to control them once more. But what would you bolster? Life, death, the solar or lunar elements that have allowed your realm to thrive for so long, order, or memory; which would you amplify to accomplish such a feat?" Rhea is smug as Melody stands before her, considering her questions.

Then, with a dominance that makes me smile, Melody pulls

back her shoulders and says, "How about you leave the specifics to us. Now, the only thing I require of you is the return of Hades' power." She points to me, and she and my mother look to where I am watching their discourse. "He is obviously weakened, which I am sure you had a hand in, so how do I get him as he was?"

My mother huffs, then rushes out, "He gave his power to me freely; I should not have—"

"I didn't ask what you want, I asked what had to be done?" she interrupts, stepping toward my mother with the stone raised once more.

My mother flinches at Melody's advance and then bows her head in supplication. "He needs to take back that which was freely given."

"So in other words: you will return all the power you have taken. But because that alone will not satisfy my need to see you suffer for everything you have done to him, you will allow him to drain every ounce of whatever you have. And then, with your son at my side, I will happily walk you to your new eternity. He offered you mercy, but when asked for your help, you offered him none. You thought being a snake was bad? I promise you, Rhea, this cave is luxury compared to what awaits you in Tartarus," she sneers.

With that, Melody grabs my mother by her hair and drags her toward me, her aura pulsing with such power that I cover my head.

Once she is beside me, Melody says, "Here," and I remove my arms from around my skull, staring up at her. "You are looking a little peckish and could probably do with some refreshment. I'm sure she is not as sweet as that beautiful wine from Chios Charon has stashed away, but beggars can't be choosers." Then she releases my mother's hair, and she falls beside me.

Rolling onto my side, I take my mother's hand and pull it to my mouth, baring my teeth and sinking them into her wrist as she had mine. I drink, drawing the ichor she took from me back into myself as her body twitches uncontrollably.

When I can feel the pulsing in her arm fading, I suck harder, pulling every bit of what had been her essence and making it my own. She may have never been a loving mother, but now, for the first time in her wretched existence, she is giving me exactly what I need. Whether or not she wants to.

With a satisfied smirk on her lips, Melody sits beside me in her robe, and a large owl lands behind her, extending its wings and screeching loudly. I release my mother's hand from the shock, and it falls limply to the ground. "Is that?" I cannot force the rest of the question from my lips.

"The owl? Yes," she says matter-of-factly. "Like it's a big deal or something?" She shrugs her shoulders, laughing when the bird nudges her back with its beak. "Okay, okay." She sighs. "I guess you are kind of a big deal," she teases, and the owl tilts its head, looking at me.

"But how did you..." My eyes go wide.

"How did I unlock the stone and follow that pain in the ass here? Well, it would have been so much harder a feat if I weren't such a great keeper of records, that's for sure. Maybe that should be my new name? But next time you go on a wild goose chase, how about you tell me where you are going instead of just giving me some pretentious pet name for who you are going to see?"

I laugh, she laughs, and then Cerberus finally enters the tunnel whimpering. "He's fine you big scaredy-cat," she calls out. "Seriously, he would not step foot in here when we arrived, so I just left him standing there growling at Anástasia and Harmonia."

"How did you get past those two? They did not give you any trouble, did they?"

"Those two? The girls love me, Hades. So when I asked them to keep watch on mister fidget over there and guard the cave, they were happy to oblige."

Then, we look down to where Rhea lies practically lifeless, her once beautiful form withered from the loss of power. Her curly golden locks are straight and colorless, since all the ichor flowing within her now belongs to me.

"Are you serious about throwing her into Tartarus?" I ask, frowning, more from thinking my mother's punishment might upset her, and less from the idea of Rhea being punished.

"Gods, yes. I am not about to chance her disrupting anything, and I would be happier knowing she is contained while we go about our business. Besides, the bitch has it coming." She leans over Rhea and places a kiss on my lips. "Come on, let's get her settled so we can go back to the castle. We still have some details to go over before setting foot in the mortal realm."

"You still want to go?" I ask, my eyebrows shooting up in surprise.

"Of course we are going. Now that I have a little extra pep in my step," she says, motioning to the crimson power sparking at her fingertips, "I am ready for whatever comes our way."

I stand and help her to her feet. "That you are," I say, placing a gentle kiss on her lips. Then, I pick up my mother and we walk toward the cave entrance with an owl flying ahead of us and an agitated Cerberus grumbling behind us; a band of travelers about to step into the fire and deliver my mother to her rightful place amongst the other Titanides, forever answering for her crimes.

CHAPTER 30

WIELDER OF THE REMNANTS (HADES)

After delivering my mother to Tartarus, Melody and I walked back to the castle mostly in silence, only laughing when Cerberus would snap at Tyto as he swooped down. And of course Melody laughed again when I told her I called the bird Tyto.

"Tito? Don't you think it's rather odd you chose to give a being that emerged from a Greek relic a Spanish name?" she asks as we ascend the steps to the palace.

I scoff, "Tyto is Greek for owl. Specifically, the barn owl, like your friend here." My attention is drawn behind us where, once again, Cerberus stops to pee on the foot of each statue. I shake my head and then continue as I open the door for her. "I had been calling him Strix because he was a screech owl for me, but seeing as he has done more for you in this one emergence than he has for me, Tyto he shall be."

"Tyto. Huh, I can get used to Tyto, I suppose," she offers.

"Good, because I am shit with names, so even if you wanted it changed, I would still call him Tyto, regardless."

"You are ridiculous, you know that?" She pushes me away playfully, and I step back to her side, throwing my arm around her shoulders as we walk down the hallway. Then she asks, "So should I send Tyto to his room, or leave him out to try to make friends with Cerberus?"

Cerberus grumbles as he pads up behind us, and she looks back at him as I say, "Be nice. There is no need to be jealous; she loves you too."

"Exactly," she says, reaching behind her and scratching under a chin. "There is enough of my love to go around."

"I am fine with that, as long as I get first dibs," I insist as we pass our room. "Speaking of love, have I told you how much I love that beautiful mind of yours?"

"Just my mind?" she teases, quirking a brow.

"Among other things." I smirk. "But if it were not for your quick thinking today, things could have very well gone in quite the other direction."

"So we're taking what happened in the cave as a win?"

"You were able to get the answers we needed when I could not, so yes, a huge win for the home team." I brush my knuckles under her chin. "Here's looking at you, kid."

"Great gesture, even better movie, but wrong context, especially since I am not leaving you to flee. Whatever happens next, we will face it together. Not just *you* bearing the whole weight of the world on your shoulders, but *us* fighting for the good of all the realms."

We stop in front of the archives, and I take her face in my hands. "I like the sound of that." I smile warmly.

"Good, because you need me."

"Do I?" I lower my hands to her hips.

"Seeing as you have made zero indication you figured out what I proposed to use to control the remnants, yes. You won't get through what happens next without me." She raises her chin.

"So sure of yourself," I tease, squeezing.

"And why shouldn't I be? I am just a lowly demigod, who not only defeated a Titanide today but saved an Olympian from the final death."

"Which I cannot thank you enough for, little one, but please do not let your sudden influx of power go to your head. I may have underestimated you, but Aphrodite will not." I search her eyes for understanding.

"No, I know." She sighs, looking down and then back up into my eyes. "It's just... this all has to be happening for a reason. And maybe she has had a hand in a lot of it, but she can't possibly know the lengths we'll go to in order to stop her. If she did, one would think she would side on the err of caution and stop Persephone."

"But she has not," I add, kissing the tip of her nose.

She sucks in a breath. "But she has not, and that tells me her hubris knows no bounds because, what if she can't stop her? What if, despite her efforts, Persephone remains not only at large but in possession of the stone?" Fear flickers in her eyes.

"Well, then where she fails we must succeed, because Rhea said we would need all six stones to stop whatever she is planning," I say, dropping my hands and motioning for her to enter the room.

"True. But I feel there is more to her plan than just obtaining the power of the remnants, if she has even considered that as an option." She steps past me and into the room, moving toward a chest, but not the one I thought.

"Oh, she has considered it. Hell, she put the wheels in motion all those years ago," I say as I watch her open my artifacts. "Maybe not with the foresight to know that she could unlock them all, but at least expecting to wield the ruby and the Infinity Stone," I explain.

Then, without offering an explanation as to why, Melody grabs the wrapped fabric bundle containing the Necklace of Harmonia.

"What... what are you doing?" I reach out to take it away from her, and she pulls it back.

"She said we needed something made by the gods that we could repurpose as a conduit. Six stones that will need to be worn to control the remnants." She holds out the bundle. "What better way to do that than with a cursed necklace, created by a god to spite Aphrodite in the first place."

I take it from her. "There is that beautiful mind of yours at work again." I grip the piece confidently, then say, "But until we have the final stone, our conduit will be incomplete."

"She never said we needed them all to wield the power," she states, placing her hand under the bundle and pressing it up to my chest. "She only said that the remnants needed a conduit. So make one. Make the piece we need, unlock the Kingmaker Emerald, and then we will place the stones we have, leaving room for the one we are missing." She pats the fabric reassuringly.

"That is great and all, but have you figured out which of the powers we should bolster to release the excess?"

"I am so glad you asked," she says, stepping back and turning in a circle.

"Well, I am waiting," I urge.

"Memory," she says, making those ridiculous finger movements she uses when she says *magic*. Then she steps toward me once more.

"Memory?" I sigh. "Exactly where do you think we can release that much power for memory that will not have negative consequences?"

"The Mnemosyne," she says confidently.

"The Mnemosyne? Why the Mnemosyne?"

"Think about it, Hades. The Mnemosyne is the one place where we can release the power of memory that will benefit the Underworld. What better way to honor those within Elysium than with their memories?" She is excited about the idea, but I need to explain why that would be less advantageous than she thinks.

"Melody, those within Elysium are spared their memories so that they are not tormented by the life they can no longer live. It is a small mercy that has been afforded to them. Can you imagine the fallout from returning their memories as they are?"

"Yes, I can. Which is why I know it will not be the catastrophe you are claiming it will. You stripped them of their memories, Hades, and they may very well be happy being ignorant of their past lives, but I refused to be stripped of mine for a reason. There were people and experiences that molded who I am, and if those were taken away, I would feel that loss, even if I didn't know to miss it. There would just be this hole where I once was. A longing for something that I could never grasp." Her eyes are pleading.

"I..." I cannot force the words out, despite knowing I need to say them.

"I know you are scared," she says, rubbing my arms. "You don't need to tell me for me to see it. It is written all over your face. But you are being selfish," she states adamantly.

"Selfish?" I contend.

"Yes, selfish. You are being selfish because there is only one soul in Elysium whose returned memories would cause your guilt to compound. I know I am right, so you do not need to argue my logic. And you know my words hold truth, so spare us both the effort of whatever retort you are about to give." She squeezes my arms, her eyes wide and offering understanding I do not deserve.

I relax my shoulders in defeat. "I will do whatever it takes."

"Good, because taking their memories was never the mercy you believed it to be. You are doing this for them, Hades." She steps to my side and leans into me, avoiding the necklace I still have clutched tightly to my chest. "But more importantly, you should do this for yourself. So that when you visit, because I know you do, you are looked upon with eyes filled with love and recognition, not ones filled with confusion as to why you are giving them so much attention."

A tear slides down my cheek. I had not realized she moved me to tears, because I had been fighting back the emotions since she said the Mnemosyne to begin with. But she is right; the Mnemosyne is the safest bet. And looking into Adonis' eyes and seeing his love staring back at me would not be nearly as torturous as what I have seen up to now—hesitation, disquiet, indifference. "I think I like this plan." I smile genuinely.

She taps me on the shoulder. "But first, you need to recreate that creature of chaos in your hands so we can place the stones, because we haven't much time to do so. We already lost a full day. Any more and we will be cutting it too close and that would be a mistake. Right now we have the upper hand; let's not lose that momentum."

"Fine," I say, kissing the top of her head, "but only if you design the piece; put those art skills to use, and all that jazz."

She laughs. "Oh, you are highly overestimating my design skills, but if you insist."

"I do," I rush out, "because to wield the stones, you have to wear the conduit, so you might as well like the piece. Now, shall it remain a necklace, or would another item suffice?"

Her eyes twinkle, her hands sparking with crimson light, and then a pencil and a piece of paper appear in her hands. And, because I am such a smartass, before she can say it, I wiggle my fingers and mouth the word *magic*.

CHAPTER 31

NEW IDENTITY (HADES)

"Are you sure you can do this?" Melody asks as she shades in her drawing. I look over her shoulder to where she holds the pencil, the concentrated strokes moving back and forth across the page. I nod. "Because I saw your work on Persephone's crown, which wasn't awful, but it has nowhere near the detail this piece will require."

"Her crown was haphazardly made, and I was worried less about the overall design than I was about getting it done."

"Still." She raises her eyes from the page to my face, halting her sketching as she looks for reassurance.

"It will turn out fine."

"Okay, because I don't want to spend all this time designing something pretty if it is just going to look like stones pressed into melted gobs of gold."

I take the drawing from her, studying the ornate baroque style flourishes. "This is remarkable," I offer, holding out the sketch for us both. "Truly, you have done amazing work, and the piece will be stunning." I run my fingers around the design, noting the elements she has used: leaves, flowers, scrollwork that wraps around some of the stones like a heart.

"I stacked the stones the best I could." She points to where each stone is nestled beneath curves and between prongs. "And I know this piece will be larger than anything I would wear, but I am less worried about how *remarkable* it is and more about it doing the job it was fashioned to do." She lays her head on my shoulder.

I brush my lips across the tip of her ear, breathing her in. "If what my mother said holds truth, then the Necklace of Harmonia is the only item we have that could fulfill our great purpose."

"True. It is not like we have anything else made by Hephaestus, or any other god, for that matter. So this will work, Hades. I am sure of it." She turns her face to mine, and I lean down, placing a kiss on her lips when she tilts her chin up to meet me.

Pulling away, I raise my hand, cupping the side of her face and brushing her cheek with my thumb lovingly. "You know I love this, right?" I ask.

Her cheeks flush, and her eyelashes flutter. "I do," she says. "We got off to a rocky start, but I think things are really turning around."

"And all it took was a couple of fights and a few death threats to get us here," I tease, and she pulls away.

"Well, now you've ruined it." She chuckles. "I thought we were having a moment there, but then you had to go and bring up death."

"As much as it pains me to say this, death brought us together. If it had not, you may have never known what you really are, or the power you possess. Where death is the end for so many, it seems to only be the beginning of something more for you."

"Yeah. Though I am not sure Persephone would agree with you. I mean, why didn't she pull my soul into the stone?"

I set down the drawing and slide out of bed, moving around to her side where she sits on the edge with her knees drawn up. I brace my hands on her knees, and she looks up at me. "When I tracked you to that place, there was only your body and a man. Oh, and lots of police and the two bodies Persephone left behind. He told police he followed you from the hospital where his wife was a patient, and that when he confronted you, you got aggressive."

"But there was no dagger?"

"No," I answer.

"Because the Subjugation Stone was in the pommel when Persephone died, right? I know it was there when she killed the others before Aphrodite arrived, and when she killed Elliott and Jen. Yet I found it beneath her bed." Her eyes widen. "Unless?"

"Unless?"

"Unless she willed it away after Aphrodite revealed herself, and that was what differed from when her soul entered the stone compared to the others."

"I suppose no Subjugation Stone means no control over the soul trapped within," I say assuredly.

"Exactly. And that is why she was able not only to possess the person wearing the stone, a.k.a. me, but knew to trap the new souls without entwining a piece of her own."

"So every soul placed within the stone since Persephone's death, except Jen and Elliott, could very well be fighting to make their way to the surface."

"And if that happens, then we will have no way to track the stone. At least with Persephone in control, we know what to look for. But if another soul emerges..."

"If another soul emerges, then what drives them may vary, and we would be searching for a needle in a haystack." I sigh. "We have to act fast and safeguard the Subjugation Stone somehow, so she cannot call it to her once more."

"I know," she says, taking my hands off her knees and kissing the knuckles. "You get started with the conduit, and I will gather the potions we need and find something to bind the stone to me." She drops my hands. "I don't think you will finish before we need to leave, but if we can at least have the base piece done, then we can hopefully come back and finish it with the Infinity Stone." She reaches over and picks up her drawing, turning back to hand it to me.

I take the paper from her and step back so she can rise. Then, we both move to the cabinet and grab a change of clothes. "We need to make a quick stop at the grotto to wash up, but then we can get started." I slip on my sandals and she does the same, following me to the door where I place her sketch on the table. I pause, looking down into the basin. "Uh, Melody?"

"Yes?" she asks, stepping beside me and trailing my gaze to the basin. "Oh, that. Yeah, so when you were going all aggro on your mother, it kinda made me sick."

"Sick how?" I ask, confusion written on my features.

"Well, first your mark on my leg burned, and then I got all light-headed, before eventually spewing my dinner." She points to the pile of sickness. "If it weren't for the flecks of ichor, I'm not certain I would have put the pieces together and realized you were in trouble."

Pointing to the pile, I say, "That is a conundrum for a different day, but remind me when this next part is over to circle back to why you were affected by me using my power."

"I mean, it was hard to ignore. But, yeah, definitely need to revisit all of that," she says, circling her hand over the table.

Melody finished bathing before I did, then went to take care of her personal needs before heading to my archives. Once I finished, I walked into the room, still drying my hair with a towel, and watched silently as she gathered two transfiguration potions and a memory transference draft.

She is more thorough than I was when I went to the mortal realm to find Persephone, and ultimately her, so to pull her from her hyper-focused state, I brush my hand across her shoulder to gain her attention. "You have got this all figured out it seems." I beam proudly as she stares lovingly up at me.

Leaning back on her hands, she cranes her neck. "Better to be prepared than caught with your pants down. Once we get there, we don't have the luxury of making trips back and forth, so if I think it is something we can use to execute our plan, I'm bringing it."

"Besides the potions and drafts, what are we bringing?" I motion my head toward the chest before her.

Lifting items from the chest, she says, "The Subjugation Stone, for sure, and I was considering the Mustēria Stone, but wasn't sure if Tyto can form in the mortal realm or not. Oh, and I dipped the Subjugation Stone in a binding draft, so it might be sticky." She hands me the stones, and I take them, noticing a healing gash on her other palm.

I choose not to mention the new wound on her palm as I squat down beside her, setting my wet towel on the ground next to the chest. She watches as I twirl the stones in my hand like a pair of stress balls, stopping to grip the Mustēria Stone between my fingers. I hold it up and allow the light to glint off the surface.

Just as I am about to offer my reply about the Mustēria Stone, Tyto flies into the room and lands in front of the chest. Then, Cerberus skids to a halt just inside the door and barks, causing the bird to twist his head behind him and ruffle his feathers while he lets out a loud screech.

Cerberus yelps, backing out into the hallway, and Tyto turns back around, his body shaking as if he found humor in the whole scene the hound made.

"Well, if we do not take Tyto with us, we better put him away so that Cerberus does not destroy the castle trying to get at him." I chuckle, taking a seat beside her, then handing her back the stones.

"So he can go?" she asks cheerfully.

"He can go," I say and she throws her arms around me, leaning against my chest.

"Oh, good. I was hoping to have him there just in case, especially if he can form and offer us guidance to that which we seek."

I rub her arms. "He will form in the mortal realm, but we have to be very careful that he is not seen. Can you imagine what mortals would do if they caught sight of him?"

"I can see it now," she muses, eyes twinkling. "His big ass rounding a corner with his light trails looking like something from *Tron*, while an unsuspecting mortal cowers as far back against a wall as they can manage."

"Yeah, no. That would not be good. We are already going to be fucking with poor Charity and Marcus. I would hate to have to mess with the minds of others if we can avoid it," I say.

"Then avoid it we shall," she insists.

Rising, I offer my hand and help Melody up so we can go back to our room to finish packing. But before we leave, she pats the bird on the head as an agitated Cerberus grumbles his opposition, and then returns Tyto to the stone where he will wait until the next time he is needed.

I take her hand, and we walk down the hallway with Cerberus at our heels. "Planning done, and now for the travel portion of our adventure. I do not suppose you know where Charity and Marcus live, do you? It would help if we could pinpoint their location so we arrive right where we need to be."

"I do, actually. I was a guest at their wedding, so the night before we all met at their place to go out since they weren't having a formal rehearsal dinner," she explains.

"Once we are ready to leave, I will have you picture it in your mind, and I will deliver us there. Then, we will have to sneak into their home and drink the potions while they are still conscious, before we knock them out to take their place. They can be in bed asleep, and actually that is the best-case scenario, so going in this evening would be most advantageous."

Reaching our room, I push open the door and we step inside. I pick out a simple set of dark gray linens, and Melody selects a satiny cobalt blue dress that hugs her curves. Neither of us will be in our clothing for long, but it will be good to have our own garments for the return trip.

I stole Aaron's suit after Melody's funeral and tore it to shreds as I took my true form while falling back to the Underworld. I landed naked as the day I was born and had to will my robes to me before searching for her. Good thing I did, or I would have scared her senseless by showing up bare at the edge of the river. I do not know if my nakedness would have hindered or helped in the making of her decision, but that thought is a foregone conclusion, yet still one that makes me chuckle.

Hearing my amusement, Melody turns to me and asks, "What is it?"

"Oh, nothing." I laugh again, and through the snickers, I say, "I was just thinking about when I came back here after your funeral."

"Oh, yeah. What about it?"

"Well, I was still wearing Aaron's suit, which was nothing but tattered fabric by the time I descended, and would have shown up naked for you if I had not thought about being clothed beforehand."

"Is that so?" She saunters up to me, running her fingers down the fabric crossing over my torso and to my waistline. "That would have been one hell of a first impression," she coos, placing her hand lower and tapping me.

My cock twitches and I grab her hand. "Settle, little one. A moment cannot be spared, remember?" I lower my gaze with mock disapproval.

"Fine," she exaggerates, stepping back. Then, she turns away from me, stepping to the edge of the bed before she says, "And because I am certain fucking as mortals will be lackluster at best, I will be a *good girl* and refrain from having my way with you."

She is bending over the bedside table, arranging her items in her satchel, when I step up behind her, allowing my length to brush against the top curves of her ass. She tenses, and I wrap my arms around her, pulling her back into me before plopping sideways onto the bed.

"Hades!" she shrieks. "You said we were in a hurry." She tries to wiggle out of my grip, which does nothing to lessen the ache in my cock.

"I did, but you also said you were going to be a good girl. Good girls do not bend over and flaunt their perky asses when there is work to be done." I nuzzle into her neck and, despite what I really want, finally let her go.

She rolls off the bed and stands, smoothing down her gown. "Now, if you can keep your hands to yourself, we can finish here and get this show on the road. Can you think of anything we are forgetting? Anything we haven't considered?"

"The plan is: go in at night, turn into the happy couple, make sure they are comfortable before we take a sample of their memories, and then wait for the following night to attend the opening."

"Sounds good," she says, "and we shouldn't need to go too far back into their memories. Arrive on Thursday night, call into work for them until Monday, sorry Charity and Marcus, gallery, and then dinner. With any luck, we will trail Persephone, snag the dagger, and place the Subjugation Stone in the pommel before trapping her within the Infinity Stone, all in time to get back to the Underworld before you are called."

"That is the best-case scenario," I point out. "Worst case, it all goes to shit, nothing goes to plan, and I have to find a way for us to get back in a hurry to regroup. Thoughts on that possibility?" I pose.

"Even if faced with that worst-case shit show, thanks for that by the way, as long as Marcus and Charity are unharmed, and we get back here in one piece, we can plan our next moves. I just can't let anyone die this time, Hades." Worry lines crinkle her forehead as her brows curve inward.

"Keep things positive. We will succeed, no one else will die, and you and I will come back here and have a glass of wine with Charon while we dish out the tea. Deal?"

"Deal," she says, offering her fist for me to bump. I do, and then she pulls it back, blowing it up.

"Everything except that last part." I chuckle. "No explosions if we can help it, but maybe just a little *magic*." I wiggle my fingers, and she mimics me. "Good girl. Now get that cute ass moving. We have about an hour to eat and finish the base of the conduit before we head out."

Things did not go according to plan. We did get the base of the necklace done before we left the Underworld, but Charity and Marcus have a dog now, which we had not prepared for. Melody was quick to pull out the Subjugation Stone and force him to calm the fuck down however, and now, Jasper and I, because of course their dog's name is Jasper, are friends. At least we were once my smart girl willed him to see us as his owners, that is.

With no other hiccups, Melody and I enter their home on the ground level, and because there is no kennel in sight, we leave Jasper out to wander, checking his food and water situation before ascending the stairs. We know the next couple of days will be busy, and want to be responsible pet owners and all that. Especially since his will otherwise be occupied.

Quietly going up the stairs, we find our happy couple in the shower, having a little playtime from the sounds of it, before they call it a night. So, not wanting to hassle with the undertaking that getting them out of the shower, dried off, and then into bed would be, we allow them to... *finish*. And once they are both finished, they get out, do what I assume is their nighttime routine, before tucking in.

The house is still as we stand in their guest room for about thirty minutes, staring at the most god-awful floral everything I have ever seen as we listen for signs of movement. I reach out to feel the bedspread, but Melody slaps my hand, shaking her finger *no* at me while she scowls with her lips pursed.

I mouth *what*, pointing to the doily-looking lace that is patch-worked on the coverlet, and she just rolls her eyes at me before crossing her arms over her chest. Then, when I walk over to the lamp and mess with the fringe hanging from the rose-colored lamp-shade, I can hear her huff of irritation behind me.

When I turn to face her, smirking, she mouths *seriously* before pointing at the door. I flip the fringe once more just to piss her off, and then pick up a picture frame off the side table and hand it to her.

She takes the picture and then pulls out our potions, handing one to me. We remove the stoppers, throw back the contents, and watch as we each transform into the couple within the frame. Then, I take her discarded gown and fold it neatly, placing it beside my garment on the side table.

Once we are sure our couple is asleep, we walk down the hall naked and stand outside their room, listening. With the sounds of quiet breathing coming from within, we enter their room, and I subdue them, but not by knocking them unconscious or anything. I mean, they are still breathing, but it is such a deep sleep that it is like I placed them under anesthesia. They will wake up refreshed, but with a wicked headache once we are done.

While I stand staring down at Charity and Marcus, Melody digs through their closet to pick out some clothes for us. I am hit in the back of the head with a pair of sweatpants, and pull my attention to where Melody stands motioning for me to get dressed.

"They are out," I say. "No need to mime at me, little one. Use your words."

I am getting a rise out of her, and it is odd to see a scowl on such an unfamiliar face. Tight, shoulder-length brown ringlet curls cover her entire head, and a smattering of freckles cross the bridge of her nose before continuing onto her cheeks. She is a pretty girl, this Charity, but nowhere near as pretty as my Melody. Where Melody is petite compared to me, this couple is about the same height and size.

Charity has very large breasts and curvy buttocks, with thick thighs and impressive calves, while Marcus is rocking a dad-bod. He is not what I would call overweight, but as I stare at this new form in the full-length mirror on the closet door, I cannot help but suck in and then release my one-pack to watch it jiggle.

I saunter up behind Melody naked, where she is still fussing with throwing on some clothes. I step into her, rubbing my belly across her back, and she stiffens. She straightens, turns to look at me, peers down at the thing I am swinging playfully between my legs with my hands on my hips, and says, "Absolutely not."

"What? She obviously enjoys it," I say, tilting my head toward the bed. "Come on, Muffin," I say, using the pet name we heard Marcus moaning earlier. "Daddy needs to butter your hot cross buns."

She throws a shirt in my face and exclaims, "You're fucking disgusting!"

I pull the shirt over my head, smoothing his equally curly dark brown hair down, and then walk over to the nightstand and pick up Marcus' glasses. "Oh, that is better," I say, walking back toward Melody with his little thing still swinging proudly. "Now I can see you."

"I've seen enough of you, and *that* will not happen, so put your damn pants on."

"We have all night, baby," I say, walking over and picking up the pants she threw at me from off the floor while holding the bent-over position. "Hey, *Charity*?" I call out.

She looks over and gasps. "Titans save me, I did not want to see your great beyond, *Marcus*," she chastises. "Put on the fucking pants, or so help me!"

"Okay, okay. Killjoy. Marcus looks like the type of guy to say killjoy, right?"

"Why don't you take the damn draft and find out if you are so curious," she says, tossing the vial at me. I catch it, and we open our vials, downing them at the same time. She makes a face, squeezing her eyes shut as if the taste is bitter, and I go to the bathroom to gargle my mouth out.

When I walk out, I say, "My tongue tingles," and she laughs at me.

"Yeah, well, I would rather have a tingly tongue than the crazy tickle that just happened to my brain just now. And can I just say, ew! These two are fucking gross. Did you see what they did with the chocolate pudding last week?"

"You mean how he had her toe paint it all over his body, before they took turns sucking it off?"

She makes a gagging motion, and I laugh again. Then she admits, "I can confidently say that a foot fetish is not in my wheelhouse."

"Not with those sausage toes." I point to her stocky feet. "But *you* have the cutest little digits, and I didn't mind putting them in my mouth in the slightest."

After a good chuckle on behalf of our pair of sleeping beauties, we grab their phones and are happy to find that they already have tomorrow blocked off from work. I guess they decided to spend the day together before going to the gallery, because based on their calendars, they had not had a date night in over four months.

I hold up Marcus' phone just as Melody is realizing the same thing with Charity's schedule and say, "Gotta keep the magic alive."

"I can think of better ways to spend a day off work," she offers.

"So, with the whole day open tomorrow, is there anything in particular you would like to do?"

"Is it morbid to want to see where I died and where my body is buried?" She raises a quizzical brow.

I walk over and wrap my arms around her. It is so odd, not only looking into a strange face, but hearing a voice that is not hers. "I do not think it is morbid. You are curious, is all."

"Curious or not, do you think it will be a mistake to go to that place? Or to the cemetery?" She stares into my brown eyes through my glasses, and I get lost in Charity's bright green ones.

"The mistake would be leaving this realm without doing so, in my opinion. Because when will you get the opportunity again?"

"I guess that all depends on how things shake out while we are here."

"That it does," I say. "That it does." We are walking down the stairs when I ask, "Do you think there is any pudding left?"

Conduit

Epirroí Stone
"Subjugation Stone"
Apeiron Stone
"Infinity Stone"
Kruptós Stone
"Mustēria Stone"
Eos Stone
"Aurora Sapphire"
Anastasis Stone
"Renascence Ruby"
Basileios Stone
"Kingmaker Emerald"

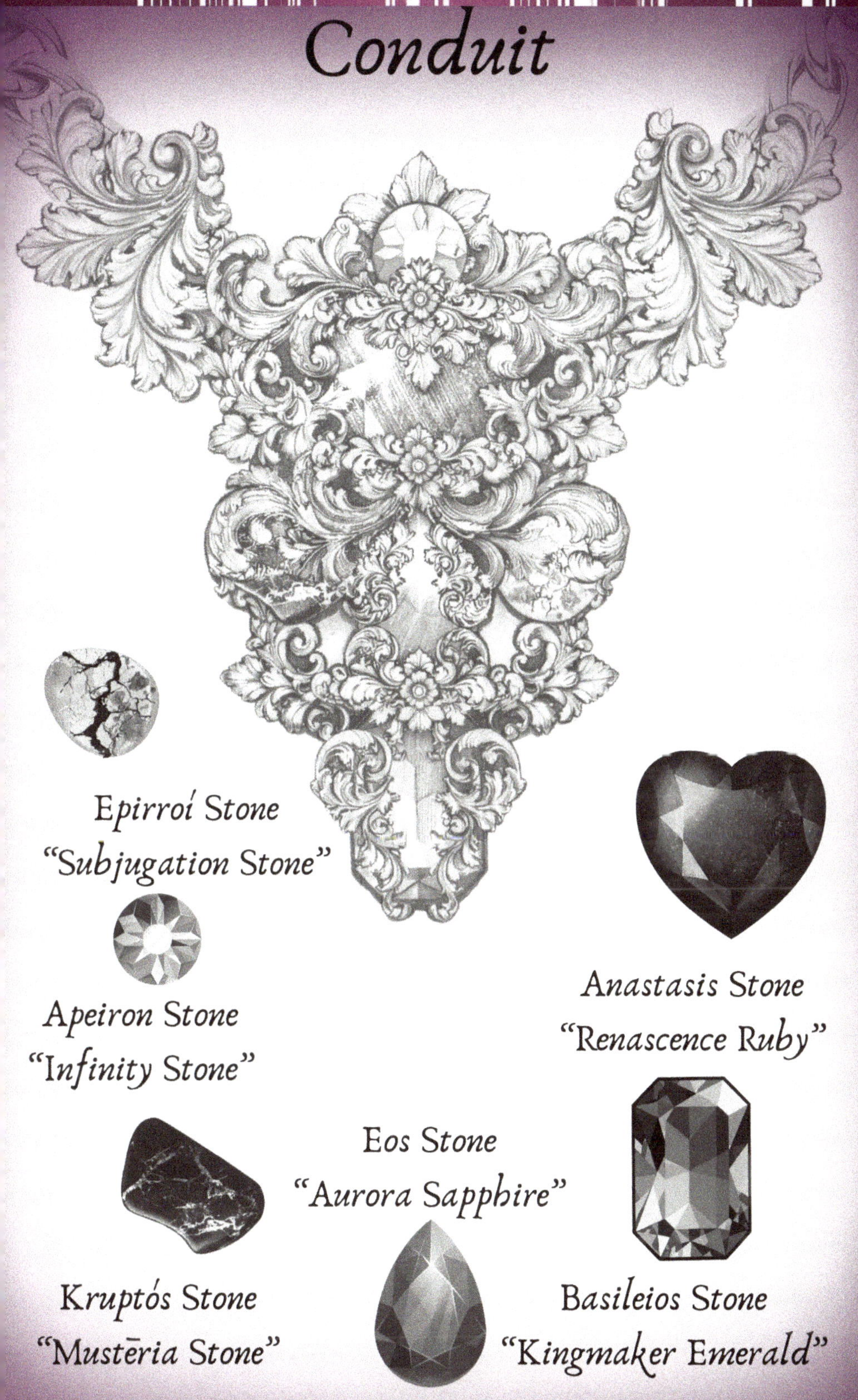

CHAPTER 32

RETURNING TO THE SCENE OF THE CRIME (MELODY)

The next morning when we pull up to the property, the academy looks ominous with the subsiding storm in the distance. More so than when Hades last saw it, he says. He notes that the dirt road is drier now than when he drove up to pure chaos almost four weeks ago, as if an unimaginable power shields the grounds from the elements somehow. Where the back roads through the county were wet during our drive, with the tires of our 4Runner finding every puddle, it is completely dry as we make the turn, stopping just before the driveway of the house across the way.

"The same car is parked in the grass out front, looking like it has not been moved an inch," he says, "and the horse trailer." He points to where the brush is higher, and it is hidden from view of the road. "I do not recommend we step foot inside the gate, what with the *no trespassing* signs and all, but it should be fine if I show you from the road. That is, as long as Farmer Dan does not come out waving his piece all around."

"Farmer Dan?" I ask, stepping to the t-post and barbed wire fence, staring over. "Who the hell is Farmer Dan?"

"No clue," he says. "That is just what I call the guy who lives in that house," he explains, pointing to where a small, white house peeks out from the overgrown bushes.

"I don't think he would take it too kindly if he heard you calling him Farmer Dan, *Marcus*."

"I know, *Charity*," he exaggerates. "That is why I am keeping a close eye on the front door to avoid any unnecessary confrontation. So if I say get in…"

"I get in and we go," I state, nodding my head.

"Good girl," he coos.

"Shut up, Marcus," I tease.

"Fuck you, Charity," he claps back.

Then he meets me where the grass has grown mostly up the fence line, peering into the property where the dilapidated stone building stands despite the storms it's weathered since the doors closed over ninety years ago. Several of its doors are missing, as are most of the windows and shutters on the second floor, and the wooden planks that used to be eaves are now splintered, making me wonder how the top floor hasn't collapsed into the one beneath it. Plus, it has a metal roof, which is worn, but looks to be the sturdiest thing about this haunted place.

"I can't believe I died here," I say, sniffling.

"I know, baby." He wraps one arm around me, unable to circle me fully, and I do the same. This embrace is different, still comforting, but it makes me miss the real him holding the real me.

Wiping my nose, I turn back to the car, take the three steps to my door and pull it open, climbing in. He watches me from where I left him standing and then kicks a rock before coming around the back of the vehicle and entering on his side.

After slamming the door shut, he looks over at me, and I ask, "Can we just go?"

"Of course," he says, pushing the start button and turning on the vehicle. "We can do whatever you want." He reaches over the center console for me, but I pull my arm back, wrapping myself tighter.

"Just drive, Marcus," I whimper. "Put your foot on the gas and get me the hell out of here." My voice is strained, and despite just getting started, I am already so over this fucking day.

He puts it in drive, and we lurch forward, kicking up dust as we leave the place some man ended my life because I, as terrifying as I was, was *aggressive.*

With the sound of the tires drowning out the purr of the engine as we go from hard packed dirt, to the crunch of loose gravel, and eventually the smoothness of blacktop, the whirring cars passing at regular intervals has me asleep shortly after we get on the main road.

I'm not sure what route we took, or where the fuck we are when I finally wake up parked outside a building that looks like a middle school. It has a brick exterior, seems to be just the one level, and the parking lot is relatively full for two o'clock on a Friday afternoon. *Apparently, this school does not allow parents to line up early for pickup,* I think, scanning the parking lot and then pulling out Charity's phone.

I have one text message from Marcus that came in about ten minutes ago, saying he would be right back, but I am bored and consider getting out of the car when I see him coming down a side-walk out to the parking lot.

He walks a little bowlegged, trying to keep his thick thighs from rubbing together, and I almost have to do a double-take because I forgot what bodies we are in. I lower my sunglasses as he climbs in, waiting for him to tell me exactly what it is we are doing... wherever we are, but he is silent.

His features give nothing away as he starts the vehicle and we head out of the parking lot. But then, as we turn onto the access road, I look over just in time to see the words *in-patient* on a sign before he presses on the gas.

"Wait! Stop!" I call out, but he doesn't slow down. He just keeps on driving down the street, the turn signal clicking as he turns left, back toward the highway. "I wanted you to stop," I say.

"And I did not," he says angrily, getting into the turn lane so he can take the on-ramp.

"Um, hello, I have questions," I say in a condescending tone.

"That I am choosing not to answer at this time," he replies flippantly, not bothering to look at me.

"You know, I thought we had gotten past this asshole phase, but apparently a new body means we are back to square one," I berate.

He is silent for quite some time, and my anger builds as I stare out the window, watching traffic blur by. Then, after about fifteen minutes or so, we are pulling off the highway and headed toward what looks like the center of campus.

I grumble under my breath, having an imaginary argument with him as the roads twist and turn through town. And before I realize where we are, he turns off Center Street to access Evergreen Cemetery.

"Oh," I say quietly when we pull in.

"Yeah, oh," he mutters under his breath.

"You could have just said this was where you were going; you didn't have to be a dick about it."

"I was not being a dick!" he contends. Then, he takes a deep breath, releasing it with a sigh. "I was not being a dick, I just was not sure how well you were going to handle coming here after your reaction earlier, and thought, you know, maybe if I let her sit with her silence for a bit, then stopping here will not have her reeling as much."

"No offense, but being here is going to affect me, whether or not you let me 'sit in my silence'," I mock.

"Which is precisely why I chose not to say anything. Because given the opportunity, you would have talked yourself out of coming, and I am not letting you go back to the Underworld with regrets. Not if I can help it." His answer is genuine and heartfelt, but I can't get past him using his silence as a weapon when the one thing we struggle with is communication.

"I appreciate your honesty," I say slowly, "but I would prefer if you just talk to me next time and help me work through my feelings rather than try to circumnavigate them by making the decision for me."

"Got it," he says, pulling to the side of the road. He puts the vehicle in park, turns to face me, looks me straight in the eyes, and states, "Melody, we are about to step out and walk to your grave unless you tell me you would rather not."

I consider his words for a moment, but ultimately decide that this is something I need to do. "No, I want to," I admit. "I just wish I had known this is where we were going so I could get flowers."

He releases his buckle, turns around and reaches into the back seat, where plastic crinkles loudly before he turns back and sets a bouquet of wrapped flowers in my lap. My eyes well up with tears at his thoughtfulness, and he places his hand on my shoulder before he says, "It was the least I could do."

I sob after that. After working so hard to choke back my feelings since getting here last night, and then again earlier this morning, there is nothing I can do to suppress the waves of emotions crashing over me now.

My tears fall fast and hard, my body quaking as I suck in each painful breath through clenched teeth, and I fall completely the fuck apart while staring at what most would consider a simple gesture, but to me means everything. Because after everything we planned, and all the things we still have yet to accomplish, when it came right down to it, today was not about stopping Persephone or Aphrodite, or saving the realms from destruction. And it certainly was not about impending annihilation or his responsibility. No, he made today all about *me*, and regardless of him being a poor communicator, his actions speak volumes.

I am still sitting there, shaking as I sob when I hear him mumble, "Is that?" He pauses. "Oh, shit!" he exclaims, and I look up from the flowers. His eyes are wide and his mouth is agape, so I try to follow his line of sight. "No, not yet," he says, reaching over and turning my face back toward him. "Just look at me for a minute, please. Can you do that, little one? Just one minute so you can calm down?"

"It is hard to calm down when you are scaring me," I squeak.

"Just breathe," he soothes, "breathe."

"I'm fucking breathing, but there is absolutely no way I am going to calm down until you tell me what the fuck is going on," I grit out.

"Okay, but you promise you will not freak out?" He grimaces.

"Yes," I answer slowly, my tone just as unsure as I feel.

He points at me. "After I tell you what I am about to say, remember that you promised. You cannot lose your shit, okay. If you lose your shit, this thing we are doing could be in jeopardy." He stares blankly at me for a moment and then prompts, "Say it with me: I am Charity."

"I am Charity," I repeat, irritated.

"And you are Marcus," he says.

"Really?" I scoff, trying to look around. He stops me. "Fine! You are fucking Marcus," I rush out.

"And Desire just walked by the car," he announces.

"And Desire just—Wait, what?" I turn my head so fast I almost give myself whiplash, pressing my face to the window. "Where are they?" I plead, scanning our surroundings.

"You promised you would not freak out," he whines, sinking down in his chair.

"But that was before you said Desire was here," I argue, turning to smack him on the arm.

Desire is here. Desire is visiting my grave. My family, and my one connection to the mortal world is just right outside those doors and for some reason I am sitting here twiddling my damn thumbs instead of leaping out of this car, and I... "I will not freak out," I state confidently, finally seeing them standing beside a headstone in the distance.

"Oh, you are so totally freaking out." He sighs. "Look, whatever you do, just do not terrify them. You can hug and cry, bond over the death of a mutual friend, but under no circumstances can you tell them who you are," he insists, reaching for me.

"Because I am Charity," I say solemnly, dropping my shoulders.

"Yes, but more convincingly next time." He uses his whole body to urge me to breathe again, and it is just pissing me off.

"But I am not Charity, and that is Desire!" I raise my voice, motioning toward where they stand by my grave.

"Fine, go. But do not freak out," his words trail off as I jump down and race toward my grave.

Oh, shit! I breathe. *This body is not made for running and I... am out of breath in less than, what was that a minute? What the fuck, Charity? All this muscle in your legs and no get up and go? On everything that is holy, girl, I am adding cardio to your calendar because this is just fuck-ing... argh!*

My brain is going a mile a minute, even though my legs failed me after fifty feet, but on the outside I look calm because... I am not freaking out. I am winded, but I am not freaking out. Desire is almost within arm's reach; despite that, I am not freaking out. Huh, his pep talk had the desired effect, and now he is at my side as we walk up behind my best friend, so I look over at him and smirk when I say, "I am not freaking out. Suck on that, Marcus."

He hands me the bouquet and then takes my hand before he says, "So glad you could be mature about this situation."

"But at least I'm not freaking out," I say cheerfully, bumping him with my hip and sending him veering to the side.

It was bittersweet seeing Desire again, but oh so awkward trying to play the part of a woman they only met once in passing and share in their grief. Still, I needed this, and I would not have made it through today if I didn't have the man I do standing beside me. So, despite all the crappy things I thought about him during the most infuriating drive through town, I do not know what I would have done without him here to support me.

I mean, I got to see Desire today. And as I did that man stood patiently as we chatted, held my hand while we cried, and after I wrapped my arms around Desire for what was probably the last time, that same man gave me his strength and held me up as I made that painful walk back to where we were parked.

Then, after he helped me inside, he allowed me to just soak it all in, embracing the silence as we made our way back to Marcus and Charity's because that was what I needed. So, regardless of all the times I've heard him say he is selfish, but it is something he is working on, today just showed me he doesn't have to work so hard anymore. And as independent as I am, I am glad to know that if I need him; I have him. As a friend and as a partner.

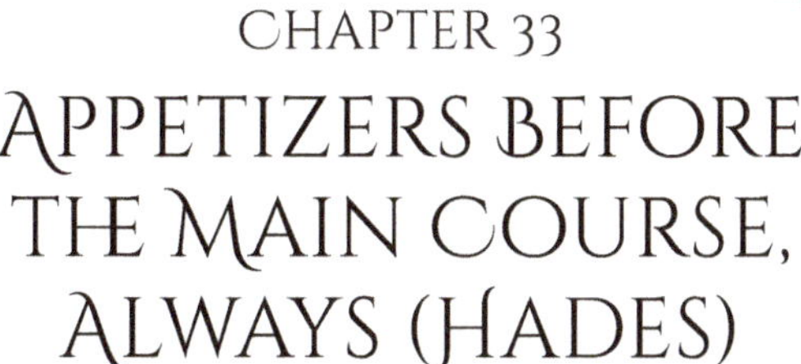

CHAPTER 33

APPETIZERS BEFORE THE MAIN COURSE, ALWAYS (HADES)

Melody is all shaking hands and agitated sighs as she does her makeup in the bathroom mirror, applying and reapplying her lipstick three times before she decides on a color. Her final choice is a dusty pink, which compliments Charity's fairer skin tone much better than the red she tried on earlier.

Not having the heart to tell her that her signature poppy hue, while it looks amazing on her caramel skin, had Charity's ivory looking pale as a ghost, I went back to the closet, because if she was happy with it, who was I to stop her? She figured it out on her own in the end, with no input requested from me, thank the Titans. If asked, I would have said she looked fine, even knowing that was not what she was asking.

I, too, am finally happy with what I have chosen—pressed charcoal slacks and matching sport coat with a navy button-up and a patterned tie—having changed three times in the last ten minutes because almost every dress shirt in Marcus' closet had me looking like *Winnie the Pooh*. I mean, who keeps clothes that fit that poorly in the first place? Unless, of course, Marcus has a New Year's resolution for a slight slim-down that he does not already have programmed into his meticulously organized phone, but I highly doubt it.

As I straighten my tie in the mirror, I say, "Not too shabby, my friend. Look at those smoldering eyes and that baby face." I smooth down my jacket. "With a properly tailored suit, you could get all the ladies, Marcus. Oh, wait, I almost forgot." Then I walk into the bathroom and smack Charity's ass, giving her a rakish grin. "Almost ready, muffin?"

Her dark green dress that hugs all of her curves plunges low in the front, and her ample breasts have so much cleavage showing from the bra she chose I want to bury my face between her peaks. She turns, facing me as she frowns. "Does this look okay?"

I step into her, taking her hand so she can feel how *okay* Marcus thinks her dress is, and she giggles as she pulls away, blushing. Her cheeks flush beautifully, giving her a youthful glow as she bats her eyelashes. Seriously, though, I am so ready to get out of these bodies and back into our own, because referring to myself using another man's name and talking in third-person is making me a little loopy. Not to mention that calling her Charity just is not sitting right with me. *But that ass*, I think, giving her another good smack before I step away.

Once she feels properly primped and coiffed, Charity grabs her phone off the nightstand and heads downstairs. I will do the same, but not until I check my hair one more time in the mirror and then stop at the bedroom door to blow a kiss to the sleeping forms of the *real* Charity and Marcus. After I do, I say, "Wish us luck," even though I know I will receive no answer.

Closing the door behind me, I descend the stairs, meeting my girl in the kitchen. Charity is refreshing the water bowl after topping off the food dish, and I give Jasper a couple of good pats before grabbing the keys. Then, we are out the door to the garage, and as I am getting into the 4Runner, Charity joins me and I ask, "Do we have everything?"

She opens her purse, showing me her phone, wallet, the velvety pouch she found in the bathroom for the stones, and I hand her my wallet to place with all the rest of the items in the bottom of her bag, her lipstick included. But noticing she has not said much since we got home earlier, I try to get her talking by saying, "Have I told you how gorgeous you look tonight?"

She huffs. "I appreciate the compliment, but the sooner we get this night over the sooner we can get back home." Her shoulders pull back, and then she fastens her belt, flipping down the visor to check her makeup once more. "Jasper is great and all, but I miss Cerberus. Do you think he'll be able to smell Jasper on me and get jealous? I mean, if Tyto sets him off, I can just imagine what smelling another dog on me is going to do." She lifts the visor and looks to me for my input.

I chuckle as I imagine Cerberus standing there with an absolute look of betrayal on his faces before walking away in a huff. "It will be fine," I say through my laughter, fastening my belt before opening the garage door and pressing the start button. "He is a big boy, and a little competition will do him good."

"Still..." she says as I back out of the garage, halting when we get to the end of the driveway for a car to pass.

"Look, little one, I love you are concerned about his feelings, but how about we address what it really is that is bothering you instead of some possible offense our hellhound might take to you loving on another pet." I pull out of our neighborhood and onto the main road.

"Fine," she sighs, "I guess I am just nervous that our plan is going to go to shit before we have a chance to at least get the stone, let alone deal with Persephone." She is silent as I take the on-ramp, getting onto the highway. Then, after several minutes, out of nowhere, she asks, "What if she doesn't show? Or, what if she shows and Aphrodite does too, and then we have two foes and a restaurant full of mortals to consider?"

"How about we address each problem as we face it, and stop allowing yourself to get freaked out by all the what-ifs before you drive yourself mad? Can you do that?" I offer her a smile, hoping the confidence I am brimming with will flow into her, even if only a little. "We have got this, babe. Home team, remember?" I offer my fist.

She smiles and then pounds my hand, saying, "Home team," but this time without the explosion, because she knows that is the last fucking thing we need in this situation.

We spend twenty minutes on the highway before taking the off-ramp toward Bentonville, and are pulling into a parking lot behind a pub about thirty minutes before the event.

Charity removes her seatbelt and is texting her group about dinner while I fiddle with the steering wheel controls, searching for some music. I find a top-100 station and leave it playing quietly as emotional support background noise.

"They said there are lots of drinks, but looking at the menu..." she trails off, scrolling up on her phone.

"Yeah?" I lean sideways in my seat, spreading my legs to air the boys out a bit. These pants are great when I am standing, but crammed into a vehicle and bunched up with my thighs squashed together, not so much.

"Okay, so there *are* some chicken options for your delicate stomach," she says, looking over just as I am adjusting myself. I meet her stare with a grin.

"What? He was getting pinched."

"You sure? Because from here it looked like you were playing with yourself," she says, not believing my explanation for a minute.

"I do not need your opinions on the matter, unless you are

offering to help ease some of the restriction I am experiencing," I retort with a smirk, wiggling my eyebrows.

"You can't possibly—"

"Oh, I can *possibly*, and he would be most grateful if you would just..." I reach over and grab her hand, moving it to my lap.

"Someone could see!" she exclaims, looking out the window for any passersby. She does not remove her hand, though, and that has Marcus' cock jumping beneath the zipper.

"So what if they did? I could easily explain that after *four* months my wife finally graced me with her presence for date night, and she was having an appetizer before the main course." I place my hand atop hers, rubbing over my bulge with both of them. The zipper does not feel great, however, so I hope she will quit fucking around and release the beast already.

"I think you forget I am not actually Charity and you aren't Marcus," she argues, continuing her rubbing even after I lift my hand and grip the headrest.

My left hand lowers to press the power controls, and my seat reclines. "Even so, I have Marcus' body, and it and I are both feeling a little lonesome without having lips wrapped around our cock at the moment."

"Fine," she huffs, draping her body across the center console, "but if we get caught, you get to be the one to explain." She loosens my belt and undoes my pants, pulling my dick out of the hole in my boxer briefs. Then, wrapping her puffy lips around the head of Marcus' cock, Charity sucks.

"As if my sated gaze and your smudged lipstick or mussed hair would need any explanation," I tease, holding back a groan as I grasp a handful of curly locks at the base of her neck.

She bobs up and down, massaging my balls over the fabric, and thank the Titans Marcus is a grower, not a shower, because as I smother her face in my lap, she finally gags. "Good girl," I moan. "Choke on that cock and show Marcus how much you love it."

She mumbles, "Mm-hmm," around my dick, and the vibration sends me over the edge before I can warn her, and I come.

Holding her down on me, I spill everything I have into her mouth, which is hopefully not a lot, seeing as Marcus got a release last night before bed. But hearing her fighting for her life in my lap, last night's activities obviously did nothing to lessen the accumulation.

I let go of her hair so she can escape, and she comes up gasping, her hand clasped over her mouth to hold in the excess. Her eyes are wide and teary, and she sits in her seat while I reach into the back for a roll of paper towels Marcus keeps behind the passenger side.

"One minute," I grunt, fumbling to reach the roll without smearing the remnants of my climax all over. I get cum on my shirt, but at least it is near the bottom and somewhere I can hide it with a simple tuck into my pants and the buttoning of my jacket.

Once I grab the towels, I unravel a couple of sheets, handing them to her, and pull off some for myself once I am sure she has plenty. I then wipe off everything that has not soaked in already, while she spits out what remains in her mouth, glaring across the vehicle at me.

At least I have the intelligence to look apologetic, though I am smug as shit on the inside for getting my way, as she opens the center console and pulls out a grocery bag, placing the wadded-up towels inside. I do the same, then pull out the mouthwash I know Marcus keeps under the grocery bags and napkins in the console, offering it to her.

She takes it begrudgingly, tosses some back, and lowers her window to spit outside. The cool air trails in, reaching my depleted cock, and he shrivels even more than he already had. I put him away, fastening my pants, and then look over as she raises the window and say, "Thanks, babe, my pants fit way better now without him getting in the way."

"Uh-huh," she mutters, staring into the visor mirror as she reapplies her lipstick, her eyes darting to me briefly. There is mischief in those searing green eyes, and I know I will pay dearly for this later. Not gonna lie, I kind of look forward to it.

CHAPTER 34

HALF-PAST SEVEN (HADES)

At exactly seven o'clock, we are standing in front of the gallery. The speakeasy and gallery opened at four, so patrons have already been going in, each one looking at us as they pass. But despite our curiosity, we stand awaiting our party just outside.

At seven o' five, the tall, slender woman in a white silk button-up and fitted slacks, who has been checking reservations, peeks out to let us know we can wait inside if we would like. We thank her, saying our reservation is at eight, and that after a quick viewing of the exhibit with the rest of our group, who are running fashionably late as usual, we look forward to seeing the place. She nods her understanding and then closes the door.

Chilled to the bone from waiting, at ten-past seven, we eventually step inside out of the crisp December air, through a large glass door covered by a metal awning and into the modern gallery. As we walk around, there are two large windows on the front wall, one on each side of the entry door and looking out to the street, with white walls and trim complimenting the chestnut-colored wood, possibly laminate, flooring.

The space is illuminated by track lighting, perfectly positioned to spotlight the varying pieces displayed on the walls, and there are several textile and tapestry pieces hanging from the ceiling, while the work of the other local artists are placed sporadically throughout. We stop in front of one piece, and Charity reads the description below while I stare at it dumbfounded.

"What am I looking at?" I mumble out of the corner of my mouth. Charity finishes reading and snickers, covering her amusement by faking a cough. I pat her back. "Well?"

"Leftover feminine products," she whispers.

"What? Seriously?" I whisper back. "But why?"

"It represents the struggle the artist feels regarding her monthly cycle and reproductive functions," she says with her hand over her mouth to muffle her reply.

"I do not get it," I say, shaking my head and moving to the next piece.

She steps beside me and scoffs as she says, "Well, you wouldn't because you lack the anatomy associated with said struggle. Periods suck, Marcus. The hormones take control and turn you into this whole other person for half the month, and then of course there are the physical components that compound that struggle, but I digress. I get it, the concept is lost on you. Moving on."

Now we move in opposite directions, taking time with the pieces we like and passing on the ones we do not, meeting in the middle once we are done perusing the exhibit. We have just taken a seat on a bench along the front wall under the window at half-past seven when another of our party arrives.

Stepping inside, Janessa, a stunning woman in a shiny black pantsuit with her lace bra visible underneath, apologizes for being late while she massages some warmth back into her arms. The movement has her breasts pressed together and on display in the deep-v of her jacket, and I avert my gaze, pretending as if I am admiring a piece hanging from the ceiling.

Charity stands, introducing us, and I try not to stare but the woman is gorgeous. Instead of a quick hello, my eyes trail up from where she shakes my hand to the luminous almond-colored skin of her exposed neck, eventually stopping when I get to her deep set honey brown eyes twinkling with excitement. Her hair is intricately braided into an updo, and my attention is thankfully pulled from her to the door when two more enter behind her.

Finally, letting go of her hand, I am embarrassed by how long I have been holding her captive, and she pretends not to notice, but I know she did. My cheeks go hot at the thought, and then I watch as she and Charity greet Matéo and a Laelia something or other whose parents were florists if I heard her correctly when she explained her uncommon name.

I do not even remember asking her about the uniqueness of her name, though I must have since she is addressing me, and I miss the question she asked in return, seeing as my attention keeps straying elsewhere. Not on my wife, Charity, as it should be, but on her very alluring friend, and the reason we are gathered at the moment.

"I am sorry, what was the question?" I give my attention to Laelia, who snickers politely.

She repeats, "I said, what do you do, Marcus?"

"Oh, nothing fancy." I chuckle. "I work in logistics. Unlike all of you, I do not have an artistic bone in my body."

Charity steps up beside me, placing her arm through mine, and teases, "I'm sure they never could have guessed that."

It is now forty-five minutes past the hour, and our reservation is in fifteen minutes, so Janessa walks us over to her piece—a black-and-white photograph of an elderly woman. She explains that the woman with soulful eyes and weathered skin, with so many smile lines that her life must have been incredibly full is her grandmother.

Staring intently at the photo, I then read the name of the piece— *Yon Famn Solid*—and turn my attention to Janessa as I ask, "Do you speak Haitian Creole?"

The conversation ceases, everyone taken aback, and now all the eyes of our party are staring directly at me, and I am embarrassed all over again.

Janessa tilts her head to the side, considering me. "I do. Do you?"

"No," I state plainly, "it is just that the title is familiar." I shrug my shoulders, trying to make it seem like it is not a big deal. But apparently it is, and now Janessa is walking me through the process she used to develop the film, and is so animated as she uses terms like developer, stop bath, and final wash as if I have a clue what she is talking about. Still, I remain focused on her eyes and keep the interaction respectful, despite the attention I am receiving from this mesmerizing woman and the tingles my body is awash in.

After she is done telling the story about her grandmother and all the great things she did for her community in Haiti, solidifying her as the epitome of a yon famn solid, the hostess announces our reservation and we are led to the painting hanging over the hidden entrance to the speakeasy.

Charity sidles up and whispers, "If I had to guess, you feel it too."

My eyes widen as I gawk at her. "I thought it was jut me."

She shakes her head, grinning. "Nope."

"But how?"

"Ask her about her grandmother and the Lwa." Then she winks, and I follow her through the passageway and into the speakeasy.

CHAPTER 35

A WOMAN MARKED (MELODY)

I have been to more places than I can count that touted the vibe and decor of their establishment as being tropical. They all fell short, looking cheesy, underdone, and more like a hut on the beach where the only other tropical thing about the place was the little umbrella in the drinks. The place we just walked into, however, is high class, inviting, and should be the picture beneath the definition of a *fancy tropical bar* in my opinion.

Instead of being in a cocktail lounge in Northwest Arkansas, this speakeasy has me feeling like I was just transported to an island where I can walk along a private beach during the day, lounging under palm trees, before spending my evening relaxing in a designer gown with a drink and great conversation in a place just like this.

Right when we enter, my eyes are drawn to a large tree draping over some booths in the back and then meander their way past the crushed orange velvet barstools, sitting before a long bar where the front is dressed in bamboo wainscoting. And because that isn't enough to set the mood, hanging above the bar and lining the space are amber-colored artesian light fixtures, and there are tiki heads carved into the wooden built-ins where the most eye-catching display of back-lit bottles line the back wall.

A bartender stands dressed all in black to our right behind the bar, and as we are shown to our booth, I can't take my eyes off where he is moving his cocktail shaker up and down fervently, preparing a drink that will be served, I assume, in the conch shell sitting before him. We sit down, and as we are handed our menus I excitedly ask our server, "I'm sorry, but what is he making?"

She looks over and then smiles. "The Four Winds. It's on page three," she says, waiting for me to turn the page and then points to the drink in question.

I read the contents and then nod. "I'll have one of those, please."

"Make that two," Marcus says beside me, holding up two fingers.

"Two of The Four Winds," she says, "and for everyone else?"

The rest of our party orders their drinks, but I find it hard to pay attention to anything else going on around me when the static in the air increases as a man and woman step up to the bar.

Curly auburn waves cascade down to the bare shoulders of the woman, and her golden, glittery gown crisscrosses in the center of her back with the thinnest spaghetti straps imaginable. If it wasn't for her profile view that allows me to see her ample breasts, I would have said that I have no clue how the dress is staying up.

She is beautiful and obviously charismatic from the attention she is getting from the equally handsome man with dark hair and a tan suit accompanying her. He smiles at whatever she just said, his perfect pearly whites gleaming beneath pouty lips, and then she laughs. It is sultry and melodic, but the sound is interrupted by a high-pitched ringing that seems to coincide with the moment he places his hand on her back.

I cover my ears, and Marcus looks at me, then at the woman, and then back to me not knowing what to do. Just when I think I will faint from the searing pain, the sound making me feel like it is turning my brain to mush, it stops. And now when I look over, the man has removed his hand from her body and I don't know what the fuck just happened.

I pant, releasing the breath that had been trapped behind clenched teeth, and as I settle, the server shows up with our drinks. "The Four Winds for you two," she says, setting them in front of Marcus and me, "and the rest should be ready shortly. While we wait for the rest of your drinks, are you ready to place your order?"

Picking up the drink, I suck it straight down, ignoring the brain freeze from how cold it is as I purse my lips, wishing the straw was wider so I could have more. Then, as I finish, all eyes at the table are on me, including the server's, and Marcus does his best to distract everyone from the scene I just made by saying, "She will have another one, and the chicken. Both types—the skewers and the fried —if you please. For you, Janessa?" He motions to my friend, and now everyone has forgotten about my awkward display and is ordering their food.

The rest of the evening goes off without a hitch, as far as having a good conversation with a great group of people, plus the food was excellent, but the one thing we lack and the main reason we came— the woman we presume Persephone now inhabits—is nowhere in sight.

Just when I think we are about to wind things down and call it a night, I hear Marcus quietly asking Janessa to tell him about her grandmother and the Lwa. Matéo and Laelia are flirting across from me on the other end of the booth, paying no mind to anyone else at the table, so I listen in as Janessa talks.

"You know for someone who says they don't speak Haitian Creole, you seem to know an awful lot about my culture," she whispers.

"Call it an infatuation with anything pertaining to the divine," he says, fiddling with the straw protruding from the shell before him.

"Divine, holy, otherworldly, these are many of the terms that have led men to seek a higher power, becoming infatuated, as you say. But very few are truly pious or reverent, seeking only to wield and never to understand. Are you one such as this?" she says, at first in a lilting tone, but then with her pitch deep and full of derision when she asks her question.

"Perhaps infatuation is too strong a word, and respectful preoccupation more aptly describes my quest for knowledge," he says, leaning in to keep their conversation private.

"Respectful preoccupation," she coos. "I like that. You are a man of many words, Marcus, but words can only take you so far. It is the deeds of a man that matter most. A man's deeds are a symbol of who he is, oftentimes more so than the cross he wears around his neck."

"Well, if it is my symbol you seek, I shall show it to you. Then, in good faith, and perhaps to better your understanding... I will do you one better and offer you a second."

Her lip twitches, and I can tell she is curious, but even more than curious, I think she already knows something is different about Marcus. As I watch him picking up a napkin, I rummage through my purse, sliding him a pen across the booth, and he takes it.

With my pen in hand, he puts it to task, drawing a small circle above a crescent. It is Charon's symbol; I recognize it from not only his temple but the repeating pattern on his robes. And she knows it too, her eyes widening as she stares at his hand still gripping the pen.

Then, as he starts the second symbol, she stares at his face with her mouth slightly agape, while he keeps his head down to draw his bident. He pauses, lifting his head and staring into her eyes for effect, before crossing the first bident with a second. The staffs intersect, the second perfectly drawn without him ever looking down.

Her eyes trail from his face to the napkin, and she closes them after seeing the new symbol, releasing the breath she'd been holding with a sigh. With her lip quivering, her voice cracks when she utters, "You should not be here."

"Shh, shh, shh," he soothes, placing his hand over hers. "I am not here for you. I only seek to find others who should not be here. Others whose symbols have no place in this realm."

She nods, her throat working a swallow. Then she clears it and calmly says, "It seems there are many symbols that have no place here tonight." She moves her hand and lifts her water glass, taking a sip, and motions her head toward the woman sitting at the bar.

As I turn around, the woman is laughing at something the man with her has said, leaning toward him. But then, she must feel my eyes on her as they stand because she peers over her shoulder, meets my stare, and her eyes seem to gleam before she turns to leave. But before she does, I see exactly what Janessa was referring to when my eyes trail down, fixing on a scar in the shape of a circle with a cross connected at the bottom, visible on her retreating shoulder. And the worst part is, I have seen that marking before.

Just then, our server arrives with the check, pulling me out of my shock and our attention to her. Marcus quickly pays when I hand him his wallet, and we rush to exit as Janessa calls out behind us, "Good luck!"

Marcus and I have been wandering around in the cold for several minutes trying to find the couple who left the bar before us with no luck. I am shivering, and my fingers have gone from numb to painful, plus my feet hurt, so I know we can't do this much longer. "I don't think we are going to find them," I say, my voice shaking in time with my body.

"We have to try," he pleads. "We cannot go back empty-handed."

"She didn't show, Marcus. And it is foolish to chase after *some* woman when we have no clue if she is even part of this!"

"Oh, she is part of it," he says, voice cracking. "I saw the same symbol as you did, and if she has no part in this, then she knows someone who does!" he insists.

"How do you figure? Just because she has some symbol burned on her back? It was nothing!"

"It was Aphrodite's symbol, Charity!" he shouts, gripping his hair in his hands, pulling in frustration. "I would know it anywhere. If it was just some sycophant obsessed with Venus or girl power, it would have been a tattoo with pretty little flourishes, and she would have been wearing fringe and more crystals than a dreamcatcher," he says, pacing. "But it was a brand of ownership—a claiming— reserved for only the most devout. Like a Devotee or an Anointed, all of which are echelons in Aphrodite's order. So, no, I am not just chasing after some woman; I am chasing after answers!" He points in every direction as he turns to get his point across.

"But Lenore had no brand," I counter, crossing my arms in frustration and because I am freezing.

"Of course not. She was an Acolyte, fallen from grace, and desperate to get back into her goddess' good graces. She was unmarked because she refused the rite by forfeiting the life of her child."

"She killed her own child?" I wail before clasping my hand over my mouth and shaking my head in disbelief.

"No. Just the opposite. She refused to dedicate the child to her goddess at birth and spared her a life of servitude and eventual death. She was shunned for it."

"That can't be right," I oppose, shaking my head. "You are wrong. You have to be." I am crying now, unable to hold back my tears.

Marcus steps to my side and throws his arms around me, offering his warmth. "I am sorry I got mad. Please do not cry. It is okay," he soothes. "Look, I know you are frustrated, exhausted, and today has been a lot."

"That's not it," I say into his neck, sniffling.

"Then what is it?"

"In the car," I say, shivering. "I will tell you in the car."

Then, he opens his jacket and covers me as much as he can, and we traipse back to the car. Once there, he cranks up the heat, and I pull out my phone, sending Janessa a quick text.

> Lost the woman. Any chance you know where we might pick up the trail?

Watching my phone, it is several minutes before I see the three dots blinking and then disappear. Then, they reappear and disappear two more times. Just when I am about to give up and put my phone away in my purse, a message comes in.

> SE 6th near Cigar District. Brick buildings. Look for the symbol.

> Thanks. 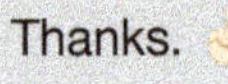

I place my phone in my purse, then hold my hands over the vent to warm my fingers. Marcus is about to put the car in drive, so I stop him. "Wait."

"You said—"

"I know what I said, but what I am saying now is you are right; we can't leave empty-handed. But before we get to that part of this evening's entertainment, there is something I need to tell you." My face falls and I pull my hands into my lap.

He reaches over and grabs my hands, pulling them over the center console where he leans down and kisses my knuckles. "We are in this together, right? You can tell me anything."

"It's..." I whisper, unsure how to start. "Well, it isn't really anything that will be helpful at this very moment, per se, but I remembered something about that symbol. More accurately, where I'd seen it before, branded in that way."

"Okay," he strings out the word, his confusion about my revelation evident. He leans sideways in his seat with his arms crossed and his head resting back on the window. "So where have you seen it before?"

"On my mother. Or I guess I should say, on Miranda, seeing as she wasn't biologically my mother—"

"Stop," he says, holding up one hand to stop my rambling. "Fast forward through all of whatever it was you were about to throw out and get to the part about the symbol."

"The symbol," I say, wringing my hands. "Of course, the symbol. So..."

"Miranda," he urges.

"Exactly. Miranda had the same scar on her right shoulder as the woman in the bar did. I only saw it once or twice growing up."

"So, the woman who raised you was either an active or past member of the order?"

"I mean, maybe. I don't know. I think I would remember her being part of an order, or a cult, or whatever the hell they are. There would have been signs, right?" I ask pleadingly.

"One would think. But they have been operating discreetly for so long, maybe not."

"Do you think it could be a coincidence?" I consider the possibility, but know he is about to refute my theory.

"That a member of her order raised you, and another, after none have arrived there before, somehow shows up in the Underworld after your death and unlocks a dormant power inside you? Yeah, I am sure it was completely random," he scoffs.

"I am not naïve, Marcus. I was just hoping I was wrong." I pout.

"Why?"

"Because if I was wrong, then there wouldn't be yet another thing I was lied to about for my entire life and I..." I break after that. I cry again, and this time I don't know if I have the strength to stop. Because first, she wasn't my mother, and now she has a past life where she was part of an order serving a Greek goddess, both of which I have no way to ask her about. "I don't even know who I am anymore," I sob, shaking.

It is awkward, but Marcus drapes himself over the divider to console me, and I rest my head on his shoulder. "When we get back to the Underworld and release the stored power of memory, then maybe we can call her forth to get some of those answers," he says, rubbing my back soothingly. "Until then, we should deal with what information we have and act on it."

I nod my head, sniffling. "Okay."

He shifts back to his side of the vehicle, and I wipe my face with the back of my hand. Trying to change the tone of the evening, in a cheery tone he asks, "So, how about we get back to this evening's entertainment? You said there was something else?"

"So I messaged Janessa to see if she could help us."

"And?"

I pull out my phone and hand it to him. "Any chance you are interested in real estate development?" I ask, pointing to the map on my phone, showing the buildings where Janessa suggested we look.

CHAPTER 36

GOLDEN TEMPLE (HADES)

Five minutes later, Charity and I are driving by two brick buildings where the entry doors face inward toward one another, and a driveway that doubles as the sidewalk runs between the two, leading to a parking lot. There are several cars parked in the back, and the same woman from the bar is entering the left building using some type of electronic access I cannot make out followed by the man.

We do not stop; we just drive by and park around the corner on the residential street until we are certain everyone has left for the evening. Considering it is now almost ten at night, however, the buildings should be empty since they are offices for a "development firm." Something is obviously happening there tonight; the question is, what?

After thirty minutes of sitting in silence with the heat blowing loudly, frustration kicks in, curiosity gets the better of us, and we find ourselves walking down the street and toward the buildings. As we pass, we see the same woman exiting, but alone, and continue on so as not to garner any unwanted attention. Then, as we crouch in the bushes, high heels echo between the buildings, announcing her retreat.

There was only one car in the lot when we strolled by, so when what we assume is her vehicle pulls out, turning right and heading in the other direction, we sneak up to the entrance and peer in the windows. The front looks normal, like it is just your regular run-of-the-mill business, because what better way to blend in with everything else than with a reception desk, a sitting area, and the company name everywhere you look.

The subtlety ends there, however, because using a name like *Hetaira Industries*, at least for me, there is no question what profession they are in. "Huh," I say, my grin widening painfully in the frigid air. "Not trying to hide what their specialty is."

"Why do you say that?" Charity asks, peering through the glass while she wraps her arms around herself. "Titans, I wish I had brought a jacket." She shivers.

"Do you want mine?" I offer, pulling my jacket off and draping it over her shoulders. "There, that is better," I say, rubbing her arms over the sleeves, "and I say that because the Hetaira were working women. Companions. The profession, some say, is as old as time itself."

"Like an escort service?"

"Makes a good front," I point out.

"Okay, but if she was an escort, where did the man go? Two went in, but only one came out."

"That my dear Charity, is a good damn question. Next question: do we try to pick the lock or do we just break in?" I tap on the double-locking doors, looking around for security cameras. There are none that I can see.

"Looks like picking it is out of the question," she says, moving to the electronic access pad. Her face twists into... it is not exactly confusion, but surprise, maybe? "Is this a biometric scanner?"

"Marcus specializes in logistics; they use a key card at his facility, so I will be of no help there." I step to where she is looking closely at the pad.

"Could be blood. Maybe they have it genetically coded or something, or is that too tech-savvy for the golden goddess?" She moves to touch it, and I grab her wrist.

"Seeing as she has stuck around through the ages, I would discount nothing as a possibility."

"You try it. Maybe it is programmed for ichor." She nods toward the device.

"Fine, but that woman did not strike me as a god. Even if she was in disguise, I would have felt her in the bar," I explain, taking off one of Charity's earrings and poking my thumb. Then I place it and a bead of ichor on the sensor. It continuously blinks red and beeps. "Nope, not me."

"Should I try?" She steps forward, waiting.

"You mean before we break in and risk getting arrested? I think that is a fabulous idea." I am shaking when I hand her the earring and she pricks her index finger, placing it and a drop of blood on the sensor. The machine sounds, the light blinking green once and the lock clicks loudly.

She grasps the handle, pulling, and it opens without issue. "Score one more for the demigod," she beams.

"I'm glad, because torching it might have drawn a bit too much attention, cameras or not. Plus, if I used my power, it would deplete the potion and I would be a little exposed."

"You think?" she quips.

We step through, and the door clicks behind us, the mechanism locking once more. "Shit," I curse, "I do not see a panel in this room. There has to be another way to unlock the doors to exit," I say, looking for a button underneath the front desk. I give up. "Perhaps before we worry about that we should look around."

"You mean before security arrives," Charity says, pointing to a round camera conveniently placed in the center of the company logo on the reception wall.

I look up and sure as shit, there it is in the center of the first "a" in Hetaira. "I guess there is no time to waste, then. Now would be as good a time as any to let your friend out to nose around."

"Good thinking," she says, opening her bag and pulling out the velvet drawstring pouch. She turns it upside down, pouring the two stones out. Then, picking up the Mustēria Stone, she summons Tyto from within, and he appears.

Our dark companion is much smaller than when in the Underworld, adjusting to the space available. Now, instead of flying, he hops around, twisting his head as he searches. He stops before the back wall with a thermostat dead center and pecks at the bookcase sitting beside it, screeching.

"Tyto thinks there is something we need to see behind that case. Care to do the honors and see if that thermostat is actually for controlling the temperature?"

Hesitantly, Charity steps before the thermostat and flips open the cover. Just like the outside access panel, the thermostat control pad has a bio-scanner. Huffing, she pulls off her earring once more, pricking a finger on her opposite hand and presses it to the sensor. It blinks green, beeps, and the bookcase clicks, shifting off the wall on one side. I wiggle my fingers between it and the wall, and it slides open to the right, showing a hidden staircase.

Tyto leads the way down the stairs, taking flight and soaring over what looks to be about a dozen steps, before disappearing down a tunnel of some kind with his trail illuminating our path.

We follow behind him, using his remaining light to guide us, but then the tunnel curves right as if leading toward the parking lot. Once we make the turn at the bend, we see Tyto standing at the end of a short corridor, pecking at a door and screeching.

"Okay, okay. We're coming," Charity announces. She steps to the door and turns the handle. It swings inward, and then Tyto takes flight again, circling above what looks to be a decent-sized rotunda with a statue at its center. It is Aphrodite, I can tell even with just the light from the owl's trail, but her gown and feet are dark and covered with some type of residue.

"If I had to guess, that is not from a dove," I say, pointing to where dark crimson pools at the base of the statue.

"As if dove blood would be the obvious choice?" she asks.

"It used to be," I say. "But seeing how much there is, and that two entered and one left, I would now say the order has turned to a different type of offering."

"But if he was the offering, where is the body?"

"No need to get twisted up on the details. We are here looking for answers, but where the body went is not one of them." Then I round the space, following the wall until I come to a large maroon tapestry with an intricate design woven into it. Tyto is sitting beneath it, twisting his head to look up at me. "Here, my friend?" The bird pecks at the fringe, and the wall hanging sways. "There is something behind this," I announce to Charity, my voice echoing around the chamber.

She joins me, and I lift the wall covering, revealing another passageway. "How far do you think it goes?" she asks, peering into the darkness and waiting for me to enter before her.

Tyto hops in about fifteen feet, and we follow, ducking through a small archway and into another rotunda. Instead of a statue displayed dead center like in the last room, there is an altar where "the offering" has been left on display. I urge Charity to stick to the outside edge to avoid the blood. "Unless you want to get your heels covered, I would follow the curve of the room. There appear to be several cut-outs along the back; see if you can find anything useful."

Charity walks the perimeter, minding where she steps, and

stops when she gets to the five cut-outs I mentioned. "There are markings above each one," she says, pointing to the two-foot squared holes that seem to be equidistant from one another.

"Can you read what they say?" I ask, rounding the other direction and stopping when I get to a table with a ledger of some sort. I can hear her mumbling to herself.

"Hey, Marcus?"

"Yeah?" I call out, flipping the pages of the ledger before me as I scan dates and names. April 1997- New York: ten girls and five boys. Eight of the girls' names have next to them either boy or girl, with a name and a date, I am assuming of a birth. Then there are two names where the unnamed baby is circled, but one of the girls' names and her baby is crossed out in red, and next to it in parentheses is the name *Miranda Goins,* which is also crossed out in red.

"Is there significance to these five places?"

"What?" I ask, my mind swimming from what I think I unearthed.

"Paphos, Cythera, Corinth, Athens, and Mount Eryx."

"Places of worship for Aphrodite, why?"

"Because there are at least ten books here in each cut-out. They look really old, so I doubt I can read them."

I do not move toward her because my eyes are still scanning the next set of dates and information. April 1972- North Carolina: nine girls and six boys. Same as the previous year listed, but no one is crossed out in red; not the women or their corresponding babies. But one name catches my eye, and her baby is unnamed and circled. It takes everything in me not to go nuclear. "Do not touch the books," I grit out, holding my anger at bay. "I will be right there." I pick up the ledger and walk to her side. "Show me."

She motions to all five cut-outs like a game show host. "Behold." Her lips are parted as she mouths *ooh* and *ahh.*

"Be serious, will you?"

"Excuse me, Mr. Grouchy Pants," she teases, calling Tyto back into the stone before placing it in her purse. "You know, this bag isn't massive, but I could probably fit some of the smaller books in here," she says, stretching her purse wide.

"Fine," I say, not opening them as I hand her one book from each of the temple locations.

"Did you find out anything from that one?" she asks, motioning to the ledger in my hand with her head.

"Unfortunately," I grumble, clutching it tightly. The leather creaks in my grip.

"Unfortunately? Why unfortunately?" She slides her purse over her shoulder and steps toward me, eyeing the book.

"There are two names in here I am familiar with," I say, holding the book up. She reaches for it, and I pull it back. "Are you sure you are ready to see what lies within these pages?"

"I'm a big girl, Marcus. I can handle it. Now let me see."

I extend my hand, and she takes the ledger, my thumb sliding out from the page I have marked. Her eyes scan left and right, reading each line, then stops, her body going rigid as her face pales.

I reach out to steady her when she sways. "Will you be alright?"

"I'm fine," she grouses, jerking out of my hold.

"You sure?"

"I said I'm fucking fine, Marcus, now drop it!"

"You can talk to me, Charity," I offer.

"Charity has nothing to say." She turns away, lowering her head to read the next line.

I place my hands on her shoulders. "And what about Melody?"

She tilts her head back. "Melody has chosen to remain ignorant at the moment and address what the fuck Charity just read when she has the bandwidth." She shrugs me off and steps to the wall, leaning against it as she reads some more.

Giving her space, because she obviously not only wants it but needs it, I pick up a book from Athens and turn to the end. The last date listed is April 1722, with a note: *temple relocated to New Orleans.* I then do the same with each other temple location, turning to the last page and seeing the month of April on each one and the corresponding year and location to which they were moved.

I have five books in my arms when Melody makes a gagging sound. "Ugh! What the fuck is that smell?"

I turn and her face is scrunched up with her nose wrinkled. Then I smell it too, but before I can panic, I jump to her side, still holding the five books, wrap my arms around her waist and say, "Hold the fuck on, Charity, because shit is about to get real."

"Wait, what?"

Just as I have her firmly within my hold, with my head cradled into her neck, the world shakes around us; the ground opens up, and Charity and Marcus fall into the chasm as Hades is called back to the Underworld with Melody along for the ride.

EPILOGUE: APHRODITE'S PLEA

"The last time I saw my mother, I had just fled to Olympus from Diomedes—Athena's hero—after being injured when trying to shield my progeny at the battle of Troy. It was foolish of me, I get that, but I am a goddess and he was my son, so what else was I supposed to do, just let him die? No, I could not. Would not. But my hubris, being what it was back then, knew no bounds, and I placed myself between Aeneas and Diomedes' spear tip."

"Now, would I have wrapped Aeneas in my robes hoping to block the blow if I knew that bitch, Athena, had made it possible for him to wound me? *Yes? No? Maybe?* Hell, I do not know. It was the heat of the moment and the mama bear in me just roared to life, and the only thing I could think was *how fucking dare he touch my cub!* But then, in the aftermath of all the chaos, I looked down to see my precious ichor dripping down my wrist and smattering my robes, and I fucking panicked a little."

"However, I promised myself that day, *Athena will not feel so wise when I outwit her and finally get my revenge.* And for a time she was enemy number two on my list, but that list has grown by more than quite a few names since then.”

“Anyway, thankfully Iris, my sweet, beautiful, quick-thinking wielder of rainbows, hauled me up, absconded Ares’ chariot, Titans how I adore him, and away we went to the mount. And there, on our blessed Olympus, Dione healed me. But then, my asshole of a father had to saunter up being all high and mighty with his *I told you so* after Athena and Hera egged him on, and I just... You know it sucks, people thinking the only thing you are capable of is love and beauty. I am strong; I will tell you that. I am, and in that moment, he became number three on my list, with Hera right there along with him.”

“Eventually the precedent and need for numbering fell away, and everyone who wronged me just got grouped together as *false gods*—the chaff who will be separated from the wheat when it is time to harvest.”

“So, after my father left, mocking me with the fanfare of those pandering at his feet, my mother reminded me of a time when she imparted to me a bit of knowledge. Something that Zeus had been hiding from all the others since the fall of the Titans, and would give me an advantage if I ever needed to ‘rid’ myself of... well, anyone— Titan or God.”

“See, unbeknownst to Hera... *and everyone else*, my father liked to have Dione, a.k.a. my mother, for a little side action now and then even after my conception. So, one time, as she was leaving his quarters, she just so happened to come across a parchment. Okay, so she was snooping, because who just comes across a hidden parchment without a little subterfuge.”

“Anyhoo, she set his chambers ablaze with a candle she left burning and, *whoopsy daisy*, parchment’s gone, information’s forgotten, and none were the wiser, except for *little ol’ me*—the recipient of said long-lost parchment many, many years later, but before I started my list with Hades.”

"That being said, I took her gift, because that is precisely what it was, and with Hades' help... well, with his ignorance. *L'amour c'est la vie*. Mwah!"

"Where was I? Oh, yes. So, under the guise of a *distraught lover*, I set something in motion that could lead to me ruling over all. And by all I mean all beings, all realms, every fucking thing!"

"Now, my dear, I did my part and answered your question *why* I am doing this. But tell me dearest, sweet, wonderful Lenore, will you be the answer to one thing that has been fucking with me since Hades went and put a wrench in my original plans when he placed *that girl* in the heart stone... by being my *how*?"

Aphrodite

Melody

THE SEEKER

OF

Persephone's

REVENGE

ANGELA M. JOHNSON

ABOUT THE AUTHOR

Angela M. Johnson is a BIPOC author of adult fantasy and romance novels living in Northwest Arkansas (NWA) with her family. She is active in her local writing community, a retired Army Veteran, mother, artist, Cosplayer, crafter, and Heavy Athlete competing in Scottish Highland Games. When she isn't writing she is chasing dopamine; collecting skills and hobbies like they are Pokémon cards. Anything from 3D printing, laser engraving, CNC carving, and other types of fabrication. She published her first fantasy novel in 2022 and has now ventured into the romance genre; releasing three novels in 2023, one in 2025, and more to come in the future.

www.notyouraveragejohnson.com